# The Murderer
# of the World

# The Murderer
# of the World

by
**Gaston de Wailly**

translated, annotated and introduced by
**Brian Stableford**

A Black Coat Press Book

ISBN 978-1-61227-408-9. First Printing. June 2015. Published by Black Coat Press, an imprint of Hollywood Comics.com, LLC, P.O. Box 17270, Encino, CA 91416.

# *Introduction*

*Le Meurtrier du globe* by "Commandant G. de Wailly," here translated as *The Murderer of the World*, was originally published as a 26-part feuilleton serial in the *Journal des Voyages* between 15 May and 23 October 1910, the fifth of the six serials that the author contributed to that publication between 1886 and 1915. It was subsequently reprinted as a paperback book by J. Tallandier in 1925 and reprinted by the same publisher in 1933.

Gaston de Wailly (1857-1943) came from a notable literary family, of whom he was by no means the most distinguished member. He published a few further books in addition to reprints of the five full-length feuilletons from the *Journal de Voyages*, but they were all in ultra-cheap paperback formats at the bottom end of the literary marketplace. All of his novels are melodramatic adventure stories, mostly set largely at sea, in the Vernian mode in which the *Journal des Voyages* specialized, but he also wrote in a very different vein for the theater, presumably after his retirement from the navy; his early dramatic work consisted mostly of one-act vaudevilles and humorous monologues, although he did have three-act "maritime dramas" produced in the later phases of that second career. It was probably for his dramatic work that he hoped to be remembered as a writer, although, by their nature, even cheap paperback books tend to remain accessible far longer than theatrical works, eventually eclipsing even meritorious maritime careers. Such are the vagaries of preservation that if Gaston de Wailly is remembered at all today, it is as a run-of-the-mill purveyor of crude pulp fiction—none of which is cruder than *Le Meurtrier du globe*, although none of the rest can compete with that novel on the grounds of sheer melodramatic ambition.

Previous members of the family who had made a name as writers included, Léon de Wailly (1804-1864) and Gustave de Wailly (1804-1878), both of whom were moderately prolific novelists and dramatists. Because Gaston did not use his full first name his works are sometimes confused with those of the latter by bibliographers, although their literary careers did not overlap. His contemporary Paul de Wailly (1855-1933) was a moderately prolific composer and musician. All of them were presumably descended from the various compilers and updaters of the oft-reprinted *Nouveau Vocabulaire Français de Wailly* first compiled in the 18th century by François de Wailly (1724-1801) and subsequently modified by Étienne-Augustin de Wailly (1770-1821) and Alfred de Wailly (1800-1869). Jules de Wailly (1806-1866) also wrote for the theater and Natalis de Wailly (1805-1886) published several volumes of non-fiction. One can only speculate as to what the more ancient members of the family might have thought of their descendant's fiction, but they would doubtless have been proud of his achievement in rising to the rank of Commandant, assumming that it was real.

What makes *Le Meurtrier du globe* interesting, in spite of its crudity, is the fundamental speculative notion that provides the novel with its title and its climax. In terms of its plot, the story is a standard chase thriller in which a small band of heroes is harassed by an uncannily powerful villain, through whose claws they slip continually in a series of hairsbreadth escapes. In that regard too, it is unusual, by virtue of the pressure of melodramatic inflation on the evil character of the villain and his various unlikely accomplices, but the eventual effect of that exaggeration is merely ludicrous. The nature of the theory that motivates the action of the mysterious scientific genius who is the object of the chase, and the project he has completed in consequence of that theory, might be deemed ludicrous too, but certainly not in any mere sense, being possessed of an admirable flamboyance that gives the novel a certain eccentric panache.

Among the many Vernian writers who flourished inside and outside the pages of the *Journal de Voyages*, Gaston de Wailly certainly cannot be reckoned one of the most stylish, nor one of the most ingenious; his prose fiction is the purest pulp—but precisely because of its purity in that regard, it does serve to illustrate clearly the essential appeal of Vernian fiction, not only by adding useful imaginative boldness to the décor and background of an adventure story, but also by raising the stakes of the potential outcome of the adventure. As in any such chase thriller, there is an inheritance at stake in *Le Meurtrier du globe*, and the atmosphere is also replete with pheromones as heroes and heroines learn to adore one another while dodging the customary routine of shipwrecks, howling mobs, kidnappings and imprisonments, but what really adds spice to the race is the fact that, as the title suggests, someone, somewhere *wants to murder the world*—and the key twist that makes the novel truly exceptional is that the would-be murderer is not the arch-villain, who, in spite of his all-out over-the-top nastiness, is striving as hard as he possibly can to prevent that murder.

The sophistication of thriller fiction in general, and of the modern "techno-thrillers" directly descended from Vernian thriller fiction in particular, proceeded by leaps and bounds after 1910, losing a great deal of its naivety during the Great War of 1914-18, when the destructive power of technology and the difficulty of countering its effects was demonstrated in no uncertain terms. Novels of the same general type as *Le Meurtrier du globe* continued to be written throughout the middle part of the 20th century, often with a similar crudity of style, but they could no longer be written with the same innocence, in terms of the mechanics of plotting, ethnological improvisation or moral judgment.

Between 1914 and 1919, attitudes to science and technology changed, throughout the nations involved, and notions of good and evil changed too, with the result that the mingling of the two in subsequent speculative fiction routinely enjoyed a synergistic amplification. Because of that, *Le Meurtrier du globe* is bound to seem primitive, even to a modern eye that appreciates the material produced during the *interbellum* heyday of American pulp fiction, but its very crudity does give it a certain mind-boggling veneer, which might not be charm, let alone quality, but definitely has a certain reckless bravado.

This translation was made from a copy of the undated Tallandier edition published in 1926. The original contains numerous footnotes, in which the author gives French translations of words he has rendered in the text in English, or explanations of terms in French naval slang, almost all of which are redundant in a translation. I have only preserved one or two of them, although I have frequently amended the author's English within the text in order to correct it, or to render it more plausible in context.

Brian Stableford

# *Prologue*

## *I*

That evening, the Hôtel Continental was exceptionally animated. A crowd of mostly young and intelligent people, vibrant with warm and generous gaiety, filled the large hall beneath the sparkling chandeliers.

"Centrales"[1] of today, yesterday and the day before yesterday, with their families and occasional chosen guests, were sharing the delicate joy of a fine expected pleasure, anticipated in total security, promised by the theater curtain masking a stage erected at the back of the hall. Laughter was prepared in advance on all lips, and hands were getting ready to applaud. That was because a comrade, the son of a great Parisian director, and a clever and zestful author, had written one of those special revues that year, Aristophanean in its liberty, in which, among the incidents of the school, reflected in the Gallic fashion, the tics of the various teachers would be wittily parodied. They would be the first to salute their young charges with their bravos, joyfully and without resentment.

A good audience! The raising of the curtain had been announced for nine o'clock, and it was half past nine, but no one was bothered by that delay. Chatting, laughing, exchanging handshakes, evoking memories, confiding successes or hopes and talking cordially about absentees, occupied the young and old comrades sufficiently to wipe out any hint of impatience.

One replete individual installed in the front row, however, did not seem to be participating in the general forbearance. Senator Dupeyroux, to whom the committee had offered the

---

[1] The École Centrale in Paris, founded in 1829, is the oldest and most prestigious school of engineering in France, long renowned for its production of technological innovators and entrepreneurs.

presidency of the celebration that year, was squirming incessantly in his seat, making it clearly manifest that even senatorial patience has its limits. Unable to stand it any longer, he stood up abruptly, traversed the hall, in spite of the deferential objurgations of two young Centrales bearing the badges of stewards, and went into a small reception room serving as a vestibule and controlled entrance to the hall, transformed for the occasion into a theater.

He addressed himself to the chief steward, who was busy checking the invitations of a few latecomers

"Well, he hasn't arrived, then, your famous Mining King?"

"Monsieur Williamson is certainly a little late, Monsieur le Sénateur."

"I'm certainly a supporter of courtesy, even exaggerated, with regard to foreigners," affirmed the "conscript father," in a slightly acidic tone, "but since we're all subject here to the pleasure of that republican monarch, I'm wondering why your committee didn't offer the presidency to him rather than me!"

Embarrassed, the steward busied himself with the classification of variously-colored pieces of cardboard.

"That's all right," the elect of the restricted suffrage went on. "I incline before the modern majesty of the dollar and I'll go back inside to set an example of patience. Oh, by the way, I asked for a place to be reserved next to my seat for my new secretary. I'd be obliged to you, as soon as he arrives...he's a tall, dark-haired young man, with the bronzed complexion of an African explorer..."

"Is Monsieur le Sénateur now involved in colonial politics?"

"It's the best thing..."

"For the future of the country?"

"For bringing down recalcitrant ministries. My secretary, a precious fellow, very knowledgeable, is named Rolland."

The young commissioner raised his head. "Rolland? An explorer? Claude Rolland, perhaps?" he enquired.

"Do you know him?"

"He was a comrade of my older brother at the École Centrale."

"Bah! He's an engineer and didn't say anything to me about it! It's a pearl of knowledge and modesty that I've found there. Look—here he is!"

Claude Rolland had, indeed, come in, very late but with his excuse on his arm: Mademoiselle Edmée Rolland, as tall and slim as her brother; as blonde as he was dark; better than pretty, beautiful—but with a slightly grave beauty that seemed poorly adapted to the tender shade of her abundant, slightly curly and hectic hair. In particular, she had two superb large blue eyes, gentle and profound, and, at the same time bright, with a determined and energetic gleam.

Claude introduced her to his new "boss."

"I understand," said the latter, bowing a trifle ponderously to the young woman, "why you've renounced the glory of your distant expeditions for Mademoiselle your sister; she's charming!"

"Our mother, who was our only remaining parent, having passed on, duty recalled me to Edmée..."

"Only your duty?" questioned the young woman, mildly.

"And my tender affection, Sister, as you know very well!" Claude replied, in his masculine but musical voice.

In a gallantly pretentious fashion, Dupeyroux added. "You'll doubtless hold it against me, Mademoiselle, if I take possession of your brother in order to talk about our great report?"

"Not at all, Monsieur—the interests of the State before all!"

"Always at your orders, Monsieur le Sénateur," said Claude. And he called: "Furet!"[2]

"Present, Commandant," said a blond and thickset fellow who had come in behind the fraternal couple, and had remained respectfully to one side until summoned.

---

[2] *Furet* is the French equivalent of the English "ferret."

"Take charge of our coats," the young man said to him, throwing him his overcoat, "and I confide Mademoiselle Edmée to you."

"Have no fear, Commandant," said the other, hastily rejoining the young woman.

Dupeyroux took his secretary by the arm.

"My dear chap, that's the second time that fellow has called you Commandant, but..."

"I'm not. This is the explanation: Jean Guitard, nicknamed Furet, is a brave and skillful sailor, who has navigated numerous rapids on the great African rivers under my orders. That's when he acquired the habit of calling me his Commandant, and he's never wanted to get out of it, any more than he consented to leave me when his official service to the State ended."

"I understand. Let's talk briefly and to the point. Where are you up to in our work?"

"The first part, the list of accusations, is already in your in-tray."

"Terrible, isn't it, the charge sheet? It's necessary that every paragraph be a stick of dynamite, in order that the whole ensemble is blown to smithereens, minister and ministry together."

"Alas, the task is only too easy; it's sufficient to content oneself with telling the truth."

"So much the better!"

*So much the worse*, thought Claude, who, not being a politician, had the naivety of thinking of the country first and foremost.

"And the second part—the reforms? For it's all very well to demolish, on condition that one takes responsibility for rebuilding. Everything is there, you understand!"

Claude Rolland understood only too well. It was not without a certain coldness, the mask of an honest scorn, that he replied: "My notes are organized; I've just begun writing them up."

"Do a good job! When will you be finished."

"In a week at the latest."

"Good—the interpellation is in a fortnight; I'll have time to work on my speech. Now..."

He was interrupted by the sudden arrival of one of the celebration's stewards, at a run, exclaiming: "Monsieur le Sénateur, we're only waiting for you to give the signal."

"Your rich Yankee has arrived, then?"

"A moment ago."

"Impossible—we'd have seen him!" said the chief steward.

Laughing, the comrade who had just arrived explained: "Weren't we told that he's the greatest eccentric in North America? He came in through the rooms reserved for the performers. He's flatly refused the seat that was reserved for him next to Monsieur le Sénateur and demanded two chairs for himself and his groom, a puny chap with an insolent and stuck-up manner, and has sat down in the passage leading from the wings to the reception room. That way, he can leave easily if the performance bores him. He's an eccentric!"

"In that case," said the chief steward, "we can't give him an entrance?"

Dupeyroux, who was already heading back into the hall, stopped, and in a tone shot through with irritated jealousy, said: "You'd arranged an ovation for that fantasist?"

"Out of professional admiration for the foremost geologist in the world!"

"Oh!"

"It's not saying too much, Monsieur le Sénateur. Every time that astonishing man, a prospector without equal, points his finger at the ground and says: 'Dig a shaft there,' they find the coal, the oil or the minerals predicted. Never a hesitation, never an error—hence his colossal fortune."

"Legend... or bluff!" protested Dupeyroux, shrugging his senatorial shoulders. Then he went into the hall of the celebrations, followed by Claude Rolland.

Their appearance was saluted with the rhythmic salvos of an ovation, which the vanity of the parliamentarian attributed to himself, although it was actually addressed to his comrade, whose intrepid youthful glory as an explorer reflected on everyone and made the École proud.

The performance had scarcely been running for ten minutes when a person of rather rude appearance, with a long bushy beard and no moustache, wearing a long frock-coat and a vast hat, arrived on the threshold of the little control room, debating in a low voice with one of the hotel footmen. He seemed the complete type-specimen of the Yankee, as popularized by caricaturists in the Old World.

"Very close to the stage, on the right, with his groom," the footman indicated, before making off, with an anxious expression.

The bearded man head toward the door of the hall with meter-long strides, where a steward stopped him.

"Green card? Or pink?"

"No ticket. Just off the train, no time to get one. No need, anyway. Jonathan Loeb, chief of the Knights of Labor,[3] member of the general staff of the Salvation Army..." As the steward pursed his lips with courteous irony, the red-bearded man said, in a surly tone: "You still have the right to smile at Salvationists in France; you'd bow if we were in America, or even in India."

"Unfortunately, Monsieur, we're in Paris, where those titles don't have the power to impose orders."

---

[3] The Noble and Holy Order of the Knights of Labor, founded in 1869, was one of the largest and most powerful American labor organizations of the late 19th century, but it dwindled rapidly in the 1890s, eventually disappearing in 1939. Modeled on the Freemasons, of whose august society the newcomer is obviously also a high-ranking member, it maintained a secrecy of membership in order to prevent employers taking reprisals. It had considerable support within the Catholic Church, but was regarded with suspicion by left-wing labor unions because of its staunch Republicanism.

"And this one?" said the tall, robust individual, standing up straight. He rapidly placed his open right hand, with the fingers extended and together, on his stomach, and then raised it to his forehead, made what is known in military terms as a half-turn, and immediately returned to his original position.

The commissioner looked at him, amazed and amused. "Are you in pain?" he asked.

The newcomer sketched a scornful gesture.

At that moment, a pale young man irrupted into the same vestibule. He had a curly moustache, a fur coat over his arm, and was clad in an evening suit of the very latest fashion: an accomplished specimen of the "dandy" or "snob," one of those elegant high spirits of Parisian high society who, without any entitlement whatsoever, are at all the premières, welcome in almost all salons, and make up the most specialized or reputedly most exclusive social cliques.

He came in casually. Proclaiming in a serenely shrill voice: "I'm late, I'll wager? Damn it, I was in such exhilarating society..."

He stopped dead. As he turned in the direction of the great hall, after having thrown his invitation negligently on to the green baize table of the chief steward, his gaze had just alighted on the tall and singular transatlantic individual, who, looking at him fixedly, put his hand to his stomach and then to his forehead for a second time.

"Damn it!" muttered the elegant latecomer, between his teeth. "That's the first time that I've encountered..."

And, awkwardly, because he was somewhat intimidated in spite of his aplomb, he took a step toward the man with the red beard and the small, steely eyes, placing his right hand, with the fingers extended, in front of his throat, and then touching his right shoulder, before letting it fall slowly again to dangle alongside his thigh.

The hollow and rigid features of the man who had named himself Jonathan Loeb to the Centrale steward relaxed in satisfaction. "Good, an apprentice," he murmured.

With a stiff gesture he extended his hand to the pale young man, and their handshake, devoid of any warmth, was nevertheless long enough for an observer to have the sensation that they were carrying out some kind of secret ritual.

"Delighted to meet you," said the American, coldly.

"What can I do for you, Monsieur?" asked the dandy, in the same tone.

"Get me in, although I haven't had the leisure to get myself a ticket."

"Difficult..." Suddenly, he slapped his forehead. "But no, in fact," he said. "The Senator who's presiding is..." He finished the sentence whispering in the American's ear.

With an abrupt gesture, Jonathan Loeb took from his pocket an enormous worn leather wallet, and took a card out of it, on which he wrote, below his name:

*Chief of the Supreme Council of New York.*

And then: *Necessity to attend celebration.*

He slipped the card into a gummed envelope, sealed it and handed it to one of the young stewards, saying: "To the senator president immediately. Interest of a superior order."

The steward, with a rather poor grace, rang for a messenger, whom he charged with carrying the missive to its destination.

Loeb turned to his pale and perfumed companion and said, in a brusque and trenchant tone: "Thank you. If I can ever be useful to you in my turn..."

"Of course. I'm glad to have run into you. I'm expecting to visit the United States soon..."

"Pleasure trip?"

"No, it's a matter of establishing the death of a relative who disappeared."

"A long time ago?"

"We last had news of him, by chance, twenty-five years ago."

"Difficult. Tell me anyway."

"Permit me first to introduce myself. Grégoire de Montalpé, well known in leisured Parisian society, great hunter of stars...the terrestrial kind: an astronomy full of charm but costly. And, well, it's a good time for me to get a feel...."

"A feel?"

"That is to say, to get my hands on a certain inheritance."

"I understand. This disappearance, only dating back twenty-five years..."

"Will tie up the funds for another five years. I can't, however, wait that long."

"French, presumably, this disappeared individual?"

"No, Russian. Muscovite genealogical branch, extinct with him, I believe. Oh, if you could help me to get the death of this Lobanief certified..."

The Yankee shivered from head to toe. "What did you say?" he articulated, hoarsely.

"I said Baron Lobanief, aristocrat of Valchow."

"Him!"

"You know him?" said de Montalpé, stupefied.

"I've been looking for him for twenty years! That's the man that it's important for you to discover?"

"Not alive, you understand."

"Trust me—vengeance is a sure guide."

"Vengeance?"

"Listen! The Russia of today is almost mild, but that of old...! My father was a Jewish serf. His overlord, young Lobanief, had him exiled to Siberia, where I was born to hate. When my father died I quit the icy inferno to search for our torturer. The latter, disgraced, had left the country. I followed his trail—too old, alas!—across Europe and then the Ocean. In Chicago, one day, I found evidence that he had passed though, but then I lost the trail, and I spent my last dollar without being able to pick it up again. Then..."

"You abandoned the game?"

"Never!"

"Without money, though..."

"What need do I have of money when I have an army at my service?"

"Don't understand."

"I have the soul of a leader. I became a Knight of Labor, in order to become one. Of the Salvationists, countless all over the surface of the globe, I'm really in command, as chief of the general staff, although the Marshal and his wife reign…and collect.[4] As a Freemason, I'm at the head of all the rites recognized in America. Strengthened by that triple occult sovereignty, the master of a million men of all nations and social classes, to convert into loyal agents, I've extended my nets."

"But you haven't found him?"

"Not yet."

"That's because Lobanief is dead."

"It's because he isn't. Tombs are loquacious; living lips know how to keep quiet. Not all, however."

"You have a clue?"

"Yes—a report from a Salvationist has identified a man who, thinking himself alone, has twice pronounced the name of the man I hate."

"And that man…?"

"Is in this hall. Nothing is as propitious as the neutral terrain of a celebration to make contact with a power who is almost unapproachable elsewhere."

"He's a prince, then?"

"He's a king—one of our American kings, sovereign by grace of the power of gold."

---

[4] The Salvation Army launched in the U.S.A. in 1880 was established by Salvationist emigrants from Britain, under the command of Commissioner George Scott Railton, but it functioned thereafter independently of the British military hierarchy organized by William Booth, with its own command structure. General Booth was still alive in 1910, when this novel was written, but would not have had any effective authority in the U.S.A. The "Marshal" to whom Loeb refers is fictitious, and the organization as he imagines it bears no resemblance to the actual one.

"The famous Williamson, perhaps?"

"The very same."

## II

That conversation was interrupted by the appearance of the bellboy coming back to invite Loeb, on the senator's behalf, to take his place in the armchair next to his presidential seat.

Loeb hastened forward, followed by de Montalpé, and the spectators, disturbed in the midst of their amusement, were surprised to see that caricaturish individual cutting through the joyful crowd unceremoniously, welcomed with marks of the greatest consideration by the most auspicious of the conscript fathers. The latter were quite scandalized to see that their advances were welcomed no better than a downpour at a picnic.

That was because the unpolished Jonathan had experienced a great disappointment: the chairs that had been indicated to him as being occupied by Williamson and his groom were empty.

Did Loeb's arrival have anything to do with the sudden disappearance of the Mining King?

Not at all. Williamson was completely unaware of Jonathan. Since the curtain had gone up on the Aristophanean and truly quite witty Centrale Revue, his broad face, carefully shaven, whose colors remained almost juvenile in spite of the approach of his fortieth year and his blue eyes, devoid of any gleam, had not expressed the slightest interest and had remained phlegmatically disinterested, although the audience was crackling with increasingly enthusiastic bursts of laughter.

Suddenly, his closest neighbors had seen him stand up tranquilly and go away without the slightest gesture, accompanied by his inseparable Toby.

Loeb and de Montalpé had scarcely left the vestibule when the chief steward was surprised to see the celebrated mining industrialist come in by another door. "Our revue doesn't have the good fortune of pleasing you?" he asked, contritely.

"It bores me."

"To judge by the welcome our audience is giving it, however…"

"Too much laughing," declared the billionaire, in a plaintive voice. "It makes me feel ill. I'm as nervous as a woman."

He spotted an armchair, pushed it into the middle of the room, and made a sign to his groom, who brought forward a chair, on which Williamson put his feet, saying: "Cocktail!"

"Yes sir!" replied the stiff and starched flunkey, pivoting on his heel and disappearing through the service door.

Nonplussed, the steward thought he ought to intervene.

"Pardon me, but the hotel bar is only a few steps away, if you…"

"I'm all right here."

"It's just that…it's not really…the place, and…"

Very calmly, in a soft voice, as if wearied by the effort of making it audible, he said: "I don't mind. I have a horror of convention…like that revue at which they're laughing…leaving business behind, I have a poetic temperament…too many men in that theater hall. I like women's voices, for their charm…I'll wait here until it's finished."

"Your desires are law…"

"I know," said the billionaire, conclusively.

His eyes half-closed, Williamson remained still, and it was in silence that he absorbed, with indifferent slowness, the drink that his groom brought him.

Although the untimely arrival of Jonathan Loeb had not caused the exodus of the nonchalant billionaire, it had had the effect of forcing Claude Rolland to give up his seat next to the senator. As there was not a single free seat left, he retired to the back of the hall. Several stewards hastened to try to find him a place. He did not want the entire assembly to be disturbed on his account, however, so, offering the pretext of needing some air, he headed back to the little reception-room-cum-vestibule, where he certainly did not expect to find the other American. The chief steward informed him, as best he could, about the singular person who had forced the explorer's retreat, adding that he thought he had understood that Loeb had come with the intention of seeing Williamson.

"Pfft!" said the latter, emerging from his mutism without interrupting his absorbing occupation. "Doubtless some mendicant. Everyone in New York knows perfectly well that I never give anything."

"Rich as you are, Monsieur, I can hardly believe that," protested Claude.

Williamson looked at him sideways. "Charity," he declared, flatly, "creates paupers and ingrates, so it's acting badly. Life is a battle; so much the worse for those killed in action."

"That's a cruel theory."

"It's true. Anyway, I'm too warm-hearted to give alms."

Rolland and his comrade the steward looked at one another, legitimately surprised.

"That's...quite a paradox," the explorer could not help exclaiming.

"Not at all," affirmed the billionaire, in an icy tone. "I've very sensitive; hearing plaints makes me feel ill."

That was too much for Claude's natural generosity. "You prefer," he said, sarcastically, "to plug your ears."

"Yes...I'm so good!" And Williamson's voice softened with intimate emotion to add: "No one since Adam has been as good as me!"

"Theoretically!"

"Practically. I pay those I employ well and punctually. At Christmas, I even give them imperial gratifications."

"And in case of catastrophe, unexpected misfortune, you..."

"Wait. I like regularity. Anything that troubles it makes me feel ill. This year, one of my engineers—a Frenchman—in order to save the honor of his family, he said, asked me for an advance on his salary..."

"You refused, evidently," said Claude Rolland, with increased sarcasm.

"No. I can't refuse—I'm too good. I just invited him to seek employment elsewhere."

"Mining King, perhaps," Claude whispered to the steward, indicating Williamson. "King of Egotists, for sure."

From her place in the celebration hall, Edmée had seen her brother make his rapid exit, and as she did not know the reason for it, the incomprehensible departure had astonished her greatly. Claude was everything to her; she loved him as much as she was proud of him. Not seeing him come back in, her astonishment was transformed into anxiety, which increased with all the customary rapidity of the feminine imagination. No longer able to contain herself, she left in her turn, followed by the faithful matelot, in search of news.

"Oh, there you are! I was afraid you were ill," she said to the explorer, emotional but reassured.

Williamson had turned his head negligently. "Is this your wife?" he asked.

"Who is this gentleman?" Edmée asked.

"Williamson, the rich Yankee," he relied, in a low voice. To the American, he said: "Mademoiselle is my sister."

"Good! Charming! How much?"

Claude started, and his face went red with anger. "Monsieur!" he said, menacingly.

"Oh, don't get upset…it's just habit…I was joking."

"In a singular fashion!" The young man took his younger sister's arm, and headed back toward the hall.

"Hey!" said Williamson. "You interest me. Come here!"

"Me?"

"With your sister."

"Not in this life, damn it!"

A sullen veil covered the clean-shaven features of the Mining King. "You're annoying me," he said. "In that case, I'm leaving."

The chief steward ran to Claude, his expression pleading. The latter stopped.

"All right," he said. "Out of regard for my young comrades." With a rather ill grace, he sat Edmée down, and asked the Yankee: "What do you want with us?"

"To know who you are."

"Claude Rolland, civil engineer," the young man announced, dryly.

"And the explorer that all Paris is talking about at the moment," the young woman added. Like her brother, she had a warm, musical and captivating voice.

"You have a delightful tone of voice, Mademoiselle," Williamson remarked. Addressing Claude, he said: "Explorer? Yes, I've heard mention of you. To get yourself massacred for the profit of others is very brave, but very stupid. Would you like to be the director of one of my mines? How much?"

"Nothing."

"You're refusing?"

"I came back to France to devote myself to my sister."

"Mademoiselle will accompany you."

"Your behavior just now would forbid me to take her."

"You're not very flattering?"

"I'm not trying to be."

An expression of blissful satisfaction illuminated Williamson's face. In a brisk tone that contrasted with his previous phlegmatic morosity, he said: "Well, so much the better; that makes a change. Your European princes see spines curbing before them; with me, it's consciences. It flattered me for a time; now I'm blasé. I've run around the old continent after America, and it seems to me that I always have the same shop-window in front of me, by dint of always being pursued by the same offers of sale. I have four hundred million dollars; I'm tired of buying things…and people… too easily. Life obsesses me…your attitude is new to me, and I haven't been bored for the last five minutes."

Edmée looked at him with a pensive ingenuousness. "You're suffering from being too rich," she said.

"One is never rich enough. Gold gives one everything one can desire."

"Except for what it can't buy."

"And what is it that it can't buy, down here?"

"Disinterested sentiments, of course."

"They don't exist. No one does anything for nothing."

"Unless," Claude put in, "the motive is honor, or duty, or glory?"

"There's no other motive in human actions but money," the billionaire declared, almost brutally, becoming cold again. "Honor, duty and glory are masks that disguise the true goal."

"Monsieur," said Claude, "just now your words made me indignant. I was wrong, Now, I feel sorry for you."

Williamson opened his eyes wide, looked the young explorer up and down, and then emitted a formidable burst of laughter. "Feel sorry for me—me, whom everyone envies! Ha ha ha—that's funny. Is that your opinion too, Mademoiselle?"

"Sincerely, Monsieur, yes."

"Perfect! Oh, what fun I'm having! I'm indebted to you both for that pleasure. Williamson never leaves debts unpaid. Since you don't want to run one of my mines, I'll find some other way to acquit myself." He tipped back his armchair, shaken by inextinguishable laughter. "Someone feels sorry for me! Oh, I'll laugh about that for a long time!"

The racket of a storm of applause and cheers next door cut his hilarity short.

"That's the end of the final sketch in the revue," said the steward.

"Oh, already!" said Williamson, regretfully, his features resuming their expression of froideur and ennui.

Edmée stood up and drew her brother aside. "That man is very famous and very rich, Claude," she said, "but I don't think he's happy. Really, I pity him."

A flood of spectators irrupted into the reception room; among the first were Dupeyroux, who, followed by Loeb, headed straight for the Mining King, his heart in his mouth.

The latter stopped the first spectator who came to hand and, pointing at the conscript father, demanded laconically: "Who's he?"

"Monsieur le Sénateur, the president of the celebration," was the reply.

"A politician," murmured the billionaire, with a scornful grimace.

Dupeyroux bowed to him ostentatiously, but did not have time to open his mouth.

"Oh, no speeches," said Williamson. "They bore me. You want to thank me for having come? Well, shake my hand and let that be the end of it."

Nonplussed and vexed, the senator replied: "You'll permit me, at least, to introduce you to one of your compatriots, who asked me to do so? Monsieur Loeb, chief..."

A rude tap on the arm cut off the speech again. "Thanks—I'll take it from here," Jonathan declared.

"What boors these Yankees are!" muttered Dupeyroux.

Loeb and Williamson were staring at one another coldly and stiffly, at close range.

"You are...?" the latter demanded, through pursed lips.

"Your equal," said the other. "You've elevated yourself above men by gold, I by domination. You buy, I command."

"Loeb? Good. I remember...I know. What do you want?"

"To talk."

"Between eight and nine, at my hotel."

"Same time at mine."

There was a glacial silence between those two gigantic prides, without any movement, without the slightest play of the physiognomy. From the first moment of contact they had been measuring one another with a superb calmness.

Dupeyroux, in whom long parliamentarian habits had killed all sterile self-respect, pulled himself together urgently. "I have a hunt, an hour from Paris, in which fur and feather abound. If, tomorrow, for example, Monsieur Williamson would like to do a little shooting, I hope that Monsieur Loeb wouldn't refuse to join him?"

"Neutral ground," said Jonathan, without ceasing to stare at his compatriot, who maintained his silence.

"You'd have complete independence, Messieurs," Dupeyroux added. "I'll be there on my own to receive you, with my secretary, Monsieur Rolland."

"Monsieur Rolland is your secretary?" articulated Williamson, who appeared to unfreeze. "He interests me, that young man. I'll come to kill a few of your beasts tomorrow."

"Bravo!"

"Unless...." He shouted: "Toby! The New York *Herald*, quickly!"

Like a flash of lightning, the groom opened a path through the increasingly dense crowd of engineers and Centrales that were almost filling the reception room, where the Mining King was a powerful magnet for curiosity.

"What!" exclaimed the senator. "You need to consult the New York *Herald* to know...?"

"Whether it's permissible for me to be your guest? Yes. You're astonished that I, who disposes at my whim of the work and time of others, don't have complete liberty in my own actions? That's the case, however; every day, for fifteen years, I've been waiting for an item of information to which death alone will prevent me from responding."

The reception room had suddenly immobilized. People scented a mystery, and all ears had become curiously attentive, none more so than those of Loeb and his interested satellite, Grégoire de Montalpé.

The Mining King had the distinct impression that the general movement was sympathetic to him, and, submissive to a kind of subconscious impulse, since he had thus attracted an interest that his fortune of which his fortune could not, in all sincerity, furnish him a complete aliment, he raised his voice slightly, and addressed the whole room.

"Messieurs," he said, "the prestige of an exceptional wealth is sufficient for me, and I don't want, before men of science, to usurp that of scientific genius. Fifteen years ago, when I was a poor reporter, I pulled an old man out of the Hudson whom I cared for in my home. Having recovered consciousness, he began by cursing me for having thwarted his

26

suicide. Suddenly, however, after having looked at me as if he were searching the utmost depths of my soul, he asked me to tell him my story.

"It didn't take long. A foundling, picked up half-dead by English soldiers at Fort William—hence my name—I'd been brought up by them on that Canadian territory, until the day I ran away to the United States to attempt to make my living freely. Of my early childhood I had but one memory: a heart-rending cry and the ground opening up ahead of me.

"When I'd finished talking, the old man closed his eyes for a long time, and then he said to me: 'Williamson, you were well-inspired to save me. I'll make you the richest man in the world. You only have to dig the ground where I tell you to do so in order to extract mineral treasures. Now, Old Sinker doesn't lie'"

At that name, gravely pronounced, Jonathan Loeb shivered. "Old Sinker," he murmured. "The old well-digger. What a flash of light, perhaps!"

"Who's Old Sinker?" de Montalpé asked Loeb, in a whisper.

The other replied, in a troubled voice: "A singular monomaniac who, it's said, spends his life fathoming the depths of the earth, without any apparent objective."

Meanwhile, Williamson continued: "I never saw him again. I've never known where in the world he was drawing breath. But for fifteen years, without asking anything from me in return, he's indicated to me the precious deposits that have made my fame and fortune. I've often repeated that story, before this evening, in all humility, but no one wants to oppose the legend; they prefer not to believe me."

"Then…he writes to you?" asked Loeb.

"Old Sinker has never written to me."

"You see him in revelatory dreams, then?" Dupeyroux joked, ponderously.

"I receive, without any indication of provenance, a fragment of a map of the designated country, with the initial of the nature of the deposit and a red dot. That's it! I give the map to an engineer, whom I make responsible for the exploitation, and once the land is bought, I'm the master of one more superb mine. It's perfectly simple."

"So simple," observed the senator, "that any practical joker could send you to the ends of the earth to waste your efforts."

Williamson smiled. "Impossible! There's a 'sign.' For, in telling you that the man has not demanded anything of me, I was only talking about money. He imposed a tattoo on me—oh, something trivial, hardly visible—and an oath to come without delay in response to his summons when...he judged the moment had come, he said, to give me the means to be the master of the world."

"How?" demanded Loeb.

"That's his secret."

"It's the height of fantasy...or mild madness," declared the future minister, laughing. Then, on seeing Jonathan's somber face he added: "You're not laughing, Monsieur Loeb? Such pretension doesn't merit anything else, though."

"How do you know?" retorted the occult dominator, violently. "Nothing is impossible...in America."

The orator of the Luxembourg shrugged his shoulders.

The groom reappeared, carrying the great transatlantic paper, of which his master took possession unhurriedly, and unfolded it, saying: "It's purely to acquit my conscience. It would be very extraordinary if, after fifteen years of waiting, this very evening..."

Suddenly, he shuddered, in spite of all his phlegm. His finger on the newspaper, his voice rendered uncertain by an emotion stronger than his will, he articulated: "He's summoning me!"

Loeb, who had rapidly slipped behind Williamson, uttered a hoarse cry and exclaimed: "The sign! And the two letters: L. F. That's all I wanted to know: Old Sinker is Lobanief!"

That name was repeated in a triple echo, by de Montalpé—for reasons we know—but also, simultaneously, by Claude Rolland and Edmée, whose brother squeezed her wrist and whispered in her ear: "Shut up!"

De Montalpé ran to Loeb, heart-broken. "He's alive then?" he said.

"What does it matter, if I'm now sure of finding him? How much money do you have left?"

"A hundred thousand."

"Dollars?"

"Francs."

"It's enough. You'll have your inheritance and I'll have my revenge."

Transported by such a firm assurance, the elegant Grégoire seized Jonathan's powerful and bony hand: "Oh, it's my lucky star that caused me to run into you. Thanks to you, the cousins are sunk! To the lucky de Montalpé, the hoard!"

Someone touched him on the shoulder. It was Claude, with Edmée on his arm, who looked him in the eye and said, ironically: "Evil designs rarely succeed, Monsieur de Montalpé."

"Pardon me, but…?"

"Why am I interfering, no? What do you expect—I'm interested in those poor cousins."

"Bah! Petty paupers that I've never seen, and who'll never know anything."

"It would have been necessary, for that, not to inform them."

"What?"

"Our maternal grandmother—my sister and I—was named…Lobanief."

"Like mine! Damn it! They're the cousins! What a gaffe, my emperor!"

"Chatterbox!" whispered Jonathan, in his ear. "Don't worry—I'll take care of them …as well as *him*." He indicated Williamson with a glance.

At Loeb's exclamation, the Mining King had bitten his lip, but he had immediately expelled any expression of annoyance, and traced a few figures in his notebook. He tore it out and handed it to his groom. "That dispatch to Camper and Nicholson at Gosport, to send me the steamer *Astrea*." Then he went straight to Loeb. "You've discovered my secret. You can't have any interest in it?"

"Yes—that of catching up with your Lobanief."

"You won't reach him."

"We'll reach him!" proclaimed de Montalpé, incorrigibly loquacious, adopting the attitude and tone of a braggart.

Williamson looked at the reckless snob disdainfully and called out: "Monsieur Rolland!"

The latter came forward, with Edmée.

"I heard just now, while writing in my notebook," the billionaire said to them, "that you have an interest in your relative Lobanief."

"It's of little consequence to me," said Claude, "but for the benefit of my sister, certainly. Unfortunately, our means..."

"I've told you that I'm indebted to the two of you. I'll offer you a voyage."

"Us?" said the two young people, looking at one another.

"Unless your prejudices against me..."

"The frankness of your story has dispelled them," said Claude.

"So?"

After a brief hesitation, Edmée nodded her head, gravely. Without the slightest reticence, the young explorer said: "We accept, Monsieur."

Bowled over, Senator Dupeyroux hastened toward his secretary. "What? You're leaving? What about my interpellation? And your unfinished work, which is the lynch-pin? Such a defection is impossible! It would mean disaster for me…and ridicule…and...." He dared not add: *and my portfolio up in flames!*

"That's true," Claude sighed. "I've promised..."

Williamson intervened. "Can you not, Monsieur Rolland, do the work during the journey?"

"But what about the time it will take to reach me!" protested Dupeyroux. "The interpellation is fixed for a fortnight hence."

"Good. You'll have plenty of time. I'll have it cabled from New York."

"But that will cost..."

"A bagatelle. Come on, it's agreed. You two, rendezvous tomorrow at the Le Havre express, eight twenty-five. Toby, hat and overcoat..."

While the groom ran to fetch his master's hat and coat, the latter felt Jonathan Loeb take hold of his arm and draw him to one side.

"Do you know how that infernal Lobanief intends to make you master of the world?"

"What does it matter to you whether I know or not?"

"I've had strange reports regarding Old Sinker. That accursed demon is capable of anything, perhaps even stealing some frightful secret from God. Whatever infernal power he's conquered, he won't transmit it to you."

"Because?"

"I don't want that."

"I'm not afraid of you."

"While I'm alive, you won't go to meet that man!"

"I shall."

"Be careful—I'm powerful!"

"It's war, then."

"You'll have brought it on, and you'll see what I can do!"

Phlegmatically, Williamson put on his overcoat, which the groom was holding out to him, took his hat and replied: "As you please."

As he left, he darted a cold glance at Jonathan Loeb, who was standing with his arms folded and his lips pursed in a satanic rictus, gazing at him with hatred and defiance.

## III

The next day, at a quarter past eight, their baggage having been registered, Claude appeared, with Edmée on his arm and escorted by Jean Guitard, on the platform of the Gare Saint-Lazare.

The young explorer's energetic face respired an intense satisfaction. He was about to quit the office job for which he was so ill-made to lead the life of the open air and vast horizons that he loved, and not only without ceasing to take care of his sister, but for her and in company with her.

Edmée was a little anxious in confrontation with the double unknown of the adventure and the eccentric and scarcely sympathetic traveling companion that hazard had abruptly imposed on them.

As for Jean Guitard, the prospect of reacquainting himself with the pitching of a vessel and the briny air put quicksilver into his veins.

On the station platform, the voyagers found Toby on watch. He led them silently to the corridor carriage in which His Majesty the Mining King was already installed, very democratically for such a rich individual. Claude and Edmée, who had expected that he would have mobilized some special carriage, were a trifle disillusioned.

"Monsieur," said the explorer, greeting Williamson, "having not had the possibility of settling anything in agreement with you yesterday, I've taken the liberty of bringing my faithful manservant and former companion of my African excursions. As intelligent as he is devoted and brave, a clear-headed sailor second to none, I'm convinced that you'll have every reason to praise his services in the course of an expedition like the one we're undertaking under your benevolent and generous tutelage."

The celebrated Yankee raised his indifferent gaze as far as the meager height of Furet, who, utterly uninhibited, saluted militarily, putting his hand to his cap. "Good," he said, in a soft voice. "He can keep Toby company. Go away."

The two servants disappeared in response to a signal, to go to a nearby compartment. Williamson invited Edmée to come into his own and said, with an awkward smile: "Mademoiselle, on the railway, I'm accustomed to choosing the place with the most passengers, because the noise of conversations lulls my somnolent wait until the arrival. Because of you, I reserved a compartment. You'll have to chat a good deal between the two of you."

That kind of "consideration" left the young woman somewhat nonplussed, and her brother bit his lip in order to hold back a hostile reply.

Without paying any more heed to them than if they did not exist, Williamson nestled into his cushion, prepared by Toby, and closed his eyes.

Edmée arranged her meager feminine hand luggage, and whispered softly in her brother's ear: "Well, that's promising!"

The blast of a whistle cut through the mist. The train pulled away.

Until the express went through Mantes-la-Jolie station—which is to say, for about forty minutes—Williamson did not make a single movement.

At that moment, Edmée, who had only exchanged a few commonplace comments with her brother, embarrassed as she was by the obsessive gaze that she sensed gliding over her beneath the billionaire's eyelids, and very nervous, exclaimed: "All in all, Claude, you'll admit that it's a wrench to be on our way to the New World like this, without even knowing where we're going, nor what route we'll be taking and what stations we'll be passing through with that unknown objective."

"Why torment yourself like that, dear?"

"Things might be indifferent to you, as a man, but they're of the utmost importance to me, a woman. A man can. If necessary, go around the world with a simple valise for his underwear and toilet necessities, but it's not the same for a woman. On your advice, I've only bought two two-piece costumes, one of which I'm wearing. I'll have to complete my wardrobe at Le Havre, according to the circumstances—so it's necessary to know what they are. A woman can't dress the same for a crossing on a liner or a yacht. And when we're on the other side of the Atlantic, if Monsieur Williamson takes us to some sumptuous palace, as his residence must be, I can't present myself among elegant American ladies dressed like an errand girl delivering a hat. A Parisienne has the honor of the flag to defend! I need to know..."

That speech was intended for the Mining King—who, as Claude observed from the corner of is eyes, did not flinch.

"Little Sister," the young man decided to say, "I understand, and within the limits of my ignorance, reasoning by deduction, I'll try to enlighten you, at least partially.

"First of all, it seems evident to me that we'll be making the Ocean crossing aboard a yacht, undoubtedly superb, that Monsieur Williamson must possess."

"What makes you think so?"

"The suddenness of our departure on a Wednesday, when the Company liners only leave on Saturday. If we were taking one of them, we'd have set off three days early."

"But there isn't only the French line that goes from Le Havre—if it's really to New York that we're going!"

"Certainly, but the Holland-America Line stops over at Boulogne and the Hamburg Lines at Boulogne and Cherbourg."

"And the English liners?"

"Leave from England, and we're not going to England."

"How do you know?"

"Because then we'd have headed for the Pas-de-Calais. Our generous guide wouldn't have wasted precious time taking the slow route from Le Havre to Southampton."

Without changing his posture, Williamson finally deigned for the first time since the departure, to unseal his teeth. It was to affirm laconically: "Both in error: I have no yacht, and no residence."

Edmée uttered a brief burst of laughter, whose nervousness attenuated its pretty sonority somewhat. "Do you, by chance, intend to have us cross the Ocean swimming, and make us sleep under the stars on the other side?"

The eccentric billionaire threw back his fur, sat up, suddenly put an amiable expression over the customary nonchalant morosity of his visage, and explained: "A yacht is a chain. It's necessary to go to its home port to board it, or wait for it a long way away when one sends for it, which is incompatible with my humor.

"I've arranged with the world's principal naval constructors that they should always have a comfortable ship ready for my use at various points of the globe: Gosport in the English Channel, Hamburg in the North Sea, Rothsay on the Clyde for the Irish Sea, Libau in the Baltic, Marseilles and Brindisi in the Mediterranean, Bordeaux, New York and Rio de Janeiro in the Atlantic, Colombo in the Indian Ocean, Hong Kong in the Far East, Sydney, San Francisco and Guayaquil in the Pacific, and the Cape in South Africa. Thus, whether I'm in France, England, Scotland, Germany, Russia, Scandinavia, Spain, Italy, Greece, Turkey, India, China, Australia, South Africa, or anywhere on the American continent, I always have at my disposal, with the minimum delay, a means of traversing the seas, at home, to go wherever my fancy takes me.

"As for the residence, I'm not stupid enough to burden myself with a fixed dwelling, with a staff more master than the master, and the obligation of coming to anchor myself there to satisfy the demands of Society, when my desire is to breathe freely under another sky. As a true Yankee, my home is the hotel—that way I'm at home anywhere in the world.

"I have three hundred palaces combining all perfect comforts, thousand of valets whose hope of a princely tip exalts their zeal. All the museums of the continent are my gallery, so that I can enrich myself with some exceptional work whenever the whim takes me, and I don't have to take the risk of paying fifty or a hundred thousand dollars for a fake signature to a dealer who'll laugh at me while banking my dollars and showing off the daub to a heap of snobs who'll ecstasize over it and a few connoisseurs who'll consider me an imbecile.

"You seem surprised, the pair of you, to hear me talk so much in spite of my principles. That's because I understood that you'll keep quiet if I don't put in my share, and your voices, especially that of Mademoiselle Rolland, are a music that has an extreme charm for me. Your turn now."

"So, Monsieur," said Edmée, pulling a face that, unknown to her, made her even lovelier, "it's because the timbre of our voices pleases you that you decided to take us with you?"

"Why do you want me to do it?"

"One isn't so frank."

"I'm not the billionaire Williamson in order to embarrass myself with hypocritical formulas."

"So it's not only to do a favor for worthy young people like us, too poor to be able, without assistance, to take care of their interests?"

"I never do favors, on principle."

"And to attract their sincere gratitude?"

"That word represents something non-existent."

"Admit, at least, that my womanly pride might be wounded on seeing myself reduced to the role of a music-box."

"I'm very fond of music-boxes. I have several of them in each of 'my' hotels, and they're all marvels. I give myself concerts, all alone, in my room, to put me to sleep…as your legendary Montaigne used to put himself to sleep in childhood. As regards feminine pride, I have the right to ignore it, never having encountered any example of it."

"I shall therefore impose on myself, from this moment on, the most absolute silence. And if my voice is agreeable to you, I shall have the regret, for the sake of my demonstration, of deriving you of it."

"Oh, you're always annoying me!"

"The music box having become voluntarily silent, you may abandon us, if you wish, at Le Havre station."

"What about your fortune?"

"I wouldn't even pay for your fortune with a single humiliation."

"What if I take you at your word?"

"We'll take the first train back to Paris, won't we, Claude?"

"Certainly, my dear," the explorer agreed.

The Mining King fell silent for a long moment, making a grimace of irritation. Then, suddenly, he said: "In that case, you'll accompany me to the end, because I retract what I said and apologize. You're both so strangely new to me, who has thus far only encountered servile complaisance. I'll take you all the way to Lobanief, and tell him what independent individuals you are. And I'll hear your charming voice, Miss, even if I have to talk myself from here until New York to get you to reply to me. Is it like that that it's necessary to speak?"

"Yes, Monsieur," said Edmée, intimately flattered by the small victory that she had just won. "To demonstrate your kind dispositions, tell us about our strange relative, whom we're going with you to meet."

"No, not that—not here at least. When we're between the sea and the sky, yes; here, there are too many ears, in spite of the noise of the machinery—free ears, I mean."

"At least you'll tell us where we're going to meet him?"

"No."

"May we know why not?"

"The best reason in the world—because I don't know, and will only learn myself when we make landfall."

"Which is where?"

"I can reveal that even less than everything else," Williamson declared, his expression preoccupied, darting an anxious glance through the closed interior door at two passengers who were going along the corridor of the carriage.

"I have no luck!" exclaimed Edmée tapping the floor of the carriage with a petulant foot.

"Listen, Miss Rolland—I may call you that, may I not, since we're going to a country where English is spoken, and it's easier for me to pronounce than your incommensurable

Mademoiselle—I shall have a great deal that is very curious to tell you concerning…the man who is summoning me. I told the exact truth yesterday at the Continental Hotel in relating publicly the rescue that was the origin of my great situation, but I didn't reveal the profoundly strange circumstances that had led the unique individual to whom you are distantly related to the waters of the Hudson. That story, I promise the two of you, but only when I judge that prudence will permit me to tell it to you. Between now and then, grant me the credit of a little patience and…let's talk about anything except the objective of our voyage."

And all the way to Le Havre, Williamson, who had been traveling the world in fantastic zigzags for fifteen years and had seen everything, with an eye that had only gradually become blasé and indifferent, revealed himself to his companions as an agreeable conversationalist full of memories and verve.

It was a sudden metamorphosis, with which Edmée's keen feminine intuition made her understand that she was not unconnected.

Animated by that unexpected success, she made her own contribution of wit. As that wit was one of the most lively— she surpassed her brother in that respect—Williamson, enchanted, declared that she alone had more humor than all the daughters of Eve that he had encountered during his existence as a rich nomad.

On arrival at Le Havre, the Mining King, having engaged in such a copious and light-hearted dialogue, had a glint in his eye and color in his complexion. Toby was open-mouthed; he no longer recognized his master. How could he have recognized him, when the true Williamson—the one behind the mask—was unknown to everyone, including himself?

Terrible events were about to furnish that repellently enclosed soul and that triply-immured heart with the opportunity to release themselves from their prison.

# Chapter I
## *Battle is Joined*

By a miracle of feminine magic, it was an almost amiably loquacious Williamson who set foot on the platform of Le Havre station in the company of Claude and Edmée Rolland. There is nothing like the taciturn for not knowing how to stop, once they have broken their customary morose mutism.

That abnormal state explains why the Mining King, who had promised himself to maintain a particular vigilance, did not perceive that when he left the station, two men, one of whom was very tall, with the peak of a traveling cap pulled down over his eyes and a muffler covering the lower part of his face, followed the three new arrivals at a distance, climbing into a vehicle that followed their own, and, having seen them get out at the Hôtel de Normandie in what is now the Place Gambetta, had themselves taken swiftly to the extremity of the harbor, to the point where the jetty begins, level with the Hôtel Frascati.

There, the taller one said to the other: "Go back to our sleazy hotel—you'll get in my way otherwise—and don't come out before I come to fetch you. Above all, on your life, not a word to anyone of what I've allowed myself to tell you on the way about Old Sinker!"

"Unnecessary recommendation," the other replied. "I'm not naïve enough to go telling tall tales of that sort!"

"Go!" commanded the first, in a rude voice.

While the hired vehicle conveyed his companion to the Rue de Paris he muttered: "It's as well that that fellow's a Frenchman. He's not worthy to be a Yankee."

Turing stiffly on his heel, he went at a long stride to the Chamber of Commerce, where he addressed himself to the watchman.

"Has the steam-yacht *Astrea*, announced on your list, been sighted?"

"Not yet," was the response.

Retracing his steps, the interminable individual went to pace back and forth along the embarkation quay for the boats from Le Havre to Honfleur, Trouville and Caen. From there it was easy for him to keep watch on the exit from the Rue de Paris to the harbor.

In these two individuals you will have recognized Grégoire de Montalpé and Jonathan Loeb. The previous evening they had left the Hôtel Continental on the heels of Claude and Edmée Rolland, accompanied by the faithful Jean Guitard, alias Furet, who were following as they retreated by the Mining King, escorted by the inflexible groom.

Then, while the "Williamson camp" had put off their departure until the following morning, Loeb had demanded that de Montalpé, exceedingly but futilely recalcitrant, impose on himself the fatigue of a seven-hour train journey on the slow train leaving the Gare Saint-Lazare at forty-five minutes past midnight, the eleven-thirty express not leaving them enough time to make the most summary preparations.

What was Loeb going to do in Le Havre, where no liner was leaving for America or England, and why had he wanted to get there ahead of Williamson? That can be partially explained by the following dialogue, between him and his companion and travel-cashier, the previous night, on the train.

"Why have ourselves jolted around all night—a real party what!—when there's an express in the morning!"

"Williamson will take it."

"Exactly. It's the best means of not losing track of him."

"We haven't only to follow the Mining King. If we get ahead of him at Le Havre, we might have a stroke of luck—not probable, but possible."

"What?"

"That of finding out what ship he's using to cross the Atlantic."

"That's easy, since the transatlantic liner that will leave on Saturday is in dock at..."

"He won't take the liner."

"How do you know?"

"I know; that's sufficient."

"Then we're going to lose track of him when he leaves Le Havre."

"Yes."

"In that case, it's not worth the trouble of hurrying."

"Yes, one of two things must happen: either I'll be able to take action in Le Havre, in which case we can wait tranquilly until the French ship leaves on Saturday, or I won't, and it'll be necessary for us to go to Boulogne, Cherbourg or Liverpool in order not to miss the first Dutch, German or English ship...for it's vital, at all costs to reach the American shore twenty-four hours before him."

"A race! And a long distance! Oh la la! I'll be worn out! Try, then, to take 'action' in Le Havre."

"I will, if chance favors me—as it probably will."

"And from New York, where are we going?"

"Straight for that demon Old Sinker."

"Otherwise known as Lob..."

"Shut up! On your soul, never pronounce that name."

"On the train, who do you think...?"

"What do you know? Anyway, if it ever emerges from your mouth without my permission, I'll cut out your tongue."

"What? No stupidity!"

"Take that as read."

"Sure! And where will we find him, this...Old Sinker?"

"That's the sole point that I need to elucidate. It doesn't worry me, I've discovered, in two minutes, all the rest of Williamson's secret."

"When?"

"Before your very eyes a few hours ago, at the Continental."

"What secret?"

"Capital: the sign and...something else."

"What sign?"

Loeb took a copy of the New York *Herald* from his pocket, bought immediately after he had left the Centrale celebration with de Montalpé. The American newspaper was folded to display the personal ads. With his finger pointing at the right place, he showed the newspaper to his companion.

"This one!"

"Oh! That's odd, that...but...it's a globe run through by a dagger."

Loeb furrowed his bushy eyebrows gravely.

"I've had strange reports about that damned Old Sinker! Many years ago, he said something terrible, something corroborated in a redoubtable fashion by that sign, devised by him for his secret correspondence with the Mining King."

"Get away! The hieroglyph is naively clear! A man who, you told me, spends his life digging holes in the ground..."

"O futile Frenchman, who stops at appearances and explains everything in a word, without ever delving deeper!"

"What do you want me to delve into? The holes that your Old Sinker digs? No thanks—I'll leave subterranean enterprises to the moles."

"Know that the man in question has said: 'The earth is malevolent to humans; it deserves to die.'"

"For the good of humanity? That's a lunatic's reasoning! To summon the end of the world to embellish existence, when it would simply destroy it? If he really used that incoherent language, my excessively-alive relative has a spider in his skull."

"Make no mistake—Old Sinker is a genius. That he's inspired by Hell, I don't doubt, but he's nonetheless capable of anything."

"Not of icing the planet, I imagine!"

"Who knows?"

That was too much for de Montalpé, who nearly choked with laughter, and exclaimed: "Oh yes! The sign! The dagger-thrust...in the fashion of our apache cut-throats! Ha ha ha! That's a good one, my dear!"

Loeb was not laughing. He looked at his traveling companion with a gaze in which irritation attenuated the scornful pity.

When de Montalpé had recovered a little of his serious-ness, he concluded: "Anyway whether the fellow is as made as they say, and whether all Yankees are the same way, or not, is an irrelevant question. The only thing that interests me is whether, alive or dead, genius or madman, he'll let me get my hands on the inheritance in suspension…before the final dead-line. That's the only serious thing; I'm risking everything I have left on you, and I expect that still holds, eh?"

"More than ever. My hatred will answer to you for that."

"Good! That's talking in human terms. Let's leave it there, if you please, and try to get some sleep. If we don't have time to get some tomorrow night, it's only prudent to get a little in advance. Good night! Oh, no—cutting the throat of the world…that's a good one."

Shaken by a slight residue of hilarity, the elegant Grégoire went to sleep, while Jonathan Loeb, his eyes fixed, pursued some somber dream, wide awake.

When, after an ample lunch, such as one obtains in good provincial hotels, Williamson, Claude and Edmée emerged in a carriage from the Rue de Paris on to the waterfront, with Toby, as stiff as a stick, beside the coachman, Loeb took cover swiftly, and then, seeing the adverse trio get down on the edge of the north jetty, followed them at a considerable distance, but in such a fashion as not to lose sight of them.

As he went past the post office, which forms the corner of the street and the quay, Jean Guitard, alias Furet, came out, having gone in to expedite a few postcards that Edmée wanted to send to her friends before departure.

At the sight of the tall silhouette of the Yankee, the mar-iner shivered. Without being exactly well-informed with re-gard to Loeb, he had discovered or divined enough to esteem the presence of that individual in Le Havre abnormal at the moment when Williamson and his young masters were pass-ing through.

Moving adroitly, he observed him, and soon saw him go to the edge of the dock, take a pair of binoculars from his pocket and study the sea, and then turn around abruptly and draw away at a rapid stride, heading directly away from the sea.

Furet then hastened to rejoin his masters on the jetty, where, following the billionaire's example, they were busy observing a ship that was heading toward the harbor from the open sea under full steam.

"The *Astrea*, Commandant?" he asked Claude.

"Yes. What a mover, eh? She'll be in the harbor within three-quarters of an hour."

The mariner tugged gently at the young mariner's sleeve, drawing him to one side.

"You have something to tell me?"

"Yes, Commandant. You know the individual who took your seat beside the senator last night…?"

"Jonathan Loeb. Well?"

"He's here and he's spying on us. He saw the *Astrea* and veered away from our wake."

Rolland immediately informed Williamson of the fact. The latter shrugged his shoulders. "The effort will be futile," he said, pursing his lips disdainfully. And he resumed observing the ship.

Forty minutes had not gone by when the superb yacht, rigged as a three-masted schooner, approached the jetties at half-speed, stopped in the outer harbor and then moved slowly to the level the Quai Notre-Dame. There she moored on a cathead anchor and, there being no danger of any encumbrance because the tide was going out, immediately made her dispositions to turn around and head westwards, in case she had to sail at a moment's notice.

Several small boats presented themselves to bring mooring ropes, and their assistance was not refused by the mate who was responsible for the maneuver, while the commandant, the launch having been lowered, had himself taken to the shore.

Williamson and his companions, who had quit the north jetty and were following a course along the quay parallel to that of the *Astrea*, but at a lesser speed, had scarcely arrived at the corner of the Quai Notre-Dame than the commandant of the yacht set foot there.

The Mining King advanced toward the officer and introduced himself. "Williamson!"

"Captain Burner," replied the impeccably-dressed and extensively-braided mariner, saluting.

"Good. Are you ready to put to sea?"

"Immediately, if you give the order."

"What! What about my clothes, my indispensable purchases, my preparations?" said Edmée, in alarm, to her brother, on whose arm she was leaning elegantly. The latter gestured to her to be quiet.

Captain Burner explained to Williamson: "I'll make the observation to you that we'd only gain an insignificant amount of time in the crossing by making ready to sail now. The embarkation of baggage and the formalities will take at least an hour. Only two hours would remain before low water, which means that as we headed out to see we'd encounter the incoming tide, with a head-wind, which wouldn't permit us to make much progress. By sailing this evening, an hour after high water, we'd have the current to take us out of the Channel, and there's a chance that the fresh breeze blowing in mid-Channel will have calmed by sunset."

"So be it. Ready to sail at..."

"Eight o'clock."

"Did you hear?" asked Williamson, addressing Claude and his sister, who nodded. "Free time until then. Oh, wait a moment, Miss Edmée!" He turned to the captain. "When I cabled for the ship, I asked that a chambermaid be embarked...?"

"She's on board."

"Well chosen?"

"The best available, given that we only had three hours to search, at night. Not young or pretty, but she's sailed before, which is an important point, and has references. Does the Miss want me to disembark her?"

45

"No thank you, Captain—I don't have time to make her acquaintance while running round the shops. I'm very grateful to Mr. Williamson for his attention, and most of all for having thought of it. What is her name?"

"Grace."

"Ah! A promising forename."

"More than it delivers, I warn you, Miss," said the Captain, who was a handsome man, still young, sketching a smile. "Grace Strangestorm. Look—there she is."

The mariner pointed at a tall individual with a jaundiced complexion, clad in black, who appeared to be very busy listening to what a man in an oilskin and coifed in a mariner's sou-wester was saying to her.

Edmée pulled a light face. "She has a rather tempestuous name and doesn't look very lively," she said, laughing, "but for the little use I'll make of her, she'll still be sufficient."

"I'll go aboard with you, Captain," said Williamson. Addressing the fraternal couple, he added: "Until this evening. We'll have supper as soon as we're out of the harbor. Be on time for casting off."

The Mining King got down into the launch with the Captain, and Edmée, on Claude's arm and escorted by Jean Guimard, headed back to the Rue de Paris cheerfully, in quest of her numerous and various purchases.

At eight o'clock precisely, the steam-yacht *Astrea* churned up the waters of the harbor with her double propeller, *en route* for a night at sea and the waves of the Atlantic.

At the extremity of the north jetty, two men watched the nocturnal departure. When the yacht began to salute the slight swell that welcomed it at the port entrance with its prow, one of them articulated in a hoarse voice, with a satanic rictus on his lips, a "Bon voyage!" replete with hateful irony.

His companion, warmly wrapped up in a fur coat with the collar raised, said to him, in a tone of mediocre satisfaction: "They've gone, though, all the same."

"Let them go."

"What about us?"

"We'll wait tranquilly for Saturday's steamer."

"You've taken action, then."

"Yes, since the imbeciles left me the time to do so, when they could so easily have slipped through my fingers by taking to the sea when their boat arrived, Oh, Monsieur de Montalpé, if the old crackpots of the mysticism of Albion didn't exist, it would be necessary to invent them. When they put their minds to it, they're worth ten men. By Jove, I need to laugh this evening. There's a music hall here—let's go, as men satisfied with a good day's work, to finish the evening joyfully there."

# Chapter II
## *The Catastrophe*

Whoever has not spent at least a few days traveling on a great yacht is ignorant of the most perfect delight that fortune reserves for its exceptional elect, as well as their parasites...on condition, of course, that none of them are subject to the disagreeable symptoms *sui generis* that can be produced by the sway of the swell.

Williamson and Claude were vaccinated against all the choreographic fantasies of the waves. Edmée, who was entering for the first into enduring coquetry with Neptune, would perhaps not have been insensible to the serious rudeness of the sea, but the latter, by the eighth day of the voyage had not yet wearied of giving evidence of a gallant clemency with which few voyagers can flatter themselves that they have been favored to such an extent.

There was only a little fatigue on departure, for the breeze, as Captain Burner had hoped, had softened while the *Astrea* waited in port for the tide, and when, on the afternoon of the next day, the yacht doubled the isles of Scilly—which the French call the Sorlingues—situated south of Land's End and making a pendant with our Île d'Ouessant to mark, in the north, the extreme limit of the Channel, she found a calm in the Atlantic that was not belied by the following days.

The voyage was a genuine enchantment, and, the human mind having a tendency to consider a fortunate beginning as a favorable augury with regard to ensuing events, everyone aboard should have been manifesting a confidence full of security.

"Everyone," however, would be saying too much. It is necessary to make an exception for the chambermaid of the young and lovely passenger Edmée Rolland, the tall, thin, jaundiced, mature and sectarian Miss Grace Strangestorm. Was it the predestination of a tempestuous name that influenced the character of the nautical maidservant? At any rate, correctly stiff and opposed to any physical movement, she was mentally the most unquiet, the most exalted and the most troubled and troubling of creatures.

"It's the most extravagant type of old Anglo-Saxon spinster that, in complicity with hazard, you've given me for a chambermaid, Monsieur Williamson!" Edmée said to the Mining King that evening, when, between him and her brother, she had stretched herself out comfortably in a padded wicker armchair after supper, in the vast saloon of the yacht, offering her finely-shod Parisienne feet to the sunset.

"What has she said or done now, your Grace?"

"It amuses you when I relate my little arguments with her, and the continual surprises she causes me?"

"You recount them with so much humor, Miss Edmée, and your voice takes on even more charming intonations. I can assure you that if your chambermaid provokes astonishments in you, they bear no comparison to those you provide for me. You're both changing and fixed, prettily cheerful and, at times, as serious as a man…and with that, so intellectually correct and independent! I've never seen that before."

"That's because you haven't taken the trouble to look."

"All the women I've encountered before you have always put on a performance in my intention, either of laughter or of sentiment. You, you're just yourself, as if I weren't here."

"That's doubtless because your millions of dollars don't dazzle me."

"That's extraordinary. You're an enigma."

"Not very difficult to decipher…isn't that so Claude?"

"Little Sister, your portrait can be painted in three strokes: good and brave heart, honest and frank character, served by a keen wit and an open intelligence. There is, besides, the spontaneity of a true young Frenchwoman, which you are in the fullest sense of the term."

"I protest," declared Williamson, *ex professo*. "Miss Edmée is an exceptional individual."

"For you, perhaps, who have only seen human societies under the mirage of your…how shall I put it?…your royalty, but not for the young men of my homeland. Ask Claude! Come on, Monsieur Williamson, I don't have any pretention to being a phenomenon, and it annoys me considerable to be considered as such, for I have a horror of phenomena, of whatever nature they might be. So, if you'd like my…ancillary story…?"

"Please."

"Well, here it is: you know that the respectable Grace doesn't give me a minute's…grace on the question of my salvation. I've already told you that she wakes me up by intoning a psalm, helps me to get dressed while talking to me about our final destiny, and in the evening, never lets me go to bed without warning me about the eternal torments of Hell. I wonder why I don't dream, every night, about horned devils, and damned souls that have our faces writhing in the flames. Fortunately, I have a tranquil conscience as well as a sound stomach, and, in consequence, no tendency to nightmares. But now preaching no longer suffices her zeal for my eternity; she's passed from somberly lugubrious exhortation to action."

"How so?"

"Listen, Brother. This morning, woken up by the first rays of the sun sliding through my porthole, delightfully rocked by a gentle swell, I experienced a desire to linger in bed a little later than usual. So, when Grace entered discreetly, I watched the woman through barely-parted eyelashes, who contemplated me in silence with an expression simultaneously ecstatic, dolorous and…ardent. When she was quite certain of the profundity of my sleep, she unhooked, with a rapid gesture, the lifejacket that a forethought with which I have no argument had placed aboard within reach of passengers.

"What an odd idea!" exclaimed Claude.

"The action did, indeed, demand an explanation. As she beat a retreat with the fruit of her larceny, I called out: 'Why, Grace, what are you doing?' She turned round without making any attempt hide the…*corpus delicti*.

"'Miss,' she said to me, gravely, 'our existences are in the hands of the Lord. His divine wisdom has fixed their term, and it in His hands alone that we should put ourselves with regard to our final hour down here. An object such as this one is impious, in that it marks a pretention on our part to oppose the verdict of Heaven. If Our Lord sends us to shipwreck, it's because he has decided to recall us to Him, and out obedience to his decisions forbids us to do anything to exempt ourselves from His will.'

"And she went out deliberately, taking the lifejacket with her."

"The woman is mad!" protested the Mining King. "I'll give the order to have the flotation apparatus in your cabin replaced immediately."

"What's the point, Monsieur Williamson? We'll soon be arriving in America, the weather is superb—and then, why disturb the poor soul in her crazy mysticism? I can assure you that I surprise, at times, the expression of a martyr...although it's true that at others..."

"At others?"

"Perhaps I shouldn't say this, and you might accuse my changing humor of being in haste to demolish the saint as soon as I've put her in her niche. After all, *honni soit qui mal y pense*...but ten times in the last three days, I've surprised my austere quakeress[5] deep in conversation with a crewman—a tall fellow with a somber air, whom I've often seen at the helm."

---

[5] The author inserts a footnote at this point translating "Quakeress" as *Trembleuse* and adding the remark: "a Protestant sect further exaggerating our Jansenism," which is by no means an accurate characterization of the Society of Friends, the most sober and determinedly pacifist of all Christian sects. Edmée, as a devout Catholic, might not know the difference (extreme as it is) between a Quaker and a member of the Salvation Army, but it is not an error that reflects well on her or her author.

"A helmsman! Wait a moment, Sister. Dark-haired, isn't he, will a full beard, sort and bushy...and a scar on the right side of his forehead."

"That's the one."

"I've noticed him too, and I asked the Captain his name, which is Smith. He's apparently very serious in service, but has one foible, which is that of not wanting to go to his bunk when his watch finishes. He claims that he finds it stifling in the crew quarters, and as he's found it uncomfortable there twice he's been authorized to sleep on deck."

"I understand, then, why Miss Strangestorm is always sure of finding him there," said Edmée, smiling maliciously.

"An idyll in tarpaulin," said the billionaire, with a mocking expression.

"It's more likely, I presume," the young woman retorted, "that he's a neophyte that my chambermaid is catechizing, doubtless with more success than me, given that I'm as far from fanatical excess as from incredulity."

Williamson shrugged his shoulders slightly.

"The foundation of the feminine character being hypocrisy..."

"Thanks!"

"I've told you, Miss Edmée, that you're an exception! Thus, for this Grace, I believe her to be quite capable of allying the most exalted religious mysticism with...with..."

Edmée came to his aid, laughing. "With preoccupations as terrestrial as they are profane?"

"That's right."

"Well, I don't share your opinion. I have the conviction that Grace lives as little as possible on earth, and hat her ardent eyes, which seem to be getting more hollow by the hour, are solely hypnotized by visions of a sacred beyond. Since we've been aboard, she hasn't belied her role as a living Bible, except on one point, on the subject of which you know that I share her curiosity."

"The agreed point to which I need to go in case of a summons from Old Sinker?"

"Yes, Monsieur Williamson. I understand that, once we were embarked, you wanted to keep the secret for the first few days after we had quit Europe, but now that we're so close to disembarking and heading toward the unknown rendez-vous...for it's true, isn't it, that we're approaching New York?"

"Miss, when Captain Burner took a point at midday, we were at 70° 55' 45" west longitude...."

"From the English Greenwich meridian?" specified the young engineer/explorer.

"Naturally."

"Well, as Greenwich, 5' 45" east of London, is 2° 20' 40" west of the zero French median, that's 73° 16' of west longitude..."

"Exactly, but as the United States, like almost everyone in the world, has adopted the Greenwich meridian..."

"Oh, I don't have any self-respect invested in it, Monsieur Williamson—except that, as I've brought a French chart of New York and its maritime approaches, I'm underlining the differences aloud in order to engrave them on my memory and rectify my own calculations with regard to the English baseline. Forgive me for having interrupted you."

"I was saying that at midday we were at 70° 55' 45" of longitude west...of Greenwich. As, since then, we've been heading due west and making an average of sixteen knots, and as the distance between two consecutive degrees of meridian, which is, at the equator—employing your metric measures for convenience—one thousand eleven hundred meters, is no more, at our latitude, than about forty-four miles, or eighty-one and a half kilometers...that means that presently, at nine ç 'clock in the evening, we ought to be...well, calculate it, Monsieur Engineer."

"I've already done it, while you were talking," said Claude, completing a rapid operation in his notebook. At this moment we're 75° 30' of longitude west of Paris, or 73° 9' 45" of longitude west of Greenwich."

"Good. Now, as New York is, in round numbers, at 74° west longitude, in English terms, the distance that separates us is ten minutes less than a degree, which is..."

"Fifty-one and a third miles, or ninety-five kilometers, just less than a hectometer."

"Still as far as that?"

"Oh, it's child's play, Miss Edmée. At our speed of sixteen knots we'll be there in...in...Oh, I'm too lazy to calculate. What is it, Mr. Rolland?"

"Three and a quarter hours."

"With the result that we'll be entering the Hudson in the middle of the night. And I was so looking forward to the spectacle of that arrival! I shan't see a thing."

"Unfortunately, that's true, Miss, but on the other hand, we have every chance of passing unnoticed and leaving New York before anyone catches wind of our presence on American soil—and I have serious reasons for considering that as good fortune."

"Then it's almost as if, from now on, we're on our way to the unknown rendezvous point to which you're taking us?"

"That's exactly right."

"In that case, I don't understand what interest your excessive prudence has in keeping it from us any longer."

"In truth, Miss, you're logic personified."

"So you're finally going to tell us?"

"Shortly. But as it would be rather difficult to explain, insofar as you don't have all the geographical details of North America presently in mind..."

"Not precisely, in fact..."

"I'll need..."

"A map?"

"Yes. And I don't know if I'll find one easily on board, where the collection of marine charts is certainly complete, but as regards terrestrial map...."

"I have what you need."

"You?"

"Not me, but that illuminate Grace Strangestorm. Outside of her minimal service, when she isn't preaching, praying or absorbing herself in some poignant meditation, she contemplates a large map of North America suspended in her cabin. Do you want me to ring for her?"

"Do…and give her the order yourself; it's so agreeable to listen to you."

Edmée pressed the call button and Toby appeared immediately, in his immaculate high collar.

"Fetch the chambermaid, right away."

Grace Strangestorm, more jaundiced and stiffer than ever, in her narrow black dress, soon appeared on the threshold of the sumptuous saloon.

"Do you still have that map of North America that I've seen in your cabin, pinned to the wall?"

"Yes, Miss," the Englishwoman replied, with difficulty, so much were her bloodless lips trembling, and in a hoarse voice, her throat having suddenly contracted, while her sunken eyes lit up with a sudden gleam.

"Will you bring it to us, please. We have to look at it for…something."

The chambermaid turned on her heel and departed like an arrow.

"Did you see her eyes light up with joy?" said Edmée to the two men.

"I didn't suspect that compassed creature of having such an intensity of gaze," observed Claude.

Without having made a movement, Williamson muttered between his teeth from the depths of his armchair: "I don't like such a violent and inexplicable curiosity—for you haven't promised, I suppose, Miss, to take her with us when we disembark?"

"I haven't even given it a thought, but in her holy ardor for the salvation of my soul, perhaps she's hopeful."

"Well, she'll be wrong, for I beg you, if you please, not to accede to her pleas if she addresses any to you. As I'm convinced that you'll keep to yourselves what I'm going to…indicate to you, her shocking curiosity won't be satisfied, for she won't know, even if she's listening—of which I think her perfectly capable—whether it's to the north, west or south that we'll be heading before daybreak."

Grace reappeared, holding her unfolded map. This time it was without haste, very calm in her stiff dignity, that she went to set it out on the large table with castors, in old mahogany, edged with marquetry. Without Williamson, who was about to do so, having any need to order her peremptorily to go away, she withdrew discreetly, and closed the door behind her.

That attitude brought a frown-line to the billionaire's forehead, which was immediately effaced. He went to the table.

"Open your eyes, both of you, because I won't pronounce a name," he said. "I shan't articulate a single word, and you'll do me the favor of following my example."

He took a pencil from his pocket, of which he broke off the lead, and, after having taken a moment to get his bearings, he placed the point of the stick on a spot close to which the sinuous line of a river could be seen to run.

The two young people looked at him interrogatively. Only his eyelids responded positively. Then leaving the brother and sister time to take account of the designated geographical point, he put his index finger across his lips and, quitting the table—from which Claude and Edmée also drew away—he went to press the call button.

As before, Toby presented himself and received the order to summon the chambermaid. The latter returned in response to a sign, picked up the map and drew away at a measured pace, after having bowed ceremoniously, attentively followed by the gaze of the Mining King.

When the door closed again, the latter shrugged his shoulders slightly and dubiously. He would not have done so if he had seen her, once in her cabin, throw herself to her knees, her arms forming a cross, her gaze ecstatic, exhaling in a single breath: "Lord, you have finally wished it! Be glorified by your humble servant, who places herself in your divine hands!"

Then she took the map, which she had deposited on her bunk, folded it up carefully, inserted it into a flat metal case which she slid into her corsage, and leaving her cabin silently, went up on to the deck.

In the saloon, Edmée said to the billionaire: "I'm very grateful to you, Monsieur Williamson, for granting my wish. Now that I know what fatigues await us I ask your permission to take advantage of the brief hours of travel that remain to us to prepare myself for them with a little sleep."

"That's reasoning and acting sagely, Miss Edmée. Unless something unexpected occurs, I don't think you'll have to leave the ship until three or four o'clock in the morning."

Edmée Roland retired to her cabin and, glad to have avoided her lugubrious preacher for once, went to bed and, very happy with a life that was both opulent and mildly adventurous, did not take long to fall asleep with a smile on her lips.

"The night is splendid. If it would interest you as much as it would me to see the lights of the American coast appear on the horizon, come and smoke a few Havanas on the bridge."

"Delighted to follow you, Monsieur Williamson, and believe that, for my part, I wouldn't have missed it."

On the bridge they found Captain Burner, who, by reason of the imminent landfall, had come to take up his command post. The mate and the first lieutenant, the officer of the watch, were with him.

"Well, Captain?"

"I proclaim, sir that you can never have made such a fine crossing. Since emerging from the Channel we've scarcely seen a cloud, and one couldn't ask for a more splendid night to conclude the voyage."

"You haven't seen anything yet?"

"Not so far, but it can't be long. And look, there's a light fore and starboard, emerging from the water. Perfectly…blinking at fifteen second intervals. That's the floating light at Sandy Hook!"

"My compliments, Captain. It's impossible to make landfall with more magisterial precision."

"Commanding a ship in these conditions in very easy; everything has gone as one would wish in the marvelous voyage."

"Including my famous work," said the senator's former secretary, smiling. "Thanks to the constantly calm sea, I haven't suffered any interruption or inconvenience, and I can guarantee that Monsieur Dupeyroux will be content. If, with that redoubtable document, he doesn't acquire the morocco that is the object of his ardent desire, he'll have been very maladroit—and if, by following the indications once in power, he doesn't achieve fortunate results for the country, it will be because he really doesn't want to!"

"On that subject, Monsieur Rolland," declared the billionaire, "as we're only going to be passing through New York by night, I've given your manuscript, and a check, to Captain Burner, who will take charge of cabling your copy tomorrow morning, as agreed. Tomorrow evening, the future minister will be in possession of the political weapon that you've forged for him."

Claude thanked him, and as, when the cigars were lit, the conversation on the bridge became general and animated, he took advantage of it to stretch his legs by taking a turn around the deck. Almost at the foot of the iron ladder he found Jean Guitard, who, with his hands deep in the pockets of his blue bell-bottoms—since Le Havre he had been exchanged his suit, too terrestrial for his taste, for a matelot's uniform—was pacing back and forth, head down, like a wild beast in a cage.

"What's the matter with you?" asked the young man, amused.

"I'm eaten up with boredom, Commandant, and bogged down in a dull anger. It's high time the crossing ended, or I won't be able to contain myself any longer, in spite of my desire not to cause you any annoyance…and watch out, if Furet brings his fists and his kick-boxing into play!"

"Good God! Who's upset you?"

"All of them…and one in particular."

Come on, calm down. Tell me about it—that will help."

"Commandant, you know as well as I do how it is between French *mathurins* and English *bluecoats*. The *entente cordiale* only ever existed in regulation manifestations and on the surface, in mutual receptions during political visits of squadrons. Apart from that, their mariners and our mariners are as friendly as cats and dogs. All those here, since I've been assigned a bunk in their quarters, have had less regard for me than if I were cockroach; none of them talk to me, and in their midst I'm more in quarantine than an infectious case stuck in an isolation ward. At least, when I'm obliged to ask them for something, in the good English that I've learned on your instructions, most of the *rosbifs* content themselves with looking at me and replying *yes, no, over there* or *I don't know*—but there's one of them who affects to turn his head and switch his tobacco plug from side to side without unclenching his teeth. Oh, the dirty caulker!

"I've had to hold myself back several times from ramming his fat belly all the way to his throat with a good kick in the…figure! Three days ago I look at him in such a fashion that he understood and since then he's been avoiding me—and it's me, since then, who's been sticking to his wake."

"Why seek him out? If it's to provoke a quarrel, you know, I'd be extremely annoyed."

"No danger; I only follow him at a distance. It's because, Commandant, I'll tell you, he's got a shady manner that I don't like, the dirty dog. Look…under the bridge…"

"But that's…if I'm not mistaken…the one called Smith."

"Exactly, Commandant."

"And who seems to be paying court to the maid put in my sister's service, unless it's the other way round?"

"She came here not ten minutes ago, bringing him something that he hid in his jersey double quick."

"Some sentimental token."

"They don't have an amorous look about them, those two. I've had my eye on him since Le Havre; we were already on board when he came back, hoisting himself up on a bit of hawser that a comrade threw down to him. I understand that a man might have shore leave, but since the ship's boats were going back and forth all the time, why would the mysterious seaman do that? On top of that, he has somber and searching eyes. In sum, he's a fellow I don't like. I believe him to be capable of more dirty tricks, and I can do other than keep track of him."

"Leave it, Jean. We'll be arriving soon, and as we'll be leaving the coast as soon as we've disembarked, you won't see him again."

"That will be with please, Commandant."

"You know that we're within sight of the Sandy Hook lightship, anchored only a few miles from the entrance to New York Bay, formed by the Hudson estuary?"

"I've seen it, Commandant. Look, there it is...and, look!"

"What!"

"There's a ship in sight, just beyond the Sandy Hook lightship."

"What eyes you have! I have excellent eyesight, and I can't see anything. I'll go back up the bridge and borrow the watch officer's binoculars."

Claude did exactly that. Through the instrument, he observed that the ship in question was carrying three lights in a triangle, of which the positional lights—of which the green was visible to his right and the red to his left—formed the base and a white light the apex. He concluded that it was a steamer heading toward the *Astrea*, and following exactly the same course in an opposite direction.

He signaled his discovery to the officers, who did not even take the trouble to confirm it, the appearance of a distant ship being of absolutely no importance in current navigation.

It was not the same when, a quarter of an hour later, when the two boats were a good deal closer, a rocket went up from that same ship, streaking the night with a thin luminous track, and, almost immediately, a rocket responded almost immediately from the Astrea, bursting above the bridge into white, red and green stars.

Captain Burner leaned over the rail of the bridge immediately and shouted, angrily: "What are you doing, Smith?"

The man addressed, who had returned to the helm, replied: "The rocket at sea aft is obviously a distress signal. I fired immediately to signal *seen*."

"Who gave you the order?"

"I thought it a duty..."

"You thought wrong! It's a serious failure of discipline, unforgivable on the part of a serious and punctilious helmsman like you. And why have you fired, instead of an ordinary rocket, a particular rocket used as a recognition signal between ships of our line?"

"In my haste I mistook the compartment in the locker."

"You'll be punished! To begin with, when we arrive in port, you'll be confined to quarters until further notice."

The punishment must have been indifferent to helmsman Smith, because his lips creased in an ironic smile.

"Steer for that ship," the Commandant commanded him. Addressing Williamson, he added: "We'll go and see what they want, inasmuch as it won't take us off course. If it really is in distress, as its speed and the fact that's its steering away from land doesn't seem to indicate, it'll renew its signal rocket at brief intervals—which doesn't seem to be its intention."

For ten minutes, the two steamers continued to head toward one another. Now, scarcely half a mile separated them. To judge by the height of the position lights above the water, the ship maintaining the course opposite to that of the *Astrea* had to be a large cargo-vessel, unladen—which rendered the eastward course that it was following rather abnormal, for a ship would not use up the amount of coal necessary to cross the Atlantic without at least being compensated by the price of the cargo it was transporting.

Captain Burner thought about that, and expected to see the cargo-vessel change course at any moment toward the north or the south, heading toward some American port.

Nothing of the sort: the distance was still decreasing. Captain Burner ordered the helmsman: "Two quarters to starboard!"

The "quarter" of the compass being 11° 15' of the circle of the "rose," steering two quarters to starboard would reset a course west-north-west instead of west. According to the international shipping regulations, the cargo-vessel ought to do the same, and both of them, both steering to the right like road-vehicles on a boulevard, would mutually move out of one another's path.

But Smith, doubtless distracted, delayed turning the helm until he had received a second order from the captain. It was high time, because the ships were only a few lengths apart...

Damn! What did that mean! The cargo-vessel was steering to port instead of starboard, and, in consequence, continuing to head for the yacht instead on turning away from her!

With a brief blast of the siren, Burner emphasized his regulation maneuver to starboard, announcing it to the other vessel. The latter did not respond, and did not rectify its false maneuver.

On the bridge, everyone held their breath. Even the imperturbable Williamson went pale, and recoiled instinctively.

"My God! Are they dead or mad in there?" cried the captain.

Bounding to the apparatus communicating his orders to the engine-room—which the mechanics call the "telegraph"—he manipulated the levers feverishly, almost howling, as if he could be heard in the bowels of the ship: "Stop! Reverse engines, full steam!"

The yacht shivered in its entirety under the gigantic effort of the propellers churning the water in reverse—but what could the *Astrea*'s maneuver, still too slow, achieve against the massive cargo-vessel traveling at twelve or fourteen knots?

Captain Burner, who, until then, had been acting in conformity with the regulations, understood that, since obedience in the presence of a ship that was doing the opposite would only render the imminent catastrophe inevitable, the moment had come to infringe them audaciously.

Stiffening himself, and calling all his mariner's composure to his aid, he measured with his eye the short distance that separated his vessel from the adverse and menacing prow, told himself, in less time that a lightning-bolt takes to cleave the darkness, that, the collision no longer being avoidable, he had just enough seconds left at least to attenuate the terrible consequences of the formidable impact.

The means to do that was that as the two ships came together, to provoke a glancing collision, scraping one hull against the other—which would very nearly demolish one side of each vessel, but might perhaps only inflict rips above the flotation line, which would avoid fatal inrushes of water.

Bounding to his telegraph that captain shouted, at the top of his voice: "Full speed ahead!" and "Hard to port!"

At the risk of breaking everything, the propellers changed the direction of their rotation almost instantly, producing such a pressure that the yacht almost capsized—but the rudder, in the hands of helmsman Smith, instead of turning left, as ordered, steered to the right...

Instead of her bow, it was her flank that the unfortunate *Astrea* offered fully to the high prow of the cargo ship, which advanced with frightful speed through the darkness.

There was a sinister clamor aboard the yacht. Everyone, understanding that they were doomed, remained motionless, breathless and horrified.

Only Claude Rolland had leapt backwards, slid down the stairway to the deck, and run like a madman to the lead of the stairwell descending to the cabins. With a few catlike bounds he had reached his sister's cabin, the door of which gave way under the impact of his shoulder.

He had grabbed his sister, who was sitting up in bed anxiously, and carried her away at a run, scaled the stairway as if he had not been bearing his precious burden and emerged on to the deck at the exact movement when, with a bang, and formidable and frightful ripping sound, the prow of the cargo-vessel opened a gaping wound in the side of the ship, through which the sea flooded.

On board, in the midst of indescribable chaos, people were rushing in all directions, some running for the boats, others toward the high iron wall of the ramming ship, in order to try to scale it and find a refuge from death.

The latter were immediately disappointed in their supreme hope, for as soon as the impact had occurred, the rammer disengaged, reversing its engine. It did not, however, depart into the night entirely alone. Smith, as soon as he had delivered the fatal twist of the wheel, doubtless terrified, had run to the exposed hull and, at the moment of impact, had grabbed a rope that, surely by some miracle, was hanging down from the murderous prow, and had started climbing....

But he felt his legs seized. A supple body, with an ape-like agility, passed over his back, climbed on to his shoulders, and hoisting itself up by the strength of its wrists, arrived on the deck of the cargo-ship ahead of him.

Smith reached it in his turn, and coolly hauled aboard the rope to which he owed his salvation, and might perhaps have saved some of his comrades.

It was then that the rammer disengaged, abandoning the yacht, which, no longer being sustained and already having three meters of water inside her hull, rapidly heeled over to port.

Claude Rolland, his sister having fainted from shock in his arms, sensing the *Astrea* going down with an anguishing rapidity, judged that within two or three minutes yacht would have sunk completely. Although he had never been shipwrecked—at least at sea—he thought about the whirlpool in which it was vital not to be allow himself to be caught. He did not hesitate, but climbed over the side and, holding his sister solidly in his left arm, squeezed her nostrils and blocked her mouth with his right hand, and leapt into the sea.

Returning to the surface, he sustained the beautiful colorless face above the water, and stated swimming vigorously with his right arm.

His objective was, having got far enough away not to fear being dragged down in the turbulence the ship would produce as it was engulfed by the waves, to get closer to the cargo-ship—the only place from which help might come.

He swam courageously, but, hampered by his clothing and having an inert body to support, he rapidly became fatigued. Soon, following the din of a violent explosion, a wave that seemed enormous lifted him up...

That was all. He understood that the yacht had just sunk, and that, if he had delayed in diving into the water, he would have been dragged down with it.

At hazard, conserving his strength, he began calling for help, in case a boat put into the water by the cargo-vessel was within range of his voice.

To his second appeal, it was a familiar voice that replied, from close by, saying with the greatest calmness: "I believe, Monsieur Rolland, that we have very little chance of getting out of this. However, if I can be useful, I'm at your disposal.

"Monsieur Williamson! You jumped too?

"From the footbridge, as soon as I understood that the yacht was about to sink. I preferred to avoid the explosion that would not have left me the time to collect myself before passing into eternity. I wanted to delay the annoying moment slightly."

"It's necessary to fight until the end, and in order to fight better, don't give up hope."

"I'm envisaging the situation coldly, that's all. Oh! But you've saved Miss Edmée! Toby followed me—we can help you to sustain her."

"Thanks—I'm beginning to have difficulty."

"Don't talk any more—it saps the strength. Toby! Come here!""

"Yes sir!"

Williamson and his groom took charge of the poor unconscious Edmée, which permitted Claude, relieved, to get a little of his strength back. Futile, alas, for the shipwreck victims had distinctly seen the dark mass of the cargo-boat vanishing into the darkness. They were abandoned!

Devoid of hope, silent now and increasingly breathless, the two men and the adolescent swam for nearly twenty minutes, taking turns to sustain the inert body of the young woman. They were at the limit of their strength, especially Claude, who had expended an excess of energy since the very beginning.

Feeling himself becoming numb, the young man did not want to let himself sink without uttering one last appeal. He collected his last forces, and, vain as the attempt seemed, cried "Help!" one last time.

A sudden start electrified him, rendering him an energy of which he had thought himself incapable. Distantly, and as if involuntarily muffled, a human voice replied to him: "Shh! Don't shout! Hold on! I'm coming!"

# Chapter III
## *Maritime Disasters*

It was a Wednesday evening when the steam-yacht *Astrea*, in consequence of the collision within sight of the American coast, went down with all hands.

Two days later, the Yankee newspapers published the following dispatch:

*Norfolk, Virginia, 20 November. Entered port last night, the cargo-boat* Awful, *registered at two thousand four hundred tons, Captain Lodgehead, coming from New York to pick up cargo for Montevideo. The* Awful*'s hull was broken four feet above the flotation line and the sheet metal had been staved in between the prow and the sides of the bow. The captain declared that he had been in collision in the open sea off Cape May the previous night with an unknown steamship which, in spite of his warnings and by virtue of a maneuver contrary to the rules of navigation, had thrown itself into his path.*

*The unknown ship sank in less than four minutes, and although the* Awful *remained on the site of the disaster and put her boats to sea with all possible haste, one of which was lost, no crewman from the sunken vessel could be recovered, nor any wreckage permitting a conjecture as to the nationality and provenance of the ship, which must have gauged approximately fifteen hundred tons and appeared to be heavily laden.*

*The* Awful *will be put in dry dock today in order to repair the serious damage, and will not be able to moor at the Jamestown docks to embark her cargo for at least a fortnight.*

*Captain Lodgehead is a well-known and highly reputed mariner, and there can be no doubt that his conduct must have been eminently correct in this unfortunate circumstance.*

Although that dispatch informs us of the names of the ramming cargo-vessel and its captain, it contains, on the other hand, several serious counterfactual statements, deliberate or otherwise.

The disaster had not taken place in the open sea of Cape May, situated to the south of New York State, at the eastern extremity of the bay formed by the mouth of the Delaware, but near the entrance to New York Bay—which is to say, a hundred and sixty-five miles further north. It had not been caused by a false maneuver by the vessel that was rammed, but by the rammer. Finally, it was not true to say that the *Awful* had attempted to save the crew, since it had sailed away thereafter, fleeing that strict duty of humanity, or to affirm that no one from the *Astrea* had survived the wreck, since Smith, and...someone else...had scaled the high wall of the cargo-boat. As for the indications so opposed to reality given regarding the appearances of the sunken ship, it leaps to the eyes that they were tendentious. There is no reason, moreover, to be astonished that Captain Lodgehead, being unable, in his own conscience, to consider himself as other than wholly responsible for the disaster, desired, by means of interested precaution, to mislead the subsequent research of the Naval Department.

It is well-known that from one shore of the ocean to the other, pilots embarking in proximity to one of the terminal ports of the transatlantic liners, bring aboard fresh news in the form of the latest newspapers to appear at the moment when they take to the sea. It was naturally thus for the Compagnie Générale Transatlantique's *Touraine*, when, the following night, it arrived in its turn within sight of the Sandy Hook lightship.

The article concerning the collision that had claimed so many victims in the very area that the liner was traversing, leapt to the eyes of all the passengers, and particularly to those of Jonathan Loeb, departed from Le Havre with Grégoire de Montalpé three days after the yacht chartered by the billionaire.

He read the dispatch from Norfolk carefully and, without a word or a single feature of his thin face having twitched, held out the newspaper to his companion, marking the passage to which he was calling his attention with his thumb.

The latter read the article conscientiously and, raising his eyes to look at the Yankee with an uncomprehendingly interrogative gaze, said: "It's doubtless a misfortune, but why are you drawing my particular attention to it?"

"You don't understand?"

"I understand that a cargo-ship has sunk another, probably quite a long way away from here. It's an accident that happens all too often, alas."

Loeb shrugged his shoulders. Standing up unhurriedly, he took Montalpé by the arm, drew him out of the lounge full of passengers and then on to the promenade deck. There, he made sure that no one was close enough to overhear him, and in his hoarse and caustic voice he said: "You haven't understood, then, that you're alone in the ranks, once Old Sinker is out of the way, relative to the inheritance on sufferance of which you have need?"

"You're not going to tell me that the ship lost with all hands was..."

"His."

"It says a cargo ship, not a yacht, and places the accident off Cape May, which isn't near here, so far as I know, and, in consequence not on Williamson's route."

"Would you have wanted Captain Lodgehead to sign his ramming? I couldn't demand such a stupidity of him."

"You? It's frightful, what you're suggesting to me! Obviously, you're making fun of me. How could you have...too bad, I'll say the word...commanded a disaster to occur while we were in mid-Atlantic?"

"Didn't I tell you, on the evening after our arrival in Le Havre, that I'd taken action?"

De Montalpé recoiled instinctively.

"It...was sufficient for you..."

"Poor brain, which hasn't yet understood the power I have!"

"Brrr...I've got cold chills down my back. But I don't understand..."

"Not one word more here. Everything will be explained to you in a few hours. Let's go back to the lounge. Come on!"

De Montalpé followed his terrible companion, but almost at a distance, as a fearful dog follows its master, in whose hand it can see the cruel whip.

Not another word was exchanged between them until the *Touraine* was moored at its arrival dock. As soon as the gangplank had been set up, they were among the first to descend to the shore. On the quay, in the first rank of the waiting porters, there was a man in a check suit with a scarf around his neck and a bowler hat pulled down over his eyes, to whom Loeb made an imperceptible sign.

That man, rendered almost unrecognizable by his change of costume was the helmsman Smith. He followed the two travelers at a distance, taking the ferries and trams at the same time as them, and rejoined them when they stopped, in an Avenue near Central Park, outside a door above which two luminous words were legible: *Salvation Army*.

Loeb rang the bell.

A thin, ageless woman, clad entirely in black opened the door, and, at the sight of Jonathan, stood aside respectfully.

"Come with us, Colonel," said Lobanief's enemy to her, in a low voice.

"At your orders, General," she replied, closing the door and triple-locking it.

An elevator carried Loeb and his three companions up to the third floor. There, with a key extracted from the depths of one of his pockets, he opened a door, turned an electric commutator, traversed a severely-furnished antechamber and went into a drawing-room that Williamson himself would not have denied, so much expense did the furniture and wall-hangings solemnly proclaim.

Jonathan threw his damp overcoat and hat on to a silken pouffe, sat down and put is his dirty boots on a sofa, and, without wasting time inviting his companions to sit down, addressed himself to Smith:

"Well?"

"It's done, Master."

"Lodgehead?"

"Received your encrypted order cabled from France and didn't hesitate, grave as the requested action was. He hastened the unloading of his ship, put to sea on Wednesday evening, just in time to meet the *Astrea* at sea, which I identified to him by means of a rocket, and which I offered sideways on to his prow by means of a false maneuver."

"You were able to get aboard the *Awful* immediately?"

"Thanks to a rope lowered from the bow."

"Alone?"

"One man, whom I wasn't able to recognize, took advantage of it, passing over my back, but the most scrupulous search mounted on board proved that he hadn't taken refuge there. He was climbing like a madman, and must have fallen back into the sea when he reached the smooth part of the side, by virtue of the shock produced when the *Awful* disengaged."

"What's this lost boat the newspapers are talking about?"

"An unconscious and quite natural impulse on the part of two crewmen who, without waiting for orders, wanted to put it into the sea to help the shipwreck victims. In his haste, one of them, according to the other, cut the supporting ropes, and the boat, falling nose-first, must have sunk immediately, for there was no trace of it when we turned south."

"It definitely sank?"

"There's not the shadow of a doubt about it?"

"So the loss of the *Astrea* is definitely total?"

"Absolutely. Complete surprise, explosion of the boilers, and lightning disappearance, having not had time to embark a single boat. I'm the sole survivor."

"Do you hear that, Monsieur de Montalpé?"

The Parisian dandy was unable to reply; he was literally frozen with horror. Loeb, as cool and calm as if it were a matter of a child's toy boat sunk in the pond in the Tuileries, went on: "Pass on to Grace Strangestorm."

The woman in black started abruptly.

"Yes, Colonel Camden," said Jonathan, lifting his booted feet on to the arm of sofa, "it is indeed a matter of the adjutant-major that you accommodated last year. A fortunate hazard dictated that I found her embarked aboard the *Astrea* as a chambermaid. Reply now, Smith."

"Oh, the worthy girl," said the helmsman, with a hint of emotion. "From the departure onwards she knew that she had to die before reaching the American coast, and didn't betray herself by an instant's weakness!"

"A martyr to our faith! Our Lord will give her a throne of light in Paradise," murmured Miss Camden, in a tremulous voice.

"She obeyed, as was her duty," Loeb articulated, dryly. "But she had a particular and capital mission. Did she complete it?"

"She told me to give you this." Smith held out to the chief of the Great Council the flat metallic box that that the chambermaid, a Salvationist officer, had given him less than an hour before the catastrophe.

Loeb, to the disconcerted amazement of his subordinates in the sect and the secret society, who had always been seen draped in a mantle of rude calm and brutally authoritarian coldness, so economical with his gestures, the living negation thus far of any impulse sentiment, bounded to his powerful feet and fell upon the proffered object like a wild beast on its prey, took possession of it, and held it momentarily in his vast, bony hands, which were trembling, his features contracted and his staring eyes flashing.

With a prompt gesture, he tore off the lid of the box and, running to a side-table, he pulled from its protective sheath the very map that Grace Strangestorm had "lent" to Williamson and his friends.

He did not even look at the map. Taking a knife from his pocket, he nervously sliced through a corner and, that section showing that the map was double-ply, he carefully slid his blade between the two leaves, which he separated from one another, with the aid of a slit rapidly made along the four sides. Leaving the map, he took the sheet of the lining, held it up before his anxious eyes and, observing a single minuscule black dot thereon, uttered a kind of roar of triumph.

"Finally!"

Heedless of the silent attention of which he was the object, he first extended the map on the table, placed the lining sheet exactly on top of it, set the tip of his knife on the black dot and leaned on it heavily, saying, in a tone of grim joy: "There!"

Then, with a single gesture, he tore the sheet away from around the blade, threw it on the ground, and avidly leaned over the point on the map pierced by the tip of the knife. Having done that, he straightened up, replaced the knife in his pocket, folded up the map methodically, put that in his pocket too, and, resuming his customary mask of harsh coldness, turned round.

"Grace Strangestorm fulfilled her mission superbly and executed the orders of the commandment. If it had been possible for her to survive, another double stripe would have been her legitimate recompense. Where she is, I can do no more for her, Let's not mention her again.

"You, Smith, make arrangements to be in New York on the twelfth of January, the day of the great convent. I'll speak to you and the Great Council, and you'll see how grateful I am for services as exceptional and secret as yours.

"For the moment, go to the house of Barthleit, the surgeon, and tell him that I'm going to send him a client who mustn't be seen by anyone. It's you who'll introduce him in the manner that will be indicated to you. Go.

"You, Colonel, return to your apartment and remain at my disposal."

As soon as Jonathan and de Montalpé were alone, the later exclaimed; "Damn! You have means and ways of action, you! You did well not to let me glimpse them in Paris or Le Havre, for I'd never have gone along with it."

"Monsieur de Montalpé," said the Yankee, slowly, string at his companion, "know that when one enters into the direct zone of attraction of Jonathan Loeb, one always 'goes along' and one 'goes along' as far as he desires."

"Hang on!"

"Have you forgotten your oath of apprenticeship?"

"Oh, those oaths only engage one for form's sake. It's a simple means, a precaution, a guarantee—insurance, if you wish—against the contingencies of life, in our epoch of political and philosophical evolution."

"You can see that Smith, who thus far hadn't put a foot wrong in his duties as a mariner, didn't understand it that way."

"You Americans, perhaps, but in France..."

"You're no longer in France, and to employ your language, you're under the blade of my guillotine."

"You think so?"

"I demand passive obedience."

"Permit me..."

"Without restriction."

"I'm not a Grace Strangestorm. I have no vocation for martyrdom, myself."

"I don't know what I shall have to demand of you, but whatever it is, you'll obey whether you like it or not."

"Threats! You know, after your trick regarding the collision with the *Astrea*, it's necessary not to take such a haughty tone. There are judges in the United States."

Loeb uttered a dry burst of laughter, as trenchant as a blade. "Jonathan Loeb makes his own law—otherwise, he wouldn't be the 'Powerful.'"

"Ta ta ta. What if I took it into my head to spill the beans?"

"You'd lose your head, Monsieur de Montalpé, before having had time to open your mouth dangerously."

That was said in a tone that made the dandy shiver. Adopting a tone of coldly ironic bonhomie even more frightening for his interlocutor than the harshly authoritarian one in which he had begun, he went on: "That said for our guidance. I'm certain that you won't ever force me to resort to such extreme means. So, a truce on idle words, with which we don't have time to waste. We're awaited at the surgeon's."

"You have an operation to be carried out?"

"On you."

"What? But I'm not ill. I don't want..."

"Don't worry. It might be a little long, but not too painful and not at all dangerous."

"Oh! No joking..."

"I never joke."

"What do you want to do make of me?"

"A satisfied heir, as I promised you."

"Are you going to explain?"

"No. Get your coat and hat, and let's go."

"But..."

"Enough! I think I've made you understand that I expect to be obeyed without question!"

Grégoire de Montalpé was prodigiously anxious, but also checkmated. He dispensed with any further protest, and, pale and with an ill-assured step, followed the master out of the drawing-room.

Before going out, Loeb had rung. He found Miss Camden on the landing and said to her: "I won't be coming back here before midday, before leaving New York for an indeterminate time. In case anything important comes up, telegraph me at..." He stopped, reflected, and then, while tracing a few brief lines on a page of his notebook, he went on: "No, not you. With an adversary such as Williamson was, it's necessary to guard even against the improbable. Miss Camden, you're coming with us."

The Salvation Army Colonel could not dissimulate a sudden pallor. In the end of Grace Strangestorm she had had a further proof of the risks involved in being charged with "missions" by the redoubtable Major-General. High-ranking, however, she had the example of discipline before her. She contented herself with objecting: "What about the Temple? And the service of the Army Corps?"

Loeb tore out the sheet of paper and handed it to her, replying: "Here are the orders. Pass command over to Major Klebbs. He's second to you on the general staff in New York?"

"Yes, General."

"Wait for us at daybreak at the Western Railroad Station on the right bank of the Hudson. No luggage: we'll make arrangements on the way."

In a tone that had become firm again, the Colonel replied: "Yes, General."

# Chapter IV
## *A Miraculous Rescue*

Shortly before nine o'clock in the morning, having crossed the Hudson River by ferry, Loeb, followed by Grégoire de Montalpé—who was very pale, his back arched, his eyes feverish and his features revealing acute suffering—arrived at the Western Railroad Station, where he signaled to Miss Camden, who had been standing sentinel for some time, to come and join him.

As all three of them went into the hall, heading for the ticket window, a young and thickset individual with leather gaiters, coifed with a large "cowboy hat" and enveloped in one of those vast ulsters that are the glory of Anglo-Saxon travelers, suppressed an exclamation on seeing them and, pulling his hat swiftly down over his eyes, murmured between his teeth: "Thunder! It appears that I'm fated to run into that bird, here, as in Le Havre. It's a pity that I daren't give chase, since, when one hasn't been seen, it's necessary not to try to get too close. But have no fear—if it only depends on me, your account will be settled, and you'll lose nothing by waiting, word of a matelot!"

You will have recognized Jean Guitard, alias Furet, the faithful mariner so attached to his former expedition-leader, Claude Rolland.

How did he come to be there, very much alive, and not at the bottom of the Atlantic with the yacht *Astrea*, Williamson and his dear masters, Claude and Edmée?

That is what will be explained without delay.

Let us go back to the moment when Williamson, Claude and Toby, sustaining Edmée's inanimate body, exhausting their last strength struggling against the cold and fatigue, in order not to let themselves sink, heard a voice call out to them in the darkness, telling them to keep quiet and hold on for a few minutes more.

We have seen the poor shipwreck victims, at the end of their tether, recover their courage and hope at the same time. Galvanizing their exhaustion, if one might put it like that, they turned in the direction of the voice, which continued its encouragements, saying: "Come on, one last effort! I'm coming! I'm pushing a float in front of me made of three oars tied together. That will give you a rest while waiting for something better."

Alas, how distant that voice sounded! Would the unfortunates have the time and the strength to meet up with that providential aid?

They thought it was still far away when a few brasses away, in the slight splashing of the black water, one of the ends of the blessed bundle of oars suddenly appeared. Breathless, kicking with their heels, they reached it and clung to it, the unconscious Edmée in her brother's arms and her head slumped on his shoulder.

"Good! Just in time!" was all that Williamson said, uttering a sigh of relief.

"There," said their savior, in a low voice. "Everybody stop moving; it's a matter of not letting the cold get us now!"

"You, Jean?" said Claude, finally finding the power of speech, and already having recognized the mariner's voice.

"Yes, me, Commandant. My God, the poor demoiselle! Not dead, at least?"

"I...I don't think so."

"Give her to me, so that I can hold her up. I've been able to hear you for some time, Commandant, but one doesn't move very quickly when one's swimming with a boat in tow."

"What? You've brought us a boat? Oh, you're a brave fellow, Master Furet! I can't see it. Where is it?"

"Not a quarter of a cable away. Except that it's only sticking out of the water by three fingers. It's full of water. You understand why it took me such a long time to tow it this far."

"Full of water? That's very inconvenient."

"It's very fortunate, in fact, Monsieur Mining King. Otherwise, we wouldn't have it, for I wouldn't still be alive and wouldn't have been able to bring it to you."

"What do you mean?"

"I'll explain in a little while. Let's get to it first. The three of you push the float toward it. I'll stay at the front to guide it."

The shipwreck-victims took ten minutes to reach the launch floating at surface level, which even the intelligent pilot had difficulty locating.

Jean Guitard recommended that his companions remain silent; they maintained themselves on the side of the boat while he hoisted himself aboard cautiously at the stern. Immediately, using his beret for want of anything else, he started emptying the water from the boat with thrusts of his arms. As soon as he judged that it could support the weight of a second person without danger of capsizing the launch, he helped Toby aboard, who followed his example, scooping with his hat, which the impeccable groom had retained in spite of everything he had gone through.

After several long minutes of effort, the water inside had descended beneath the level of the benches. Then the mariner, assisted by the groom, hauled the icy and inert body of poor Edmée aboard, and laid her down to dry out on a bench. Then they both resumed their labor.

Finally, Williamson first, and then Claude Rolland, were able to come to join them, but, without lending any assistance to their endeavor, the rich Yankee having sat tranquilly down at the rear and the engineer devoting all his efforts to the attempt to bring his sister back to life, by means of vigorous massage.

The launch was empty before he was able to bring the slightest warmth back to the young woman's lovely and supple body. She remained as unconscious and cold as a beautiful antique marble.

Claude was in despair, hot tears mingling with the sweat that was running down his face in spite of the low temperature of the November night, born as much of anguish as fatigue. Jean, his task terminated, dared not propose that he assist him in his tortuous endeavor, out of respect for decency. It was Claude who invited him to do so.

The young mariner took off his short woolen blouse with a high collar, and then his jersey, and gave them to Toby in order that he could wring them out, until not a drop of water remained within them. Opening his shirt, he applied the poor little bare feet to his chest, the contact of which was as painful as if he had placed two blocks of ice on his skin.

Claude understood the naively-set example, and did for the arms and hands what Jean was doing for the feet; leaning over the poor child, he also strove to warm up her neck with his breath.

At the rear, Williamson, numb, was shivering on his bench. Abruptly, he stood up. "By Jove!" he said. "It would be too stupid to catch pleurisy now; let's make a useful reaction."

He came forward, arrived at the middle bench where Edmée was lying and asked: "Well? Is she coming round?"

"Alas, no!" groaned the unfortunate brother, sobbing and raising his head. "She must be completely dead."

At that moment, the first ray of light from the waning moon, outlined the eastern horizon and came to strike Edmée's closed eyes and mortally pale features.

"Oh! Oh!! Oh!!!" said Williamson, repetitively. And he added, in a penetrating tone that no one had heard in his voice before: "It will be a great pity if she's dead; she's regally beautiful, that young woman!"

Momentarily, he contemplated the soft and grave marmoreal face, framed by the golden algae of her wet hair...but the cold made his teeth chatter again, and self-consciousness reclaimed its exclusively empire over him. He took note of the fact that his admiringly contemplative pity was not increasing the beautiful victim's chances of a return to existence in any way, and that no one had any desire to go and keep her company in the icy shades of death. In consequence, he took possession of two heavy oars and stared rowing with a hysterical fury.

At the appearance of the first ray of moonlight caressing Edmée's face, Jean Guitard had experienced an exceedingly sharp sensation, with which the resplendent, solemn and sad beauty of the rigid and icy features of the young woman had nothing to do. It was a sensation of violent disquiet, which was translated into a glance of extreme anxiety directed at the sea in a southerly direction—but it disappeared immediately. Under the white radiance of the nocturnal star, the ship that had caused the catastrophe only appeared as a minuscule distant silhouette cut out in black against the silvery and scarcely undulating surface of the sea. At such a distance it was utterly improbable that the little launch was perceptible, and the mariner breathed out, relieved of a dread that had not quit him for an instant during the time—nearly an hour—since the yacht had been swallowed up.

Claude was at the limit of his strength and his mental suffering. No sign of warmth was manifest in his beloved sister, and his eyes, drowned, ardently fixed upon her, could only see her through a mist.

"It's finished!" he murmured, dolorously. "It's finished! She won't wake up again."

Desperately, he struck his ear against the icy young breast, and suddenly raised his head, abruptly, transfigured, his eyes wild with crazy joy.

"The heart! The heart's beating! How faintly…but it's beating! She's alive!"

Jean held out his jersey to his commandant, which Toby had finished wringing out, so conscientiously that it seemed almost dry. Quickly, aided by the groom and not without difficulty, Claude passed it over his sister's inert torso, and, taking off his wet jacket and waistcoat. Seized her in his arms and pressed her against him, addressing touching maternal words to her, which implored her not to remain any longer in the limbo of unconsciousness and apparent death.

Finally, the long velvety lashes twitched and the eyelids lifted effortfully, allowing a vague fearful gaze to slip through. The pretty lips parted slightly, having become less pale, to allow the passage, in a fragile breath, of a few scarcely-perceptible words.

"I'm cold...where am I?"

Bewildered by joy, the young man lifted the resuscitated loved one from the bench, and sat down in the bottom of the boat, holding her on his lap, while Jean enveloped the numb gracious body as best he could in his matelot's blouse and Claude's jacket, duly wrung out.

Williamson, his reaction now complete, had stopped rowing, and was watching the unexpected resurrection with a very keen interest. Then he too took off his jacket and gave it to the groom to be wrung out, so that it could be added to the means of bringing back a little warmth to Edmée. It was the first time in his life that the billionaire had made an altruistic gesture.

Under that multiple improvised covering, she gradually warming up and he exhausted by fatigue and emotion, the fraternal couple fell asleep.

Jean and Toby, henceforth free, took up oars, following the example of the Mining King, who, to compensate for the loss of warmth caused by the reduction in his clothing, had resumed rowing energetically.

The matelot had taken up his position between the last bench and the stern of the boat, manipulating the most power-ful oar—a scull—and steering the boat as skillfully as if it were a rudder. With a few vigorous thrusts he had brought the skiff round in a semicircle, and the latter, which Williamson had moved a few cables toward the America shore, became to glide instead away from the Sandy Hook lightship.

The King of Mines perceived that.

"What are you doing, Master Jean?"

"Our duty is to make sure that none of our unfortunate companions survived the shipwreck in addition to us."

"A pointless waste of time. I listened while you were oc-cupied in recalling Miss Rolland to life. No cry for help reached me. The entire crew of the *Astrea* has gone to the bot-tom. Evidently, that's extremely regrettable, but we can't do anything about it. Let's take care of ourselves. Set a course for Sandy Hook, my lad, and..."

He interrupted himself. His port-side oar had encoun-tered an unexpected resistance.

"What's that?" he said.

The mariner had leaned over the side. Swiftly, he resized the boat's landing-gaffe, saying: "Your blade has encountered a body floating just beneath the surface. Hold on, while I hook it...come and help me haul it aboard, Toby."

"Not necessary. Just see who it is."

"It's a woman...the chambermaid...the eyes are vitre-ous; she's definitely dead, poor creature. Shall I let her go?"

"No!" said the billionaire, urgently. To his groom, he said: "Toby, help him haul her in."

"Are we going to take her to New York?" asked the mar-iner.

"Not your business...I only want..."

Without completing his thought, Williamson pulled in his oars. Moved cautiously toward the rear and, with a preoc-cupied expression, searched for the dead woman's pocket and rummaged therein. He pulled out a coin-purse, which he re-placed, and a little wallet, which he kept.

"Let her go," he commanded, "And let's get moving."

Grace Strangestorm's corpse was reintegrated with its damp tomb, and the boat resumed its slow progress, briefly interrupted.

"Tell me now, lad," said the Mining King, addressing Jean, "how you were so fortunately able to bring us this boat."

In sentences punctuated by the rhythmic effort of plying the oar, Jean Guitard, alias Furet, explained.

"It came of keeping watch on the helmsman Smith...and I wasn't wrong, as you'll see...something pushed me...and there were the sideways glances he gave me...to keep my eye on him. I was under the footbridge...not far from the helmsman's post...when the cargo-boat came toward us...and I wondered if it wasn't doing it on purpose..."

Williamson fixed the mariner with his gray eyes, with extreme attention.

The other continued: "When Captain Burner...ordered 'Hard to port!' I distinctly saw Smith...push his assistant away...and spin the wheel...as hard as he could to starboard...offering the side of the ship to the rammer."

"That Smith...good! Go on," said Williamson, phlegmatically.

"My blood ran cold...I leapt to the helm...too late for a thrust in accordance with the order to do anything to avoid the crash. I saw Smith quit the post at a run...I bounded after the bandit like a tiger...I saw him, at the moment when the *Astrea* was gutted...grab an rope dangling from the bow of the cargoship...and not by chance, no one will ever convince me of that...and quit the deck of the *Astrea*, hoisting himself up...

"With one bound, I grab the rope myself...and then that scoundrel Smith by the legs...I hoist myself up after him, sure that he wouldn't let go...I pass over his hips, his back, his shoulders...I grab the rope above him...I get to the rail of the cargo-ship first...and jump on to the deck...I run like a madman to the nearest boat...I can see its silhouette hanging from the davits...I cut the seals with my knife, tear away the tarp. A crewman's there...I shout at him, in English: 'Launch in the water, now! Captain's order!'

"The man helps me shove the boat out over the side, above the water...I jump into it immediately...and while the other unwinds the rope from a pulley-block, I cut through one of the safety-ropes with my knife...one turn of the suspension-rope...on to the second safety-rope...which runs free...the boat tips up, nose down to the sea, and I find myself taking a header into the big drink...the shock has made the comrade up top let go, and the support rope unravels...the boat falls, nose first...while I'm coming back to the surface...

"It was a very lucky that it had fallen...given that, by a chance I can't yet explain...it floated, full of water...I say very lucky because the men on the cargo-ship...which, after having backed up to disengage, put on full steam to run away...thought that it had sunk, while it and I passed under the canopy in the wake of the propeller...and they didn't worry about it any more...otherwise...

"Finally, I heard...and the rest you know...I steered for the Commandant's appeals...not making fast progress...in spite of my efforts...because it's not easy to tow something like two tons of water...understanding from the voice...that the poor Commandant...was near to letting himself sink...I tied the oars together to make the float...and while replying very quietly...in case anyone on the cargo-ship might hear...I shoved the float toward you...that's it."

Williamson had not interrupted the faithful mariner for a second time. After a moment's silence, he contented himself with saying, his voice having become calm, indifferent and bank again: "Good. You're a clever fellow." A moment later, he added: "I owe you my life. I'll pay."

"Oh, that, no, damn it!" exclaimed the mariner, his tone brusque and angry.

"Why not?" demanded the billionaire, in a tone once again surprised. "I value it highly."

"First of all, for me, adrift on the big drink, one man's worth as much as another. And then, to offer a French mariner money for having done his duty in working to save shipwreck victims, is to humiliate and offend him. Where we come from, those services, when there's a great deal at stake, are rewarded by a bit of ribbon, by which the minister distinguishes those who've proved that they're not afraid to drink a cup. And then, to tell the truth, you know, I can't say that I wasn't also thinking about you, but only in third place. My Commandant and the pretty mam'zelle Edmée, so good and not proud, came first. If, of the three of you, I'd only been able to save two, it would be you who'd be in the soup."

The plump face of the Mining King blossomed in satisfaction. "All right!" he said. "You belong to the same free-minded nation as those Rollands." He added, as an aside: "Well, I accept the debt to be settled *sine die*." Then, in a louder voice: "Understood. Enough about the past. Let's look forward. Have you been to New York before?"

"A little. I know the harbor and the rivers like my pocket. Before going into the service I was a novice, and then an able seaman, aboard a four-master that spent six weeks there for repairs."

"All right! Can we land by our own means, with this boat?"

"This thing? A little heavy, but a first-rate model. If I were sure of a crossing as calm as the one that just finished so badly, and could scrounge a little canvas, I could take you all the way to Havana in her."

"Perfect, lad. I have reasons for landing, not in New York or Brooklyn, but, for example, at Newark on the Passaic River."

"Known! Through the Kill van Kull, between Staten Island and the tongue of land at Bayonne, then the bay at the mouth of the Passaic. I can see it from here.

"Oh, very good—from now on, you're our captain."

"Fine."

"At five dollars a day. I don't want you to say no. That's what I paid Captain Burner."

"Since it's a wage, I've nothing to say. Although, for the command of a transatlantic of...two tons... Anyway, so be it!"

"Only, I don't want us to stop, or to be seen too closely, until Newark, where I want to land tonight."

"That's what I would have done without you telling me," declared the young mariner, winking. "Necessary that no one has a little act of war in store for us like last night's...have no fear. Count on me."

"You're a perspicacious fellow."

"Oh, it would be necessary to have a tarp over one's eyes not to see...the sun at midday!"

"Good. You can dispose of our arms."

"Oh! Damn it, yes—I can't do everything, can I? In our situation, it's necessary that everyone puts his best foot forward. The Commandant will play his part too."

"Let him sleep a little longer. He's had a great deal of trouble and…he's keeping Miss Edmée warm."

Toby looked at his master with astonishment. He had never heard him show such concern for anyone else.

Aided by a weak current, the boat doubled the Sandy Hook lightship, a distant witness to the loss of the *Astrea*, prudently keeping a mile to the south, at about half past midnight—an approximate time that the new captain, a very modest commandant, estimated from the height of the moon, the castaways' watches having failed to resist such a long immersion.

Seeing the mariner studying the numerous lights in view with some preoccupation, Williamson asked him: "Are you hesitating over which route to take?"

"It's more a matter of studying the routes to avoid, because they're frequented by ships. In front of us, a little to starboard, is the Gedney Chanel, marked by eight luminous buoys, which we can see a trifle confusedly, as one can see a constellation like the Pleiades in the sky with the naked eye. That would be a wasps' nest for anyone wanting to pass unperceived.

"I'll set a course for the double red light of the Scotland lightship. I know that it marks the southern channel, leading via the Swash Channel to the main channel that all the big ships entering or coming out New York take. So, from there we'll head westwards, leaving the terrestrial light at Sandy Hook further and further to starboard."

"But that will take us straight on to the coast of Sandy Hook."

"That's what I want to do. I recall that on that tongue of low-lying land closing the bay of New York to the south there are isolated houses where we can, I hope, without raising the alarm, in spite of the late hour, find indispensable fresh water and food, clothes that we need badly—especially the poor demoiselle, who was surprised by the collision in her night-dress—clothes that, along with the advantage of being dry, will have that of modifying your appearance, too obviously that of shipwreck victims. Not to mention that the jersey I've given to Mademoiselle bears on the front, in red letters, the letters S.Y.A.R.S., for "Steam Yacht *Astrea*, Royal Squadron." Might as well shout out loudly who we are."

"Well reasoned. But rescue stations are numerous in the approaches to New York. I seem to remember that there are at least two on the coast of Sandy Hook. Won't we run into one?"

"Well, only if we're unlucky—but before landing, we'll take precautions. We can't appear in daylight as we are."

"You're right again. Go on."

It was at that moment that Claude Rolland woke up. In a low voice, he called on the faithful Jean to help him. With infinite precaution, they laid Edmée, finally warmed up and sleeping peacefully, in the bottom of the boat, in order that he could add his recovered strength to that of his companions in misfortune. They succeeded in doing it without waking her, covered her up as best they could, and the rowing resumed, activated by that vigorous reinforcement.

At about half past two in the morning, after having maintained an average speed of four knots since the accident, covering thirty-three kilometers in total since ten o'clock in the evening, the launch ran aground gently on the beach, not far from a modest fisherman's hut. Jean Guitard leapt on to the shore, his pockets duly ballasted with dollars by Williamson, and set out on reconnaissance.

After half an hour he came back, escorted by a family of "toilers of the sea," bringing almost everything they possessed of spare clothing, warm and dry. The mariner was carrying a heavy acquisition of which he was prouder than anything else: a mast and a dinghy-sail, with a coil of strong new rope. In addition, the fisherman's wife deposited on the sand a heavy basket full of provisions, solid and liquid.

All of it had been acquired at a high price, which ensured the silence of the couple, delighted with that stroke of luck.

While Edmée, who had woken up when they landed, exhausted but fully lucid, got dressed on the strand, assisted by the fisherman's wife and veiled by the shadows of night, the moon having been temporarily eclipsed by cloud—her brother had brought up to date with the shipwreck, which she only remembered confusedly, the rescue effected by Jean while she was unconscious, her laborious recall to life and their present situation—the men transformed themselves into Yankee fishermen and the real fisherman and Furet set up the mast and sail.

Afterwards, Jean donned the costume destined for him, and the maritime couple, after having helped the young castaway aboard, shoved the launch out to sea.

The mariner, full of joy, adjusted the rigging, set the "rudder," and, leaning slightly under the effort of a light south-easterly breeze, the launch disappeared into the calm night extended over the plaid sea.

The first light of dawn found the vessel, carried by its sail, waiting in Gravesend Bay, Long Island for the nearby light on Norton Point to go out. "Captain Furet," as Williamson had baptized Jean Guitard, having not wanted to engage by night and without a searchlight in the bottleneck some fifteen hundred meters wide—less than a thousand of which are usable for those unfamiliar with the coast—that separates the upper and lower New York bays, guarded by four forts, one of which, Fort Lafayette, is on an islet emerging from the bosom of the waves.

As soon as it was bright enough for him to steer, the boat set off and went through the bottleneck, three nautical miles long. When it entered the upper bay, its crew, who had not attracted any attention in the estuary of the Hudson, where the navigation is so intense—contented themselves with saluting the famous Statue of Liberty on Bedloe Island from a distance, skirted Staten Island to the north, went past Factoryville and Port Richmond, and traveled the entire length of the lower bay of Newark, just in time to have a frugal midday meal in a modest inn, where they represented themselves as a small party undertaking a nautical excursion. As they had taken care to rebaptize themselves in whimsical fashion for the occasion, there was no danger that the incognito of the overly famous Mining King would he unveiled.

More than ever, Williamson did not want to be recognized. As soon as daylight had permitted him to do so, he had set about attentively examining the little wallet that he had taken from the pocket of Grace Strangestorm's dress during the night, after his oar had chanced to trouble her final slumber in her vast liquid tomb. Among a few letters of no interest and pious images, he found the identity card of an officer in the Salvation Army and a piece of paper on which a few lines had been scrawled in pencil by the dead woman—Williamson had no doubt of that, although there was no signature. They read:

*General, I have been faithful to the end to the discipline of our sacred cohort. Your orders have been carried out. Now, strengthened by duty passively accomplished, I await calmly the death that will not be long in coming, for I have just heard it said that the America coast is in sight. Pray that the great general in Heaven will give me a modest place among the martyrs of the faith.*

The paper was folded in four, and bore the subscription: *Mr. Smith, Helmsman, Yacht* Astrea.

On reading that notes, born of the imperious desire to write that few women can resist when an idea or a sentiment occupies them wholly, and which it had not been possible to confide to the man charge with conveying it to its true addressee, a flash of enlightenment had illuminated in Williamson's eyes the full extent of the web of intrigue to which he had so nearly fallen victim—aimed at him alone, he thought, although so many others, who has nothing to do with the matter, had found death therein.

He did not hesitate for a moment to add the name of Jonathan Loeb to the title of General traced by the Salvationist.

He understood that such an adversary was not to be disdained, and that when Loeb had said to him in Paris that it was war and that he would show him how he could wage it, he had not been formulating a vain threat.

The Mining King, who was fundamentally very brave, in spite of all his sybaritism and his monumental egotism, did not entertain for an instant the possibility of renouncing his expedition, or even delaying it by an hour, but he recognized the necessity of tightening his game and taking serious precautions.

The first of those, the one most immediately indicated, was to take advantage of the belief that Loeb must have that his criminal plan had succeeded—a belief that would incite him to act openly, and, in consequence, to become more vulnerable to his alerted adversary. Williamson was under no illusion; a person of his notoriety could not hope to preserve his incognito for long on American soil unless he went to ground, which he did not want to do at any price, being honor bound to respond to the appeal of Old Sinker/Lobanief. It was, however, at least necessary for him to go unnoticed for as long as possible, and that would not be easy to do, from the very start.

The castaways landed in the New World in a state of complete deprivation. Williamson had seen the liquid money that he had carried with him in the form of banknotes go down with the yacht. Ordinarily, the wealthy nomad would only have had have had in his possession the small sum—relatively speaking, of course—of a few tens of thousands of francs. Like all princes of fortune, he proceeded by means of checks, having deposits in all the great banks in the world.

It followed that the peerless billionaire became, so to speak, all proportions maintained, as poor as Job as soon as he could no longer show his face in the sunlight. That was a difficulty whose resolution was extremely delicate.

As they left the inn after the meal, the groom went away, and, taking every precaution to maintain the secrecy of the conversation, the billionaire made his companions party to his predicament, as well as the vanity of his efforts, since day-break, to figure out a way of vanquishing the difficulties.

Very frankly, he did not hide anything of the discoveries he had made concerning the plot made by Loeb and the perils to which that war to the death would expose in future those who attached themselves to his paces. He proposed to Rolland and his sister that he should leave them behind, promising that if, in spite of ambushes, he succeeded in reaching their relative, he would speak to him about them.

He was profoundly surprised by the headstrong simplicity with which Edmée rejected the idea, which she qualified as desertion in the face of the enemy, and affirmed her determination of not depriving Williamson, by pusillanimously accepting his proposition, of the devoted assistance of two supporters as valiant as Claude and his matelot.

Once again, the pretty Edmée, a simple young woman discovered by chance in the French bourgeoisie, overturned all his most stubborn theories, which he judged to have been severely put to the proof by the musicality of her voice, and then, successively, by her proud susceptibility, her disinterest, her intelligence, her impressive beauty revealed under the appearances of death—and now the young feminine soul was offering the unexpected grandeur of generously virile decisions and a reckless bravery of which his trenchant philosophy and misanthropic lassitude had disdainfully deprived the weaker sex.

Decidedly, in a matter of days, the brother, and even more so the sister, had caused that American to discover...America!

And that little matelot Jean Guitard! How that child of Gaul, to whom the prideful prince of the dollar had not deigned to pay any attention previously, had imposed his alert and clear-sighted personality on him, since the day before!

In the embarrassment of the present problem, it was the mariner, once again, who found the elegant solution, in a trice. What did he need to take care of the most urgent needs?

Three or four thousand dollars, Williamson affirmed.

The latter wishing to pass temporarily for having been swallowed up with the *Astrea*, and none of his companions possessing the slightest fraction of the necessary subsidies, was it not impossible to avoid introducing a third party into the secret of the miraculous rescue? Evidently—but it was necessary that the third party in question could advance the funds discreetly, and with the security of absolute discretion.

It was with regard to that point that "Captain Furet," had an idea that seemed to him quite natural, but which was a stroke of genius.

During his sojourn in New York a few years earlier, the young mariner, who was not a man to repudiate the pious traditions in honor among worthy maritime populations, had found himself in communication with an old priest of French origin, in whom he immediately inspired a paternal sympathy.

That priest, the founder of a mission in New York State, seeing the number of his flock increasing, had dreamed of building a beautiful church, to which he would devote all his personal wealth—modest, alas, and very insufficient—but had despaired of ever accumulating donations proportional to the goal he was pursuing, his congregation being almost exclusively proletarian or belonging to the world of small tradesmen.

"That's the banker you need, Monsieur Mining King," the matelot proclaimed. "Promise him his church, and everything he has will be yours. As for guarantees; the disinterest of a man devoid of needs, the discretion of a confessor doubly sealed by his apostolic interests. Oh, if only the good God could allow us to find him again!"

"Try," concluded Williamson, giving his new captain *carte blanche.*

Finding the priest in another district of the city, not without difficulty, bringing him to Williamson—who made the deal with royal generosity—realizating and handing over the funds, took forty-eight hours.

During his first sortie in Newark, Jean Guitard had procured a globe-trotter's outfit that disguised him sufficiently in case Loeb had retained some memory of him, after having seen him at the Centrale celebration. He had come from Newark to collect a small residue of funds when he found himself almost face to face with the said Loeb at the Western Railroad Station, departing for the interior in company with Grégoire de Montalpé and Colonel Camden.

When, having rapidly returned to Newark, the mariner gave an account of his encounter, and the time and place at which it had taken place, Williamson went pale.

*Does Loeb know where I need to go to pick up my guide?* he wondered. But he reassured himself. *The direction he's taking can only be a coincidence. And then again, even if he's going...there...he won't obtain anything. He doesn't have the sign.*

More anxious than he wanted to appear, however, he said to Edmée: "Miss, I would have liked to give you two days to recover completely, but it's important that we arrive...you know where...as soon as possible."

"Whenever you wish, Monsieur Williamson; I'm strong, I assure you."

"Good. Captain Furet, do you have the revolvers I asked you to buy?"

"Four large ones for the men and a real jewel for Mam'zelle Edmée, plus fifty cartridges apiece."

"All right! Let's eat quickly, and be on our way!"

# Chapter V
## *The Sign*

Wisconsin, as everyone knows, is a western state bordered in the north by the western reached of Lake Superior, in the west by the St. Croix River and then the Mississippi, and to the south by the state of Illinois, whose famous capital is Chicago, on Lake Michigan. Finally, it is limited to the east by the shores of that same lake, from slightly below Racine to the south as far as Marinette, on the Menominee River, and Green Bay in the north. It is a vast, flat territory, heavily wooded, except for the north, where there are high hills in the approaches to Lake Superior.

From the center of the state, situated close to the great Rapids in the Wisconsin River, if one travels east-north-east for almost two-thirds of the radius that would end at the common frontier of the states of Wisconsin and Michigan, at the point where it plunges into the waters of Green Bay, one finds a small rectangular territory some sixteen miles long and twenty-four wide, traversed in the middle from north to south by the Wolf River.

That territory, minuscule in proportion to the immensities of America, a little more than sixty square leagues, is the Menominee Indian Reservation, left to the Indians of that tribe.[6]

What a gigantic human drama—or rather inhuman; let us say "ethnic," to employ the correct term—is contained in that word "reservation," apparently so calm and innocent. "Reser-

---

[6] The Menominee Reservation now has its own website; the representations imply very strongly—and there is no reason to doubt them—that the present plot calumniates that people in its depiction of them, albeit not to the same extent as it calumniates the Salvation Army and other organizations that the author seems to consider fairer game.

vations," of which the number and extent is diminishing as rapidly as the last resides of their populations are thinning out, are the cemeteries of races.

The autochthonous Indians, driven back by the formidable white invasion, decimated by gunfire, and destroyed, most of all, *en masse*, by the treacherous and mortal "firewater," being for the most part unassimilable, have gradually been confined within increasingly narrow limits, pressed from all sides by the brutality of the inexorable conquering civilization. There, incapable of finding the elements of their existence in the native fauna, destroyed like them, the last vestiges of one-powerful tribes, sovereign rulers of an immense continent, can only count, in order to sustain their precarious and condemned life, on the parsimonious and insidiously calculated liberalities of the white man, whose invading masses are submerging them like an implacable, continuous, untiring tidal wave.

You will have an idea of the miserable existence of these rare temporary fugitives for the ethnic inundation if you care to penetrate with us into the Menominee Reservation whose situation in east Wisconsin we have just identified.

Near the center of the minuscule hunting-ground—where hunting is virtually proscribed, for lack of big game—on the right bank of the Wolf River, in a small clearing open in a vast woodland in which oak and maple abound—too much for the long security of the present and last occupants—around a fire whose ruddy glow merges with the last red gleams of the sunset, is an assembly of strange, or, more accurately, dolorously grotesque, appearance.

In the center of a great circle formed by a few hundred men and women, warriors and squaws, clad in ragged costumes half-Indian and half-civilized, a dozen old men—old more by virtue of appearance than real age—are seated around their chief.

That chief, who is only forty-six years old, although the numerous silvery threads mingled in his long black hair, falling in thick hanks over his shoulders, and the lassitude of his features seem to indicate a much more advanced age, is the only one who is almost entirely dressed in traditional costume: moccasins on his feet, bottomless leather trousers whose longitudinal seam is fringed externally with long goat-hairs for want of human scalps—the heroic era of the warpath being long gone—and a hide blouse decorated with a few emblematic hieroglyphs. But a threadbare manufactured macfarlane is thrown over his back, while instead of a feather bonnet, it is a heavy rigid bowler hat that coifs him, grotesquely.

The sachems, or tribal elders, who are assisting him do not all have moccasins on their feet. Two of them are sporting, without any pride, strong hunting boots, another "cowboy boots," a fourth a mariner's jersey under an ample cotton blouse frayed by usage, etc., etc., and the series of headgear offers a lamentable disparity. As for the "warriors" and the "squaws," one might think that a blind fairy had gathered together a lot of old costumes worn for a century, as many in New York or Chicago as on the Prairie, and made a magical distribution of them at random. One woman might wear, beneath her Indian shirt of tanned leather, a fluttering skirt, another might secure her torso within an obsolete military uniform-jacket, and more than one warrior, dressed in an incomplete three-piece suit, envelops his shoulders in a shawl as feminine as it is civilized.

Only one young woman, slender and gracious, sitting a few paces behind the chief, dressed in a perfectly correct cycling costumes in gray cloth, with a short skirt, her hair gathered into a heavy plait, might be mistaken for a "Miss" from Washington or Cincinnati, not having very much Indian color in her face.

There is nothing about all the individuals thus clad, however, so great is their gravity, so evident their suffering and so visible the dull and terrible anger that inflames them, that could lead anyone to smile.

Leaning on their rifles, the men wait, gazing fixedly at the torches and the ardent coals of the hearth of the "council." An uninformed traveler would hesitate to recognize them as the "redskins" that they really are, so pale to they seem by comparison, for instance, with the Sioux of the neighboring state.

The chief gets to his feet. In a sonorous but singular language, incomprehensible even for those who know most of the Indian dialects of the New World, and in a strong but unemphatic voice, as somber and sad as the features of those who are listening to him, he says:

"Menominee warriors, it is with grief that I see you in the miserable state to which we have been reduced by the false promises of the Palefaces, who have stolen all our lands and are completing the destruction of our race by famine.

"When I think that my voice can be heard simultaneously by all those who remain of the people that the first Palefaces who came from beyond the great lake without limits called the white Indians, by reason of the scant difference between our faces and theirs, all those who remain of a proud, wise, and intelligent nation, the most beautiful of all those which freely hunted the bison on the boundless Prairie, I ask the Great Spirit what crime we could have committed to be thus afflicted by slow and yet frightfully rapid annihilation!

"The Menominees have, however, always maintained the respectful worship of the Ancestors whose bones, piously collected, repose in this forest, our final refuge. In our nation, fathers never cruelly abuse their sacred authority, sons never show themselves disrespectful or disobedient, and squaws have always been good mothers and valiant wives.

"But it is unworthy of us to lament. The force and numbers of the Palefaces has reduced us to their mercy. Let us at least not give them the joy of hearing us complain, like women. Let us not give them either, by allowing ourselves to be dominated by our anger, legitimate though it is, a pretext for shedding the last blood of our race and coming to plant their great wooden tents on this land, our last refuge, our last homeland.

"Yes, certainly, while not leaving is enough territory in which to hunt and with which to supply our needs by ensuring the primary necessities of life, they promised to furnish us with indispensable support, and still, today, they are not keeping their word. The season of frosts is beginning, and we are hungry, and for half a moon we have been waiting in vain for food supplies.

"My beloved daughter, Snow Rose, who has lived for a long time in the stone huts of the Palefaces, has been to make claims of the white chiefs in their great city of Milwaukee. She has been assured that the convoy would be rapidly formed and sent, but in spite of that promise, the sun has set nine times since she has returned, and we are still waiting."

A man detached himself from the circle and brandished his rifle. "We can't wait, and don't want to wait, any longer!"

"Silence! The venerated sachems of the tribe have deliberated with your chief. They recognize that your anger is just, and your suffering great, and the anxieties we have for our existence legitimate, since we even lack powder in order to attempt to hunt, but they know to what misfortunes any act of violence on our part would give rise. They say: 'The promised convoy will come; we are suffering, but let us be patient still.'"

"The sachems are old men; their needs are less imperious than ours," grumbled the warrior.

"Silence, Black Bison!"

"In that case, Chief Manitoba, give me firewater so that I might forget that my squaw's teat has dried up at the lips of my new-born."

"Even if I had any, I would not give you that deadly water!"

"You have none! Gillette, where the smoking carriages roll, is overflowing with it, as with clothing and provisions. We still have enough powder and bullets—let's go take them!"

"Shut up, serpent's tongue! At the next sunrise, Snow Rose will depart again. At least wait for her return!"

"And my child will be dead, as his elder brother did, of the same cause, last winter!"

"No, your child will not die. I have a single goat with re-plete udders. My daughter will give it to you."

"So be it! In that case, I can wait."

"We shall wait," approved the unhappy Menominees, "but let the convoy make haste, or we shall follow the counsel of Black Bison."

Snow Rose stood up, and interjected in her clear voice: "You will follow the counsel of the White Avenger, who for-bids any talk of using powder against men, because men, all being victims of the Great Monster, ought not to kill one an-other. And he has promised that he is the one who will avenge all men!"

"I did not yet have the strength to carry a rifle when he shared the tent of the chief and said that. Since then, he has disappeared, and his vengeance is still is the state of a prom-ise, like the Paleface convoy!"

"Know, Black Bison, that Old Sinker has not disap-peared for me, who, throughout last year, lived on his bread and his teaching! Know that the hour is near when he will keep his promise to make you all the fortunate people, for he has told me to wait here and guide to him the one who is to be witness to his mysterious work. And look! All of you, look!"

Opposite the clearing, on the other bank of the Wolf Riv-er, five people, emerging from the edge of a nearby wood, had paused: three men, one of whom wore the woolen jersey, beret and reefer jacket of a mariner, a boy of fourteen or fifteen, whose tight costume, high stiff collar and cap gave the impres-sion of livery, and a woman.

The tallest of the men shouted in English, in an imperi-ous voice that easily carried over the watercourse, which as narrow by America standards: "Chief!"

The latter advanced to the river's edge.

"Manitoba is the chief of the Menominees!" he replied.

In the same tone, the stranger shouted: "Williamson! Come in response to Old Sinker's summons."

"What did I tell you!" cried Snow Rose, triumphantly.

"Welcome!" said Manitoba, making a sign to a group of Indians to go and meet the travelers.

The Redskins gathered on the river bank, each picking up two long poles from a large number disposed in rows close to the water's edge.

Winter had come early. Already the Wolf River was carrying large ice-floes. The Indians, plunging one of the extremities into the bed, while holding the other end in their muscular hands, launched themselves forward. In three "giant steps" separated by brief pauses on an ice-floe chosen because it offered solid supper, they crossed the Wolf River, carrying extra poles for the use of the newcomers, who passed from the far bank to the nearer one by the same procedure.

When they arrived at the council fire, the one who had already spoken asked: "Is Old Sinker here?"

"No," replied Snow Rose, "but he warned me of your arrival, and I am waiting in order to take you to him."

"Perfect, lovely squaw. When do we start?"

"Shortly after the second sunrise."

"Why not right away?"

"First, I have to go and demand the provision convoy that the administration owes us, and for which we've been waiting in vain for two weeks."

The stranger winked imperceptibly at one of his companions, who was wearing an elegant traveling costume, and who immediately came to join him, while the others remained behind.

"No need to delay for that; I'll do what's necessary to make sure that your tribe has what it needs tomorrow."

A few approving "Ahs" departed from the popular circle. No promise could assure the Palefaces of a more enthusiastic welcome from the exasperated and famished Indians.

"I'll set forth," said the chief's daughter, "as soon as I've seen the convoy arrive."

"You don't trust me?"

"Old Sinker has always told me to believe in facts rather than words."

"Oho! Since when has a squaw cackled so loudly among the Redskins?"

"If Old Sinker, the White Avenger, has chosen the daughter of the great chief Manitoba for his confidential missions, after having had her educated by the Yankees and initiated to formidable secrets, it is because he knows that her soul is prudent, her will firm and her judgment circumspect. In raising me to his level, he has given the Americanized squaw the right to speak loudly."

"I can see that," said the other, ironically. "My apologies, Miss…Miss?"

"Snow Rose."

"Good. Miss Snow Rose will not have, henceforth, any follower more devoted than me…provided that she does not delay in showing us the way."

"I shall only indicate it to Williamson. It is under is responsibility that he takes others with him. He has not given me instructions on that subject."

"The others? They are, in addition to this mariner, who is my servant, and that boy, who is Williamson's, my sister Edmée Rolland and me, Claude Rolland, cousins of the man that Snow Rose calls the White Avenger."

"You are not Williamson, you who have spoken thus far?"

"No, this is Williamson," he said, indicating his immediate companion.

"I'm the King of Mines," confirmed the other, in a soft voice.

The daughter of the great chief Manitoba looked at him fixedly. "In that case," she interrogated him, "you have the sign?"

"That I can assure you," he replied, in a singular intense tone of certainty. Swiftly taking off his overcoat and jacket, he rolled up the left sleeve of his shirt, and laid his arm bare.

The young Indian woman had gone to fetch a flaming brand from the fire, for the daylight was fading rapidly, and she approached it to Williamson's pale and thin arm.

"On the left arm," she said, "and it is indeed the sign, but..."

"But what?" demanded Claude Rolland, in a hoarse voice, furrowing his bushy eyebrows.

"Nothing. Since it's the sign, I have nothing more to see."

She said a few words to her father in the indigenous language, and then said to the newcomers: "The chief will have tents set up for you next to the fire."

"And sleep on the ground? Brrr!" said Williamson.

"When it would have been so easy to avoid that accursed chore by leaving right away!" said his companion. "You aren't taking us, I think, into regions where nocturnal travelers are in peril?"

"First, we're going to Chicago," said Snow Rose.

"By Jove! That's retracing, all the way to the Railroad, the easy road that we've just traveled. Come on, yield to our haste, since I give you my word...as a Frenchman...that the convoy you're waiting for will be here tomorrow, and let's leave immediately."

"The Menominees have learned from their ancestors to speak with cordial respect to the people of that nation, for they were, in the times when we were strong and considered, with our great allies the Sioux, the first of the men of the distant East who settled in our lands. The relationship that our nation had with them was all justice and amity, and we have retained the traditional memory."

"Then since I, a Frenchman, promise you, and affirm the certain arrival of the convoy, you'll consent...?"

Snow Rose remained silent and indecisive for a moment, moving her dark gaze from one stranger to the other, and then, in a clear and resolute tone, she said: "No. We shall leave as soon as the convoy is in sight. I have spoken."

A dark flash passed through the eyes of the taller of her two interlocutors, who suppressed a gesture of anger.

The tents were erected and, in spite of the penury to which the tribe had been reduced, Indian hospitality succeeded in assembling the elements of a meal, which was served to the travelers: a picturesque meal that was finished by the light of resinous torches, night having fallen, very dark.

The Menominee families, still seething with their contained anger, and resolved to wait for the promised convoy at the assembly-point, had dispersed in groups to the neighboring clearing and along the river bank, where they made arrangements to spend the night around rapidly-lit fires.

Having finished their meal, the white travelers had slipped inside their conical shelters, after having received wishes for happy dreams from Chief Manitoba, who went back to his own tepee in the wood.

Snow Rose had not followed her father.

Sitting on the ground, her folded arms enclosing her knees, she remained pensive next to the dying council fire, and her gaze frequently went to the tents occupied by the white men.

In the narrow tepee that they shared, crouching side by side, the pale and jaundiced Williamson and the tall, rude Rolland were not sleeping either.

"Why that preoccupied expression?" said the former, in a low voice. "The dispatch you received on getting off the train in Gillette, announcing our adversaries? What does it matter, since everything is going well, in sum? Haven't all the precautions been taken?"

"Yes—but all the same, I'd have preferred to be *en route* this evening to meet Old Sinker. To be immobilized is to leave a flank open to surprises."

"Our half-breeds, back there?"

"Will fulfill their mission well, that's certain. Each of those fellows, who are the terror of the region, is worth four men on his own. But that defensive organization caused us to lose precious time, and we're inconvenienced here by the fact that the little Indian girl is the ransom of our delay. I'm thinking of completing our safety precautions with the aid of the two companions we've brought, and in order to ward off and further difficulty coming from this night of forced rest."

"What a terrible man you are! What need is there always to be imagining dangers, instead of letting events take their course while everything is going well?"

"It's only by anticipating too much that one is sufficiently prepared. Stay here and sleep, I'll go and give instructions to our people, if the circumstances arise."

Slipping out of their common tepee, Williamson's companion went to the one to which their traveling companions had retired, and shut himself in with the mariner and the groom.

He was still there when a shout rang out and caused Snow Rose to leap abruptly to her feet.

"Chief!"

"Who wants him?" demanded the young Indian woman sharply, trying to penetrate the nocturnal darkness with her gaze.

From the other side of the Wolf River, a voice that was evidently forced, doubtless unaccustomed to long-distance dialogues, replied: "Williamson! Come in response to Old Sinker's summons."

The same sentence that had already resounded on the arrival of the other Palefaces!

Manitoba's daughter shivered violently. She was certainly not alone, for the white men who had already arrived were all standing up in their tepees.

"Wait!" commanded Snow Rose, in a trouble voice. Immediately, she modulated a bizarre sound, simultaneously reminiscent of the call of a blackbird and the mewling of a cat.

It could only be an alarm signal, for, almost instantaneously, the entire underwood surrounding the big clearing lit up, as did the river bank, with flickering torches. In less than two minutes, all the warriors of the tribe, rifle in hand, Manitoba and the sachems at the head, came to gather beside the ruddy embers of the council fire.

By the light of the torches, the same passage of the river, back and forth, as effects. In the same way as before, too, the new band of white travelers was composed of three men, a woman and a boy of about fifteen. But if the latter wore a livery similar to his predecessor, none of the three men indicated by their clothing that one of them was a seaman. And furthermore, they had a guide, who, in response to the welcome given to his clients, had not thought it appropriate to cross the watercourse with them.

The young Indian woman, her brows furrowed and her eyes flashing, advanced toward them. "Which of you claims to be Williamson?" she demanded, abruptly.

"Me."

"You're lying. Williamson is here!"

"Well, I expected that. Who is designated by Old Sinker to take Williamson to him?"

"Me."

"Very good," said the newcomer. "Will you observe the sign?" He undressed partially in order to lay his arm bare.

Nervously, Snow Rose took hold of a torch that a warrior passed to her and gazed at the minuscule tattoo representing a terrestrial globe pierced by a dagger, which illustrated the very pale flesh of the arm, almost feminine by virtue of its roundness. She looked at it with extreme attention, slowly moving her finger around the design.

Finally, with a completely changed expression, she said: "You really are Williamson? Then…the other…."

"May I see him, if he hasn't fled when we arrived?"

A rude voice replied to him, rising up a few paces behind the group formed by the chief and the sachems.

"The true Williamson doesn't flee before an impostor. Here he is!"

And, pushed forward by his tall Barnum companion, the pale and frail Williamson number one emerged into the yellow torchlight. A loud burst of laugher greeted his rather pitiful appearance.

"What! Cousin de Montalpé, you've suddenly become a billionaire and the Mining King? Truly, you don't look the part! No matter, all my compliments!"

For his part, Williamson number two, addressing the spokesman of his counterpart, said ironically: "Did you think, Monsieur Loeb, that those whose ship you sank within sight of Sandy Hook would really be obliging enough to disappear from the world of the living? As a good believer, as the great General of the Salvation Army ought to be, don't you see, in this resurrection, a miracle from On High and a sign of supernatural protection, against which such a great chief of the Servants of God ought to forbid himself to struggle any longer?"

"I only see one thing, and that's a false Williamson, who wants to deceive the friends of Old Sinker, in order to be taken to him, the devil only knows with what unacknowledged design, and that false Williamson is..."

"Him!" interrupted Snow Rose, forcefully, pointing at the young traveler with the appearance of a dandy, whom the pretty companion of the new arrivals had just called cousin, and who appeared, as the common saying has it, not to be very sure of himself.

"That's false!" thundered Loeb. (You will have recognized him long ago, and there is no point henceforth in designating him by circumlocutions.)

"That's false!" repeated de Montalpé, like an echo, in response to a fierce glare from his brusque companion.

"It's true!" proclaimed the Indian woman. "The proof was given to me by examination of the signs. The second one I've seen is very old, and had faded to the point of being half-effaced. The one I saw first was, as you know, only accepted by me with certain reservations. That's because it's so recent that the inflammation of the needles is intact, and the swelling clearly visible."

"Cousin de Montalpé," said Claude, ironically, "will have the regret of having suffered the pain for nothing!"

Loeb bit his lips until they bled. Suppressing his internal rage with difficulty, he shouted: "Are you going to put your trust in the absurd words of a squaw who is surely slightly mad?"

"It's obvious," said the brave young rescuer Jean Guitard, "that Mr. Loeb hasn't looked very closely; it's not with two beautiful big velvet eyes like those, which radiate a limpid gleam of clear intelligence, that one can accuse someone of poor sight. I'm only a matelot, Mademoiselle Indian, but as such, I've already traveled to the far ends of the earth, and, well, faith of a mariner, I've never encountered a gaze as ...beautifully impressive as yours."

"Come on, enough nonsense!" thundered Loeb. "If the squaw declares herself for the imposture, it doesn't matter to me. Before daylight comes, she'll know, as will you all, which of the two Williamsons she's going to take to Old Sinker—I'll guarantee that!"

So saying, he brutally took hold of the exceedingly nonplussed Grégoire by the sleeve of his jacket, turned him around without the slightest regard for a pretended American king, pushed him into his tepee, strode away, and plunged into the trees bordering the clearing.

In groups, the warriors dismissed by the chief—who did not know enough English to have understood very much of the scene that had just unfolded before their eyes—went back to their respective encampments.

Around the council fire reanimated by the young Indian woman, Williamson, Claude, Edmée, Jean Guitard and Toby sat down in company with Manitoba and his daughter. It was decided with the latter that the departure to meet Old Sinker would take place as soon as the band of impostors had left the area—which the chief promised to obtain, whether they liked it or not, in the course of the following day.

They were counting without their guest; Jonathan Loeb was not one of those who leave the battlefield before being victorious or dead.

# Chapter VI
## *The* Coup de Jarnac[7]

Williamson had refused, on his behalf and that of his companions, Manitoba's offer to set up tents for them. So close to his implacable enemy and hateful competitor of "Power," he judged it prudent to stay together and on watch, armed and in the open air, les propitious to surprises.

Not wanting to be reckoned pusillanimous, in the opinion of the Indians in communication with Old Sinker, he gave Manitoba and his daughter a brief account of the criminal collision engineered by Loeb of which he had been the victim, and how he and his companions had survived the shipwreck, thanks to the initiative, decisiveness, boldness and agility of the young French mariner.

That story occasioned two very different reflections of the scantly loquacious lips of the two Redskins.

"So this Loeb," said the Menominee chief, "is also a very great chief among the Palefaces, to have been able to provoke such a catastrophe at such a distance!"

---

[7] A "*coup de Jarnac*" is a violent, unexpected and expert thrust, with a implication of underhand practice, It is named after a thrust delivered by Guy Jabot de Jarnac in a duel fought in 1547 against the champion of the dauphin, which sliced through his opponent's hamstring. The move was, in fact, not illicit, but Jarnac was a Protestant, and it was described as treacherous in the Jesuit encyclopedia that was responsible for the phrase entering common parlance, before the 19th century lexicographer Émile Littré called attention to the real cheats. The phrase was repopularized by Honoré de Balzac in his essay-sequence *Petites misères de la vie conjugale* (1830-46), who, like the present author, retained the Jesuitical implication.

Snow Rose, looking directly at Jean Guitard, who had not enough eyes to gaze at her, declared gravely, in her half-Yankee half-Indian fashion: "Captain Furet is a great warrior, worthy of his ancestors, whose honesty out ancestors held in high esteem. If he were Menominee, all the squaws of the Reservation would be proud to feed the fire of his tepee."

The mariner did not understand that very well, but he felt distinguished by the beautiful and slightly strange Indian, and in truth, felt a sharp emotion in which his self-esteem was not the only thing in play.

Manitoba and Snow Rose having decided to stay with the strangers in order to cover them with the protection that their mere presence constituted, Snow Rose went to fetch a bison skin from the paternal tepee in which Claude could wrap his exceedingly weary sister. The men, smoking slowly, chatted for another full hour by the council fire.

It was, naturally, about Old Sinker that Williamson, Claude and Edmée—whom curiosity kept awake—wanted to hear from the father and daughter with the slightly ardent complexion. To get the Indians of the American prairie to talk, however—particularly about a desired subject—is a task before which Hercules himself would have recoiled.

All that they were able to learn was that the White Avenger had been the guest of the Menominees for the last time two years before, and had taken Snow Rose away with him, having previously had her educated at the girls' school in Milwaukee; that he had only stayed for an hour in Manitoba's tent, and that the young woman had been initiated by him for twelve moons in the redoubtable secrets that she was to impart to Williamson alone when the moment came; and that the prudence of the venerated and strange individual had instructed Snow Rose to guide Williamson without having revealed to him in advance the itinerary that she was to make him follow.

That was all, although it was as insufficient to satisfy the curiosity of the travelers as it was to permit them to keep the dialogue going for a long time. Thus, the first hour of the watch having passed awkwardly, the periods of mutism became so long that Edmée went to sleep and her companions had to struggle desperately to vanquish the drowsiness that was increasingly overtaking them, thanks to the warmth of the fire. All being tranquil around them, a peaceful and reassuring silence as reigning in the enemy tents as well as the entire Indian camp, Williamson proposed that they yield to natural solicitations, without departing from a prudent surveillance, thanks to sentinels ensuring everyone's security.

It was decided that "Captain Furet"—the mariner seeming immune to the drowsiness of his companions—would take the first watch. After two hours—or sooner if he feared that he was about to succumb to sleep in his turn—he was to be relieved by Claude, who would be relieved in his turn by Toby, Williamson naturally reserving the most prolonged quietude for himself.

Rapidly, the Mining King, Claude Roland and the groom lay down, rolled up in their mantles, while even the Indian chief, inclining his head on to his arms, folded over his knees, allowed himself to be carried off to the land of dreams.

Snow Rose seemed no more inclined than the matelot to imitate her father and her white guests. After making sure that his revolver was quite loose in its holster, and having paced around he sleepers for a quarter of an hour, moved gradually closer to the motionless young Menominee, who was watching him covertly.

Under various pretexts, he exchanged a few remarks with her, banal at first, and then came frankly to sit down beside her—and a whispered conversation was established between them, which became increasingly animated.

It does not require an expert in such matters to understand that a naïve and spontaneous flirtation had been established between the two young people. What they were saying must have been very interesting, at least to them, because they did not perceive that a rumor—almost imperceptible, it is true—had risen in the underwood, son to give way, abruptly, to a silence so complete that it would have given Fenimore Cooper's Leatherstocking pause for thought.

Suddenly, Redskin instinct awoke in Snow Rose.

She seized the mariner's arm, stood up, and darted her dark gaze around her in an anxious glance—only one, for it was already too late!

From all directions around the almost-extinct council fire, beings bounded like wild cats, and before the sleepers, who had stood up in response to the a cry of alarm, could even put their hands on their weapons, they were knocked down—including Snow Rose—and all resistance was rendered impossible.

No hand had committed the near-sacrilege of touching Manitoba, but the chief found himself surrounded by a dozen men as respectful as they were determined not to let him intervene in favor of the travelers who were victims of the aggression, sand when he raised an angry voice to demand an account from his warriors of such an inexplicable attack, it was Black Bison who replied: "The chief has been deceived by odious impostors!"

"The impostors are those who presented themselves first. My daughter, Snow Rose, established that before the warriors."

"Snow Rose left the tepees of her brothers the Menominees too young and too long ago. Among the Palefaces she has lost the keen senses of the children of the Great Spirit, living free in the prairies and the forests. The fact that you were all surprised a moment ago proves that Snow Rose is unable to see."

The young Indian woman had freed herself from those who had knocked her down, and who evidently permitted that liberation, which could no longer hinder the execution of the forcible strike now accomplished. She protested: "The inflammation of the swelling around the sign proves that..."

Black Bison interrupted her forcefully: "Proves only that Snow Rose was not able to discern the cause, being a stranger to tattooing. The man who protects Williamson—the first and true one—has convinced the warriors of that."

"The Menominee warriors are naïve children!"

"Let Snow Rose not insult her brothers! The Menominees do not want to be duped like her! Williamson and his friend, who is a great chief among the white men, are the friends of the Menominees, and the newcomers are their enemies, who want their death."

"That is false!" protested Manitoba, is a loud voice.

"It is so true," howled Black Bison, "that it is them, the accursed sons of pigs, who have prevented the expected convoy from reaching the hungry, and which the powerful friend of the man who calls himself the White Avenger will bring tomorrow, on condition that we make it impossible for our starvers to hinder his efforts in favor of the children of the Great Spirit! Let those filthy reptiles be tied to trees and put under guard, until the assembly of warriors decides their fate."

Manitoba and his daughter, now freed, looked at one another. Their eyes said, mutually, that to try to struggle overtly against the furious anger of the tribe would be to expose their friends to worse and immediate danger. It was necessary to appear to give in to the unexpected torment, with the hope of subsequently bringing back the unfortunates, exasperated by suffering, to saner ideas, and a comprehension of the role that an infernal cleverness had caused them to play.

"The light of the Great Spirit has been withdrawn from the hearts of my sons the Menominees," Manitoba said, "but they are right, if they believe the newcomers to be guilty of such a great crime against us, to take precautions that a near future will make them regret. But let the warriors be wise! Once those they believe to be their enemies are immobilized, let them not hasten to judge them without proof!"

"The chief has spoken well, and not otherwise than the powerful protector of the friend of Old Sinker and the Menominee nation," proclaimed Black Bison. "The great white chief asks nothing more. 'Let them be rendered incapable of doing harm,' he has said, 'and when I have proved their crime and repaired the effect of their machinations, let the Indians do justice to their enemies.'"

Without waiting for the mute acquiescence of Manitoba, the Mining King, Claude and Edmée Rolland, Jean Guitard and Toby were taken away and tied solidly to nearby trees with the aid of lassos, and a picket of a ten armed Indian guards was posted nearby, around the council fire, reawakened by the addition of a few dry branches.

The warriors went back to their respective encampments. The chief and his daughter went back to their tepee, under the suspicious surveillance of the indigenous leader of the rebellion, who, without wanting to injure the person, or even the authority, of the leader of the "nation," had substituted his will, in a specific instance, for the *vox populi*.

Not one of the victims of that aggression, of whose Machiavellian origin they were all too well aware, weakened under the blow of that new catastrophe—not even Edmée. The young woman had only uttered one cry, quite natural, when, awakened in anguish by the alarm call given by the chief's daughter, she had seen two of the red demons hurl themselves upon her, their customary grotesqueness dramatized by the darkness. Valiantly, she had stiffened al her will, and had not allowed any plaint to escape when she was brutally tied to a tree between her brother and Williamson.

The latter had suffered the surprise, just as he imagined the consequences, with a phlegm that, in the circumstances, equaled the firmest courage. Whereas Claude had only uttered one word—a name, Edmée!—absolutely forgetting himself in his fraternal alarm, the mariner, in his impotent anger, had allowed an oath to escape, and that Toby's correctness had not been able to retain a fearful: "Help, sir!" the billionaire had been content to hiss between his teeth a "Good!" synonymous with: "Well, it's gone wrong…and this time, it's serious!"

When the clearing had emptied, the mariner, who had been biting his tongue for some time to combat the urge to… say something, remembered that he had always been "the Parisian"[8] aboard the ships on which he had served, said to the billionaire: "Well, Monsieur Mining King, I believe that Loeb, this time, is well on the way to freeing you from the concern of Captain Furet's wages!"

Williamson did not reply to the mariner, firstly because a joking tone never found a reply on his part, secondly because "Captain Furet" was occupying the position furthest from the river in the line of prisoners, and it would have been necessary to raise his voice, which he never did except in cases of urgent necessity, and finally because a preoccupation—and a saddened preoccupation, to boot—was absorbing all his thought.

It was toward Edmée that he turned his head—the only thing he could move—to say, in his customary tranquil tone: "You would not believe, Miss Rolland, how desolate I am on your account for what is happening, and what reproaches I am addressing to myself for having dragged you with me into such disagreeable adventures."

"You're not doing yourself justice, Monsieur Williamson," the young woman replied, in a weary but firm tone. "Whatever happens to us—and it's to be feared that the imminent consequence of this treacherous attack will not be pleasant—you ought not to accuse yourself of anything in my regard. You insisted sufficiently in Newark that my brother and I, and our brave Jean, should allow you to depart for the interior alone, in company with our young Toby. We wanted to come with you. If our destiny is to finish as soon as the journey has begun, be sure that, like Claude and our faithful Jean, I shall hold my head up and look ill-fortune in the face."

"Miss, your words only drive the dagger more deeply into my heartsickness. You have revealed to me the existence of a kind of woman that I thought non-existent, as I've told you—and now you add to the surprise I have already had the astonishment of discovering in you a firmness of soul that

---

[8] The author inserts a footnote here to explain that "Parisian," in this sense, means a joker, no matter what the provincial origin of the sailor in question might be.

even yesterday I would have sworn to be incompatible with your sex in general, especially in the Old World."

"Because you've only seen the uninteresting flighty individuals who were attracted by the shine of your millions and your celebrity. It's among those, infinitely more numerous, who hide themselves, wounded by the overly brutal glare of an arrogant human sun, among the silent and retiring army of the proud and the modest, that it's necessary to search, there that it's necessary to take the trouble to look, in order that your judgment will not be misled, by virtue of being superficial."

"Good! I greatly regret that I might not live to follow your advice. Since hazard had involved you in it, my life, which was so indifferent to me, had begun to interest me in a fashion that amazes me."

"In that case," said Edmée, making a valiant effort to be cheerful, "I think that in philosophizing, flattering as it might be for me, you're wasting precious time. Our exceedingly precarious fate might depend on a fortunately opportune idea coming to illuminate your thought, as only you know our adversary and these demi-savages that he's employing against us. Whatever the obsession might be of the horrors that wait us, we must search until the last minute for the means of getting out of it…if there is one."

"Never despair! By Jove, from what a human race you're the issue! I'm not talking about North America, which is a composite of all the races in the world, nor of myself, who have no idea where I emerged from, but I understand the people of the Old World who say, with one of the great poets, who is only misunderstood by us: Every man has two fatherlands: his own and France!"[9]

---

[9] The author includes a reference to "Vicomte Henri de Bornier, *La Fille de Roland.*" The quotation is usually attributed to Thomas Jefferson, when he was the American ambassador to France, but it might be apocryphal; undoubtedly, however, Henri de Bornier had Jefferson's alleged remark in

After that unexpected fit of lyricism, perhaps fatigued by an effort so extraordinary for him, Williamson fell silent and began reflecting ardently.

Claude, a man of action in any circumstances, twisted repeatedly in his bonds, exhausting himself in attempts—vain, alas!—to break them.

Jean Guitard, knowing as well as any mariner how to judge knots, did not renew a first attempt of the same kind, having understood its futility. He avenged himself with mocking and vituperative sallies addressed to the savage guards who were crouching around the council fire, mute and attentive, with their rifles on their knees.

Toby, white with fear but correct, remained stiff, his dilated eyes fixed in his master, unable to believe in a prolongation of his captivity, and expecting to see him cast of hi shackles at any moment and come to set him free, and say to him tranquilly: "Toby...*cocktail!*"

Soon, a great silence reigned in the clearing—a poignant, anguished silence for the prisoners, a feline silence of predators sure of their prey for the Redskins.

That silence had lasted for more than a quarter of an hour, without anything having troubled it, when Jean Guitard felt something touch his shoulder, and a scarcely perceptible voice that had recently become as familiar to him as if he had known it for years, whispered in his ear: "Don't move, and don't say a word! Just turn your head slowly and negligently to the left. I'm behind the tree. Good, like that. Now listen. Reply to me without moving your lips, so quietly that your breath couldn't lift a down feather.

"My father and I don't expect anything good for you all, although we'll try to save you, when the stars pale in the first light appearing in the Orient.—but I don't want you to fall victim to the impostor. At great risk for both of us, I'll cut

---

mind when he put the same words into Charlemagne's mouth in his 1875 play.

117

your bonds, and while I distract the guards' attention, take advantage of it to flee."

"No," Jean replied, simply.

"Captain Furet refuses his life?"

"Without being assured at the same time of those of my companions, yes, Mam'zelle Snow Rose. Among us, it's like this: all or none. I'm deeply touched by your good intention in my regard, but I'd be a wretched dog if I took advantage of it."

"The white warrior has a great heart. I had no need of that new proof to save him. But let him reflect—I can only attempt to save one."

"Then let it be Miss Edmée, the weakest, too good and too pretty to die like this."

The Indian woman's dark gaze launched a double flash into the darkness, immediately extinguished. "It would be in vain if I freed her; she's be recaptured before taking twenty paces. It's only Captain Furet that I can save, firstly because he's at the tree closest to the heart of the woods and most distant from the fire where the guards are on watch, and secondly because, having the suppleness of a serpent, the cunning of a fox and the speed of a deer, he alone has a chance of escaping the Menominees' pursuit, and finally because…because I want him…to owe me his life."

"That's very nice, what you're saying, Mam'zelle Snow Rose, and be sure that if we can't avoid the bad quarter of an hour, not being able to prolong our acquaintance will be what I regret most in quitting life…but a French mariner fleeing alone and leaving his comrades face to face with their executioners has never been seen and never will be, you understand? You could cut my ropes and I wouldn't budge."

"If you don't lose a moment you could reach a Paleface village, warn the police and come back to get your companions..."

"And find nothing but their dismembered bodies. No, not that. Thanks, Mam'zelle, but don't go on."

"Oh!" murmured the young Indian, clenching her fists. "It's necessary that I save you, even so."

And, as light as a bird, hardly disturbing a blade of grass, she disappeared into the depths of the wood.

Another quarter of an hour went by in the lugubrious silence.

Suddenly, the five prisoners looked in surprise at the opposite side of the clearing. A man appeared there, moving with precaution. That man was the false Williamson, Claude and Edmée's cousin, Grégoire de Montalpé.

He advanced toward the group of armed Indians, and with a tempting mimicry, showed them two bottles whose necks were sticking out of the inside pockets of his overcoat.

For the Menominees, deprived by the long delay to the convoy, the temptation was too alluring. After a semblance of resistance, they yielded to it. Five minutes later, the two bottles of firewater were empty, passed round and their contents silently swallowed. De Montalpé took two more from the same hiding place, and ten minutes had not gone by when the ten guards had fallen to the ground, struck down by the effects of the alcohol.

Then, deliberately, the dandy headed for the prisoners.

"This time," he said to them, "you have no chance of escaping Loeb's hatred. Oh, he's taken his measures jolly well, that fellow. A good idea, stopping the convoy—or, rather having it stopped a band of half-breeds recruited and mobilized in a trice. If you'd come via Gillette, like us, things would have gone without so much fuss; you'd have been caught without suspecting it by an ambush set by three of the Prairie bandits, who were charged with preventing the drivers of the convoy and their escort from untying themselves—for they've been temporarily transformed into black puddings, just like you, my friends. Then, a few bullets that wouldn't miss their mark, and it would all have been over.

"The trouble is that you got off that the preceding station, Shawane, south of the Reserve instead of East, and came here along Lake Shawane, then up the left bank of the Wolf River. That meant that you didn't see the convoy, avoided the trap, and that satanic Loeb, who's a hell of a lot smarter than you, has been obliged to create a revolution among the Indians to get rid of your inconvenient persons definitively.

"You're wondering why I'm telling you all this and taking the trouble to get your guards drunk? Well, me, I'm not bloodthirsty. I want the inheritance, that's all. That Loeb has a score to settle with the Mining King—a royalty that he must be regretting rudely at present—but I couldn't care less. They can settle it between themselves—in private, of course. But it's not the same for you, cousins. I'm not a bad fellow, I don't insist on your demise.

"You can see that I've put your guards to sleep. Sign a renunciation of the Lobanief inheritance for me, which I have here in my pocket, all ready, with pen and ink, and I'll untie you, advising you to clear off…you'll be done for otherwise.

"That's generous on my part, isn't it? Life is well worth, as is sung in the *Noces de Jeannette*, 'a name at the bottom of this page?'[10] Agreed, isn't it? I can take out the piece of paper?"

"On one condition," said Claude, "and that's that we're all free."

"Ta ra, ta ta! I can see you coming with your big clogs. Once all four of you are free, good old Grégoire is knocked down, and you make off, after having taken the piece of paper back. No fear, my jewels! This is how we're going to proceed: I detach one of the cousin's arms, just enough so that he can sign, with my help. I tie him up again and do the same with his sister. Then, as I keep my word, I detach the brother definitively, and hold a revolver to his sister's head while inviting the excellent Claude to keep twenty paces away, under pain of causing damage to that dear head. When the girl is freed in her

---

[10] *Les Noces de Jeannette* [Jeannette's Wedding] (1853) is a one-act comic opera with music by Victor Massé and a libretto by Jules Barbier and Michel Carré. The highly improbable plot revolves around a marriage contract, which a reluctant groom is tricked into signing.

turn, they'll both do me the pleasure, still under threat, of going somewhere other than where I am. Is that understood?"

A violent conflict then took place in Claude's heart and mind. He honestly did not care about the fortune, but it would be extremely repugnant to him to abandon Williamson. Alone, he would not have hesitated for an instant, but what about his dear sister? Out of chivalric sentiment with regard to an egotist he had only known for a fortnight, was he about to let his beloved sister die?"

"Sign it," advised Williamson, smiling internally at a hidden thought, in which he could not prevent himself hoping that, thanks to Manitoba, he might succeed in thwarting Loeb's hatred once again.

"I need five minutes to think," said Claude.

"As you please, cousin. The fellows I've laid out here aren't going to wake up any time soon. We have the time. You can even discuss it with your companions. I'll go to the river bank, discreetly. I'm very obliging. Only, decide before I get back, or I'll go back to my apartment, and then...you can guess the rest. Without adieux, my dear."

When his back was turned, Snow Rose suddenly stood up beside the mariner.

"The opportunity is exceptionally propitious," she said. "Does Captain Furet still refuse to escape?"

"Now? Oh, no!" said the brave mariner, swiftly. "On condition that you come with me to carry out a little operation I've thought of."

"Not saving the others? If the Menominees here are drunk, the others are watching in the woods. A mass escape is bound to be perceived."

"Don't worry—I'll leave alone...with you."

"Come on, then!" said the Indian, urgently, cutting Jean's bonds.

Gliding like shadows, they both disappeared under the somber branches. Toby, who was next to the mariner, was the only one who perceived the desertion, but the unfortunate boy was too fearful to pay attention if lightning had struck at his feet.

Grégoire de Montalpé returned to Claude.

"Well?"

"Oh," said the other, "it's miserable and cowardly, what I'm doing! Forgive me, Monsieur Williamson."

"Don't sign it, Claude!" protested the young woman, bravely.

"Sign it...for her!" the billionaire pronounced, forcefully and emotionally.

"I'll sign," declared Claude, nervously.

"Well I won't!" said Edmée, closing her eyes as if to drive away the tempting vision of life and liberty reconquered.

"You'll sign too, Miss, or I'll never forgive you!"

Edmée did not reply.

De Montalpé set about freeing one of his cousin's arms. While acting attentively and prudently, in order not to give the prisoner too great a liberty of movement, which he judged dangerous to his security, he said: "You see, my dear, how well precautions have been taken for the operation to proceed smoothly. I certainly wouldn't have thought of it myself."

"Loeb knows?" asked Williamson, abruptly, his expression darkening.

"He organized the whole ceremony."

"He authorized you to get our guards drunk! Oh, be careful, Monsieur Rolland! What trap is still hidden here?"

It was, indeed, a trap, but aimed at the one who suspected it the least. Just as Claude's right arm was finally freed, a volley of guttural cries rang out on the far side of the clearing, where a band of Menominees surged forth.

They pointed at the tree left vacant by the flight of the mariner, and then de Montalpé, still occupied with Claude's bonds. They rushed upon the fake Williamson, caught—in their view—*in flagrante delicto* freeing the prisoners. In spite of his cries and protests, he was dragged away brutally and tied up in the fugitive's place.

In response to the tumult the entire tribe was not long delayed in arriving, and with the strangely picturesque horde, Loeb, the terrible architect of the mortal scheme.

With a cruelly ironic curl in his lips, he did not even deign to glance at his adversaries, so magisterially vanquished, and went straight to his accomplice, who, suddenly riveted to his tree, was writhing like a devil in a holy water stoup and howling like a polecat.

"Be quiet!" he commanded him, rudely. "You only have what your humanitarian fantasies merit. When one wages a war like the one with which you've associated yourself, one doesn't stop at the violence that the circumstances warrant, more or less. Too bad if, in fighting to the death the man who proudly titles himself the Mining King, it happens that these Rollands, about whom I don't give a damn, are swallowed up in his defeat.

"You wanted to take care of your petty affairs alongside mine and spare the accomplices at the moment of the final settlement, but you didn't think that one doesn't play games with a host one has launched into revolt and whose savage passions one has excited to paroxysm. You've been caught red-handed in complicity with the escape of the prisoners, whose death these furious fellow desire. I can't prevent your sharing their fate and, in truth, I confess that your stupidity will rid me of an inconvenient and, by the same token, compromising companion.

"Get yourself out of it, my dear, if you can. But I want, at least, to give you this information: the Indians never sacrifice their victims except in broad daylight, because they want to enjoy their suffering. You therefore have a few hours before you to prepare to be brave, or to think of a means, if any can be found, of dissociating yourself from the condemned before the fatal moment.

"With that, Monsieur de Montalpé, good night—I'm going to bed. Oh, I'll also warn you that they'll surely start with you: all the advantages, my dear! That will spare you a spectacle as painful as it would be demoralizing."

And without paying the slightest attention to the fearful supplications and desperate sobs of his accomplice—whose funds he was keeping—he drew away from the clearing, shrugging his shoulders scornfully.

For half an hour the crowd abused the prisoners, in particular the breathless Grégoire, the most culpable of all, in their eyes, for having wanted to deprive them of their imminent vengeance.

Then the Menominees returned to the wood, and took away the dead drunk guards, who were replaced by a new and wide awake squad.

And the lugubrious watch recommenced.

Great as their courage was—Grégoire and poor Toby excepted—the prisoners' strength, energy and resistance to anguish was exhausted when, without, Chief Manitoba having wanted or been able to do anything to save them, a pale pink light rose above the Wolf River.

It was daylight…it was death.

There was a rumor in the underwood. The executioners were making their preparations.

Soon, with the chief and the sachems in the lead, they advanced processionally into the clearing.

It really was the end! The prisoners exchanged in a glance—and what a glance!—a mute and supreme adieu.

Suddenly, there was a stir within the crowd that had invaded the lugubrious theater of the quintuple execution. After a moment of indecision, it moved *en masse* toward the bank of the Wolf River.

What was that distant noise, those cries, that the savages' ears perceived in spite of the distance?

The sinister preparations were suspended. A few warriors broke away, crossed the river, and went to see what was happening.

The wait lasted a quarter of an hour at the most.

Suddenly, between two thickets, moving at a rapid trot, three heavy wagons appeared, in the midst of whipcracks.

"The convoy! It's the convoy!" howled the Menominee crowd, in a delirium, no longer of vengeance, but of joy.

The first wagon approached the river, escorted by the warriors who had departed as scouts, who were capering around it frantically. And standing at the front of the wagon were...Snow Rose and Captain Furet, making grand gestures of victory!

The first wagon, now launched down the slope leading to the watercourse, comes to a halt a few yards from the bank. The mariner and the Indian woman try to get down, but they are seized by enthusiastic arms, which bring them across the river holding them high above their heads, and they make their entrance to the clearing carried in triumph.

Imposing silence with a gesture, Snow Rose shouts: "A band of half-breed scoundrels, on the orders of the infamous companion of the false Williamson, had stopped our convoy, tied up the drivers and the escort, whom three of them were guarding under the menace of their rifles. The great Paleface warrior and Snow Rose took them by surprise, killed the Prairie bandits and freed the escort. Here is the convoy for which the Menominees were waiting, and of which the infamous impostors deprived them!"

A tempest of "Ouahs!"—Indian cheers—accompanied by a hectic dance, welcomed these words. Then, while the crowd crossed the river and fell upon the wagons, under the guidance of Manitoba and the sachems, desirous of preventing pillage and organizing the distribution. Snow Rose ran to the prisoners and started setting them free.

On arriving in front of Grégoire de Montalpé, his replacement, the mariner stopped, in amazement.

It was Claude Rolland who cut his cousin's bonds, saying: "You wanted to sell us our salvation; personally, I'm setting you free without condition. I'm not forgetting, anyway, that it was your loose tongue that must have informed my intrepid and wily comrade Jean of the existence and location of the intercepted convoy, which he was able to bring here...just in time. Take advantage of that great service involuntarily rendered to those you considered as enemies. Try to get away, because I think that very soon, this won't be a good place for you to be."

More dead than alive, and as crestfallen as a fox caught in a trap, the dispirited Grégoire disappeared hurriedly into the woods.

Williamson's first action, once freed, was to come to Jean Guitard and shake his hand vigorously, saying to him, with a frank and amicable emotion: "You're a brave lad, Captain Furet!"

Jean replied, bluntly: "No trouble, Monsieur Mining King. At your service!"

If Toby, collapsed unconscious at the foot of his tree, had been able to hear and see his master, he would have been less able to recognize the old Williamson than ever.

On the other side of the river, the first wagon had been unloaded, as if by enchantment. The driver had unhitched the horses, which hastened to drink, and then drew away to browse a few hundred paces away. The poor animals were naturally desirous of a well-earned rest.

While the Menominees were uniquely occupied with unloading the precious cargo, three people who had crossed the Wolf River half a mile upstream and had then slipped back under the trees, creeping through the grass, leapt on to the three most distant horses, and, striking them repeatedly with sticks, launched them at a triple gallop eastwards.

A cry of anger rose up among the Indians, twenty of whom set off in pursuit of the fugitives. It was in vain. Loeb, de Montalpé and Colonel Camden were out of reach. It was in vain, too, that they searched for the false mariner and groom. As soon as the convoy appeared, the disguised half-breeds had fled on foot and reached safety.

On the afternoon of the same day, Williamson and his companions, having been fêted as gods by the same Indians who had wanted to torture them, departed for Chicago with Snow Rose.

# Chapter VII
## *The Immense Beast*

Some forty hours later, in three separate and successive groups, clad in overcoats purchased in various stores—Williamson having also, as an additional measure of prudence, by reason of having passed through Chicago on several occasions, donned a superb false beard—the Mining King and his companions, augmented by their Indian guide, had installed themselves in a hotel in one of the giant buildings known as skyscrapers.

Since then, they had not gone out, even to stretch their legs on the sidewalk of the broad street, for two reasons, each as important as the other.

On the one hand, Snow Rose was waiting for an indication of the route to follow, which was to be given to her, as to Williamson in Paris, by way of the New York *Herald*, but in a different fashion, which could only be recognized by her, in an advertisement that would be repeated once a week until further notice emanating directly from Old Sinker.

On the other hand, it was important for the travelers to avoid their dogged enemy, who was not unaware that they had to come to Chicago, Snow Rose having unfortunately not concealed the first stage of the journey to the man she had then believed to be the real Williamson.

In the hotel, they occupied, under false names, four separate rooms, Claude and Edmée on the eighth floor, Williamson on the ninth, the young Menominee on the seventh and Captain Furet and Toby on the thirteenth. Except when they slept or took their meals in the dining-room on their own floor, however, they all gathered by day in the Mining King's apartment.

You can see that their precautions had been carefully taken.

That day, after the midday meal, at about half past two in the afternoon, Williamson, swaying in a rocking chair, and Edmée sitting on a sofa on the back of which Claude was leaning, saw Snow Rose come in at a more rapid pace than usual.

"Well? Do you have news?"

"Yes."

"The indication."

"I've read it."

"Good. Are we going to leave, then?"

"By this evening's train, if you wish."

"May we know on which line?"

"The Great Western line."

"All right! And will it take us long to reach Old Sinker?"

"Only he knows."

"What precautions!"

"He can never take enough."

"Like us," Claude observed.

"You have only one enemy to avoid, who is also one of his; he has a legion," said Snow Rose, gravely. "There are still a great many who haven't forgotten the scenes that unfolded fifteen years ago."

"What scenes?" asked Edmée, curiously.

"I believe," said Williamson, consulting the young Indian woman with his gaze, "that I may speak now?"

"Yes," she approved, "And me too, since we're well on the way to joining him."

"Well," Williamson began, "you'll remember, my dear Miss, that I confided to you aboard the *Astrea* that I'd only told part of the truth in our presence, in Paris, about the event to which I owe the acquaintance of Old Sinker. It's quite true that I pulled him out of the Hudson, where he wanted to put an end to his days, but he hadn't thrown himself in there entirely voluntarily, and the desire for suicide had only come to him after he had sought instinctively, on the contrary, to avoid death."

"That's an opposition difficult to comprehend," observed Claude Rolland, smiling.

"It's quite simple, however. He had sought refuge in the river from a crowd that wanted to lynch him, and it was in the middle of the river that uncomprehending disgust for the material instincts of the crowd, combine with the sudden conviction that it would be impossible for him to realize his scientific dream, that inspired him with the sudden idea of ending his existence."

"They wanted to lynch him because he was a great geologist?"

"For another reason, my dear engineer. Old Sinker had an opinion on the subject of our planet that will perhaps seem strange to you, if not insane, as a man nourished on official science, but on his part, it's more than a conviction; it has risen to the level of an ardent faith, a sacred scientific religion.

"You're pricking our curiosity," said Edmée, her elegant body leaning forward.

As Old Sinker so often pricks the earth to your profit," Claude joked.

"Never sufficiently!" said Snow Rose, gravely. "The evil one can never endure too much suffering!"

Claude and Edmée looked at the young Indian in amazement, wondering whether they ought to laugh at her strange exclamation. Williamson's face, nowadays generally smiling, had also taken on an almost mystical seriousness. The young French couple fell silent, somewhat bewildered, awaiting an explanation for which the Mining King did not keep them waiting long.

He said, in fact: "You'll soon understand the imprecation of that child nourished on the faith of your relative of genius. If he was fleeing, as I've just told you, the lynching with which a furious crowd was threatening him, it's because Old Sinker had just revealed, in a meeting, that he had discovered—and he gave reasons that his audience approved at first, and found persuasive—that the terrestrial globe is not the inert mass that present-day science believes it to be, but a living being: an organism."

"What!" exclaimed Claude's sister. "Something like an immense beast, then?"

"Yes."

"That's an extravagant theory, damn it!" exclaimed the young engineer-cum-explorer.

"Wait before judging, and let me finish my story first," said the billionaire, phlegmatically. "In America, you, see, people aren't astonished by the extraordinary; they even have a tendency to admit it as soon as it's announced, with all the more reason if it's supported by strong evidence and profound knowledge. If Old Stinker had restricted himself to his demonstration he would have been, so to speak, deified by the delirium of spontaneous disciples. Unfortunately for him—and fortunately for me—he let himself get carried away by a singularly dangerous speech.

"'Yes,' he cried, 'the earth that bears us is a living being, but it is also a gigantic monster of cowardly malevolence. And will the Man who shall punish the evil mother of all his misfortunes not be the quintessential Man, the Man pushing well beyond all human power, the Man-God, in a word, because he is almost equal to a god: *the man who will be the murderer of the world?*'

"At first, there was amazement...and then a general egotistical madness. To kill the Earth was to annihilate humankind! Would not the prodigious man who had discovered the living nature of the globe be capable of becoming the murderer that he was praising so highly? The instinct of conservation exasperated the crowd. Speakers surged forth who proclaimed with loud cries the necessity of forming a Club, or a League, of World Defenders.

"Another, more practical, declared that the best thing would be to nip in the bud the possibility of such a...global assassination, by suppressing the man whom an evil genius might make the author of that capital crime.

"Frantic hurrahs welcomed that proposition. Old Sinker fled...and you know the rest."

"I know now," said the young engineer, "that American credulity in fantastic folly must be raised to the $n$th power. I knew it was extreme, but not to that immeasurable degree." And he gave free rein to the desire to laugh that, out of respect for Williamson, he had so far contained, with great difficulty."

The Earth a beast, with its mines, its productions, its spherical rigidity, its icy poles…its atmosphere! It was simply too baroque!

His fit of hilarity, which Edmée had begun to share, was abruptly cut off.

Snow Rose had bounded, as if moved by a spring, from the far side of the drawing room, where she had been standing, attentive and reserved. Arms forward, her eyes launching an angry glare, an expression of almost ecstatic faith animating her features, she came to a stop three paces from the sofa, shouting in an exalted voice: "Don't laugh! It's impious to laugh at Old Sinker's sacred dogma! It's impious to laugh at the truth!"

"Eh? That's exactly what I'm contesting. Let our amiable guide deign not to anathematize me if my common sense puts in doubt—very great doubt—the first article of the dogma to which she accords her genteel faith!"

"I believe it, because it's true!"

"Oh!"

"And you ought to believe as I do, a paltry creature whom Old Sinker has deigned to educate."

"As I'm not in your situation, you'll surely admit that…"

"No, it's necessary to believe, I tell you!"

"You'll permit…"

"It's necessary to believe, because you have no good reason to support your incredulity."

"That's not so!"

"The Earth is a living being; everything proves it."

Claude Rolland, surprised at first by the sudden fit of fanaticism on the part of Manitoba's daughter, was now very amused by it. He resolved to push her to see how far she would go in the development of what he considered to be an imaginary scientific fantasy in the manner of Verne, who had long been a master of the genre.

"My beautiful Indian," he retorted, "it seems to me that everything demonstrates the contrary."

"Because you don't know or don't want to see."

"I swear to you that I'd be delighted to see through your eyes, which must only see beautiful things."

"They see the truth, which isn't always beautiful."

"No matter—I'll risk it. Enlighten me."

"What objection do you have?" demanded the young Redskin, with a certain hauteur that suited her svelte and elegant person very well.

"First of all, my dear Master, it appears to me that our planet does not exhibit anything in its constitution that could make you assimilate it to a living organism."

"How do you know?"

"But..."

"What do you know on the Earth other than its epidermis?"

"Pardon me. I've descended..."

"Into mines? Then let's say that you've penetrated to the outermost level of the dermis—you're a long way forward! Is it the case that one of the microscopic beings that pullulate on us could claim, because it had plunged into the opening of a pore of our skin by a few hundredths of a millimeter, to know the human organism?"

"So, according to you, the terrestrial crust is the skin..."

"Of the monster, yes. It isn't me who's speaking—I'm only a poor ignorant girl, in spite of the studies I've carried out at the white girls' school. The person who is expressing himself through my voice is the Master, Old Sinker."

"Let's see, you've just made, with regard to humankind, a comparison with parasites living on our surface—a perfectly just comparison. I'll appropriate it in order to observe that the different organic parasites of humans—I won't go into detail; everyone is familiar with them from having suffered them—have, at least a constitution that resembles ours more or less

132

distantly: a head, a body, locomotive apparatus, respiratory, digestive and circulatory systems, organs to touch, vision, hearing, etc., etc., whereas the Earth..."

"One moment, if you please Is it the case that, in order to be alive, nature requires all its creations to have a form and organs similar to ours? Is it not the case that in running the gamut—already vastly extensive—of the organisms we know, and which belong to the Earth, we find many that are totally different from us in their external and internal structure, as of their ways of life, but which are nonetheless alive? It's not an educated man such as Old Stinker's friend tells me you are who needs me to tell him that one finds living beings that are spherical, like the Earth, and not offering anything more in the way of external and clearly visible organs."

"Undoubtedly, by searching in the ultimate series of the animal kingdom..."

"Well, it's not among those sketched beings that it's necessary to classify the Earth, but among those possessing a more perfect organism."

Claude marveled at finding so much knowledge in the young Indian and hearing hr speak with such surety in scientific terms. Edmée was looking at her in amazement, and Williamson was listening gravely, his eyes half-closed.

The engineer exclaimed, not without irony: "You're not classifying the planet among the vertebrates?"

"It's not, however, the projections of the vertebrates that it lacks. What about the great mountain chains? But I don't insist, that similarity not yet, so far as I know, having been proved by the Master. In any case, there's no lack of other similarities. You mentioned a circulatory system?"

"So?"

"What else are its subterranean rivers, seething in the depths of the terrestrial dermis? And take note that they're only tiny cutaneous veins carrying the excreta of the skin in the form of dissolved salts, like the blue blood of our tiny microscopic veins.

"So, for you, the blood of the Earth is water?"

"Pure in the arteries buried in depths that humans have not thus far attained, impure in the veins that we know, and which are the most superficial."

"And respiration? Does your monster breathe?"

"Yes, but more grossly than we go."

"Aha! You admit a difference there?"

"Capital, but normal. Need creates the organ. The Earth has no need of a respiratory apparatus similar to ours, not having to introduce into itself a dense gas like air."

"What does it breathe, then?"

"It absorbs the element in which it moves—the element that we call, vaguely, the ether. Ether is much subtler than air, and the Earth respires it in the fashion of our trees, which assimilate air through the intermediary of their leaves. The penetration takes place by endomosis, and the ether, like air in us, is used to aliment the eternal combustion."

The engineer smiled. *"Si non e vero, e bene trovato!"*[11] he murmured. And he added: "That suppresses the difficulty of…the lungs."

"The Earth possesses two kinds: one internal, which is everywhere, and one for the external or superficial circulation, which is the sea, where the cold veins, or rivers, discharge in order to purify them of their saline water."

"And nutrition?"

"Our rotating and floating beast nourishes itself on solar emanations, that nutrition taking place by a process analogous to the phenomenon of respiration."

"I expected as much. I confess that the theory is insidious and adroit. It has only one great fault—that of colliding head-on with the theory of the central fire, which is demonstrated by a hundred various effects.

---

[11] "If it isn't true, it's well conceived." An Italian saying, usually credited to Giordano Bruno's *De gli heroici furori* [On Heroic Furies] (1584), although it might have existed beforehand.

"In what way? It's merely a matter of reaching an understanding regarding the expression 'fire.' For us, it's organic matter possessed of a great deal of heat. Now, is it the case that, proportionately speaking, one of the microscopic organisms living on our surface, like those I mentioned to you a little while ago, wouldn't suppose that we had a central fire? Isn't it the case, for example that, progressing into our skin by infinitesimal degrees, it would find heat increasing with depth, given our vital heat and the relative coldness of our normal external habitat?"

"But what about volcanoes, which are the outlets of that chaotic central molten matter?"

Snow Rose shrugged her shoulders. "An unhealthy accident provides nothing, except for accidental purulence. Volcanoes are the bursting of boils—of which they have, in fact, the general structure, and lava is merely pus, which is no more a constituent of the body of the Earth than ours.

"Damn! They're long-lasting bursts!"

"Relative to the longevity of the Earth, a volcano that remains active for a hundred centuries doesn't last any longer than one of our sores, which disappears in a few weeks."

"You have an answer for everything."

"You've hardly raised any objection yet, and I have many other arguments to develop. Is it the atmosphere that preoccupies you? Doesn't a mare, after a long gallop, radiate vapors, especially in cold weather? Aren't all animal mouths misty in winter? Now, what is the heat of minuscule beasts by comparison with that of the terrestrial beast, and what is our great winter cold but a parallel with that of the ether, tough which the monster's frantic trajectory moves.

"Are reeking fogs—which, by the way, your theories explain so poorly—a subject on which you would care for some enlightenment? What, pray, is the meaning of your expression: 'It smells feverish?' when you go into a sick-room, if not that the invalid's whole body is giving off an odor, and is therefore carrying a mist invisible to our poor eyes? Often, the terrestrial beast also has a fever on some point of its gigantic body, and

emits the relative rarity of those special and more or less dele-
terious exhalations.

"Would you like to talk..."

"Enough, thanks!" exclaimed Claude, in a tone deprived
of gravity, but whose ironic tone had evaporated somewhat.
Come on, beautiful and knowledgeable Snow Rose, it's necessary to spare my self-respect a little, as a white European instructed in the errors of the old science.

"You're playing in the unlimited field of hypotheses like
an airplane doing stunts over its experimental field, with vertiginous rapidity, precision and a disconcerting assurance. The
objection hasn't got time to arise in the mind before it's
bowled over by an unexpected outline before which I remain
with closed mouth. That's all to the honor of the arguments
that Old Sinker has given you, and we admire the fact that
you've profited so marvelously from their education—but for
us it's very humiliating."

"You're joking about such a grave subject. You're very
French."

"I swear to you that I'm not joking. I sense, in your bizarre arguments, certain naiveties of form that, as soon as I try
to get past them, present themselves to my judgment like
screens partly masking disquieting depths. If they aren't persuasive, I confess that they cause a certain trouble in the mind,
and I'm asking you...to let me breathe."

"So be it," said the Indian. "The cup of truth requires to
be drained in small sips by those guided by a strong reason,
for it ought not to intoxicate them as it does less cultivated
minds. It ought to penetrate their cerebral substance gradually,
in order to melt into it and transform it. I'll await the opportunity to pursue my demonstration, but I won't let you off today without having deposited in your reason one argument of
scientific philosophy that I defy you to refute."

"Go on," said the engineer, reluctantly but curiously.

"From the infinitely small to the infinitely large, nature is
unified. The sublime law of universal gravitation applies not
only to terrestrial, planetary and sidereal bodies, as the genius

of Newton indicated, but also to the most infinitesimal elements of all bodies

"It was anticipated for a long time, and an as-yet-incomplete proof has been provided by the discovery of X-rays, that every solid body is formed by particles cemented together. Exactly the same thing happens in microscopic beings as in the worlds voyaging in the infinity of Time and Space, passing through a drop of water, a blade of grass, humans and mountains to planetary systems. It is the universal vortex, of atoms as for suns. Is that true?"

"Undoubtedly."

"Well, if the universe is unified with respect to movement, by what right do you claim that it is not so with regard to life? You admit that a drop of water contains thousands of organisms animated by an intense life, because the microscope has shown them to you. You think, rightly, that those tiny creatures contain creatures infinitely tiny in respect to them, and so on. You therefore consent to the existence of organic beings in the sense of the descending progression, but you deny it in entities of superior dimension to the animality wandering over the surface of what you call the terrestrial crust? So that animal life rises from the infusorium to the elephant and the whale, but stops there? Why?

"Reflect on that, and you will say, with Old Sinker, that the living organism extends from the 'minus infinity' to the 'plus infinity,' passing through the infusoria, via humans and the Earth, the sun and all the suns we perceive, which are perhaps no more than formidable atoms composing some great being decillions of decillions of miles in extent, microscopic itself with regard to others...and so on, indefinitely!"

"Enough!" begged Edmée, in her turn. "I'm getting vertigo."

"Let's leave it then, Miss, with our petty Earth, which is a very malevolent beast—which explains why there are so many malevolent ones among those which crawl upon its surface. Another time, I'll tell you about its misdeeds. I'll tell you how that monster..."

Snow Rose as unable to finish. After having rapped summarily on the door and entered without waiting for authorization, Jean Guitard came into the drawing room like a gust of wind and ran to Claude Rolland.

"Commandant, I've just come face to face with your cousin."

"De Montalpé?"

"The same."

"Hmm!" aid Williamson, getting up from his rocking chair. "Then Loeb isn't far away!"

"Probably."

"And Grégoire saw you?"

"Since I've told you, Commandant, that we nearly bumped into one another."

"What bad luck, only a few hours before our departure!" Edmée declared.

"Oh, Mam'zelle, if the Great American Shark hasn't discovered our niche, it isn't the cousin who'll let the cat out of the bag."

"You're dreaming, Jean. Isn't he allied with the man you've so aptly baptized?"

"Allied like the mouse and the cat, Commandant."

"How do you know?"

"He told me so, of course."

"You talked to him then?"

"For sure. Or rather, it's him who talked to me, because I received him like a smoker in a Sainte-Barbe!"[12]

"He's fallen out with our enemy, then?"

"He's had enough of being treated like a lame dog by him, especially after the trick that he played in Mam'zelle Snow Rose's father's place, with regard to which his flapping

---

[12] Sainte Barbe [Saint Barbara] is the patron saint of artillerymen, military engineers, miners and anyone else who works with explosives, so "Saint-Barbe" became slang in Catholic France for ammunition-dumps, dynamite-stores and so on—and also for booby-trap bombs.

tongue worked out so well for us. Then again, he thinks that the dirty dog of a pirate is using…methods compromising for anyone who sails in convoy with him. He thinks that one can't go around sinking ships and provoking worthy people to rebellion without the police getting involved, especially when it's a matter of a person like Monsieur Mining King. So, he thinks it would be prudent to get away from Loeb, to obtain your pardon, to offer you his amity and to pursue the recovery of the inheritance in concert, which he'd rather share than risk being electrocuted someday—which is the way they guillotine people hereabouts."

"And what did you reply?"

"I put on my amiable expression of a steel mask to tell him that I'd deliver his message. I came up double quick to tell you about it, via the elevator to the fourteenth floor, in order that he couldn't follow my route."

"Might this offer of reconciliation conceal a trap?"

"On your cousin's part, Commandant? Word of a matelot, I don't think so. He's not clever enough for that."

"I agree with Captain Furet," Williamson opined. "Nevertheless, it's necessary to look twice before making him welcome. His incompetence makes him a precious auxiliary…but in the hands of the adversary. The adventure among the Menominees proves that.

"In that case, Monsieur Williamson, it would be more advantageous to us to constrain him to stay with Loeb?"

"I think so, Monsieur Rolland. But in that regard, there's an accessory question. It's not the accomplice that worries me. If he's staying in this hotel, as it's his first time in Chicago, it's because Loeb brought him or sent him here. Now, is that choice a mere coincidence, or has our exceedingly skillful and powerful adversary has discovered our retreat?"

As if in response to that question, the electric bell situated beside the fire place in a metallic box sealed into the wall, connected to a pneumatic tube, signaled the arrival of a visiting card, which the Mining King went to collect, without his phlegm deigning to hasten a single one of his strides.

"He's the answer," he said, in his most tranquil voice. Without the slightest trace of emotion, he read aloud: "*Jonathan Loeb informs Mr. Williamson that he can take off his false beard and cease to cloister himself. J. Loeb, president of the reconstituted Club of World Defenders, is waiting for you to come alone to the landing of this floor, neutral and public ground, setting aside any possibility of an ambush, for an urgent conversation and an interesting proposition.*"

Claude, Edmée and the mariner looked at one another, anxious and troubled. Snow Rose furrowed her black eyebrows. Only Williamson seemed no more emotional than is the incident were happening in Tokyo or Valparaiso, and concerned someone else entirely. In his nonchalant tone, he said: "Good. I'll go."

"Let me go with you!" exclaimed Claude and the matelot, running toward him.

Williamson stopped them with a gesture. "It says *alone*. So stay here, and whatever happens, don't budge."

He put his hand to his belt to make sure that his revolver was in its holster, and, that gesture alone betraying his secret opinion of the gravity of the situation, he went out.

# Chapter VIII
## *A Drama in an Elevator*

When he arrived on the landing, Williamson scanned it in its entirety with a rapid glance. In the center, the twin elevators were in action, dispersing residents or visitors to all the floors. On the monumental stairway with a double revolution, its steps covered with a thick carpet, members of the service staff were going up and down, crossing paths with residents who were only coming or going between the neighboring floors, disdaining the mechanical elevators. On the landing itself, two of the numerous doors were not closed.

Satisfied with that entirely reassuring examination, observing that his enemy had not lied about the "neutral territory," the Mining King marched toward Loeb, who, quitting his station in front of the elevator-shafts, came striding to meet him, with his hat on his head.

"You wanted to see me. What do you want?"

"To finish."

"With?"

"An absurd situation."

"Your pursuit?"

"You've escaped me twice."

"Only because the attack was, on each occasion, badly planned."

"It's too many machinations for a simple suppression. I've had enough."

"Good. I'll be glad to have peace."

"Complete. I've come to propose an arrangement that will give it to you."

"Go on."

"First, I want you to know that I don't have any direct hatred against you."

"Your actions, however..."

"Are aimed over your head."

"Old Sinker?"

"Lobanief, yes. You understood my card?"

"President of the Club of World Defenders. I thought that was an old story."

"I've rejuvenated it."

"To make yourself a weapon?"

"Against Lobanief, whom I hate, and to whom I don't want you to bring the help of your millions and the incredible luck that favors you."

"The fact is that you're not fortunate against me."

"It doesn't matter to me that you're alive, as long as you don't get in my way."

"It's you who are getting in my way."

"Solely because it indicates mine. I want Lobanief choking under my foot, and I need your guide to reach him. You're rich enough. Let me do my work and I'll let you live."

"You can see that I'm conserving it quite well without your permission."

"Renounce joining the man who has summoned you."

"No."

"Tell me where I can find him."

"He hasn't made me that confidence."

"Then let me take the girl that's guiding you; I'll be able to force her to guide me."

"A thousand regrets."

"That's...no?"

"No—today, tomorrow and forever."

"It's you who are forcing me to kill you in order to render myself master!"

"She has other guardians."

"With you out of the way, they scarcely count Do they have the domination of men, as I do? The power of gold, like you?"

"They have intelligence."

"That's good to serve."

"Courage."

"Useful to die. Let's leave those negligibilities. It's between the two of us that the struggle is circumscribed, since you don't want to give up."

"Never."

"Do you know something?"

"I will when you've told me."

"It's that my life has been entirely guided by my hatred, and now that I'm within reach of my vengeance, my hatred is my entire life."

"Which means?"

"That I'm only living to satisfy my hatred, to the accomplishment of which you're raising the supreme obstacle."

"Conclusion?"

"Be good players. Instead of wasting time and effort in plans of attack and defense let's settle the future like good Yankees, revolvers in hand. The survivor will be free of all cares."

"That's neat. I like it. When?"

"Ah! Right away. Rightly or wrongly, I thought you'd refuse... tomorrow, perhaps?"

"Because?"

"Of...those who are accompanying you."

"Then you're mistaken. I don't want to expose them to your ambushes any longer."

"It's a point of view."

"But we can't do it here. At the first shot, people would come running. And I think it would be in bad taste to give the spectacle to...my companions."

"Yes, besides, we'd be hindered...wait! I have the means."

"Where?"

"Without leaving here."

"Which is?"

"The elevators."

"Practical?"

"You'll see."

Taking a voluminous chronometer from his fob pocket, Loeb said, in his hoarse and imperious voice: "Let's synchronize our watches."

"Three-fourteen and twelve seconds," Williamson said, having taken out his own.

"I'll set mine to your time."

"You can—it's that of the Observatory in Washington. Now?"

"At three-thirty exactly I'll take one of the elevators, alone, from the roof of the skyscraper. At the same time, also alone, you take the other from the ground floor..."

"Good. When they meet, fire at will..."

"And, arriving at the bottom before any word of the affair has spread. I'll make myself scarce, to avoid any annoying complications."

"What about me?"

"Oh, no one will cause any disturbance to the famous Mining King. Anyway, it doesn't matter—you'll be dead."

"Or you. I'll have on me a declaration certifying that there was regulation duel."

"Me too."

"Agreed for three-thirty."

"Agreed."

The two adversaries turned their backs, and Williamson, very calm, almost smiling, went back to his apartment.

He found his friends there, their expressions distraught with anxiety. Claude and Edmée ran to him.

"What happened? Condemned to remain here by your order, we were in mortal dread."

"Nothing happened," said Williamson, with a forced cheerfulness, "that isn't, fundamentally, very advantageous."

"For us?"

"Certainly. Loeb declares that he's tired of tracking us."

"Him?"

"And regrets the needless trouble it has caused you."

"He'll reach a settlement?"

"I think I can bring him to one. We'll be having a second... private conversation about the subject shortly."

Edmée, fixing the billionaire with her large profound eyes, velvety and limpid, said to him, choosing the most harmoniously soft notes of her beautiful voice: "Why, Monsieur Williamson, aren't you telling us the truth?"

"Me?"

"Don't be astonished; I sense that there's something else, or something more, than what you're expressing. I swear to you that you can confide in us, who have open hearts with regard to you."

"You have, then, some amity toward me, Miss Edmée?"

"A great deal, Monsieur Williamson, and a little more every day, because every day I discover a little more of the secret man that you hide within you, under the disabused mask of the billionaire that villainous humankind has spoiled."

The Mining King did not reply immediately. Then, adopting a detached tone, he said: "I assure you, Miss, that there's nothing but what I've told you."

"As you wish!" said the young woman, a trifle sadly, still visibly incredulous In the midst of the somewhat constrained general silence that followed, she added: "I also sense that our presence embarrasses you at the moment, and that you'd rather be alone."

"For a moment, yes, perhaps. I need to reflect on the fashion in which it will be necessary, momentarily, to engage the combat...of words...with my adversary." Seeing his companions sketch a movement toward the threshold, however, he swiftly added: "But don't go away. There's no need to return to your rooms. Go in there, into my bedroom. I'll only be a few minutes."

*He doesn't want us to appear on the landing*, thought Claude Rolland's sister. But she did not breathe a word, and, contenting herself with nodding her head graciously as a sign of acquiescence, she indicated the discreet retreat route to her brother and the mariner—and to the young Indian, who never ceased to devour the latter with his eyes.

Williamson's gaze followed Edmée until she disappeared.

When, with urgent politeness, "Captain Furet" had closed the door behind Snow Rose, the expression of the American King changed abruptly, and a crease of anxiety was hollowed out in is smooth forehead.

He sat down rapidly at a writing-desk. On the first sheet of paper that came to hand he traced a few lines:

*I declare that, having been killed in a duel, my last will is that my adversary not be either sought or troubled on account of my decease.*

He folded up the paper and put it in his pocket.
On another, he wrote:

*I bequeath all that I possess to Miss Edmée Rolland, who, with her brother, is accompanying me on the present voyage. I designate Monsieur Claude Rolland, her brother, to continue on her behalf, with the title of managing director, the exploitation of my mines and associated factories. She will not forget that Toby has served me well, the Jean Guitard has twice saved our lives, and that Snow Rose is a friend of Old Sinker.*

He put the address of a solicitor on an envelope, unhooked a telephone and said: "Hello? The hotel manager... It's you? Good. Would you care to come up tight away to the ninth floor, number 174, with three or four people that you have ready to hand. Understood? All right!"

Three minutes later, the manager of the skyscraper and the requested assistants appeared in front of Williamson. The latter said to the master of the immense caravanserai: "I'm present here, as are my companions, under a false name. I'm Williamson, the Mining King."

"I know."

"Ah! Since when?"

"An hour ago."

"Naturally..." And the billionaire thought: *That simplifies things*. Aloud, he went on: "You and these gentlemen are going to establish in writing that it really is me who signed these documents in your presence."

When the signature had been countersigned and the witnesses dismissed, Williamson put his testament into the envelope he had prepared and, handing the later to the Hotel manager, whom he had retained, he said: "You will only hand this letter back to me, in person. If I...judge it appropriate not to do so today, before nightfall, you will immediately send it or put it into the hands of its addressee. Here's twenty dollars for the errand-boy.

The hotel manager acquiesced, and left. Williamson looked at his watch. He only had four and a half minutes left. He took his revolver from its holster and examined the barrel, replaced the weapon methodically to his belt and quit his apartment, at a tranquil pace.

While all this was happening in the Mining King's room, another brief scene was unfolding on the landing of the floor.

As Loeb, having quit Williamson, strode toward the ascending elevator, he had made an authoritative sign to an individual resembling a Quaker who emerged therefrom and immediately disappeared into the stairwell. At that moment, Grégoire de Montalpé, coming down from Jean Guitard's room, where he was gone to wait for the response he expected from the latter, appeared on the ninth floor landing.

At the sight of him, Loeb frowned. "I ordered you to keep watch in the ground floor grill room," he said, brutally.

The accomplice baulked. "I revoked the order myself. I've had enough of being treated like a whipped dog in order to go after my money."

"What are you saying?"

"That I'm finally rebelling! That I'm changing uniform! That I'm leaving, if you want it in a word."

"You think so!" exclaimed Jonathan Loeb, with a dry, sinister snigger of sinister irony.

"I'm so convinced of it," said the other, raising his head like a bloody and de-plumed cock at the end of a losing fight, "that it's now a settled matter. My re-entry has been negotiated into the grace of my cousins and Williamson, whom you have failed to stop for a second time."

"Because of your stupidity."

"Not with regard to the collision at sea, though! And then, you know, please keep your insults for others. Whether you like it or not, I'm handing in my resignation. That's it!"

"Cretin!"

"Ah! There you go!"

"Peace, then! What about my permission?"

"I'll do without it."

"Listen. I'd like nothing better than for you to go over to the enemy."

"What?"

"You had twenty thousand dollars; we've spent four. Are you going to give me the remaining sixteen?"

"Give them to you? That's not going to happen."

"If you don't give them to me willingly, you'll be found tomorrow lying on the bank of Lake Michigan, unburdened to my advantage."

"What about the police?" de Montalpé countered, unable to help shivering.

"Half those in Chicago are under my control—so, no idle threats. I'll take the cash and you'll go to Williamson to betray me...if, in a quarter of an hour, that's still necessary. But remember this: you're going into the enemy camp with my permission, to serve me there."

"Never!"

"I've put down better men than you, my lad. Not having the leisure, at the moment, to take care of such a small matter, I'm content to scorn this vain attempt at rebellion, which you'll redeem by showing zeal and trying not to be stupid. You're going to run to the square at the end of the street. On the sidewalk outside the entrance door, you'll find a gentleman Ask him whether or not his dispositions are presently made, wholly or partly, in accordance with my orders. Whatever his reply is, I need it here before three twenty-five. You have exactly five minutes. Go!"

"But..."

"Would you prefer the lake or two inches of steel between the shoulder-blades?"

"Me? I'm...going. But when I get back I warn you..."

"You'll receive my instructions on the nature of your role in the Williamson camp, if they make the mistake of letting you in. Go!"

De Montalpé made a grand gesture of heroic decision...and took to his heels, in order to obey more rapidly.

Loeb shrugged his shoulders and murmured: "Oh, if he didn't represent the sinews of war...never mind. If I'm rid of Williamson shortly, all will be well. If, impossibly, the encounter turns to my disadvantage, I've woven a net around him that he won't escape."

And, striding back and forth on the landing, he waited, frequently consulting his watch.

The five minutes were up. De Montalpé had not reappeared. Leaning over the cage of the elevators, Loeb waited two more minutes, tapping his foot angrily.

He saw Williamson come out of his apartment. He only had the time strictly necessary to get to the top of the skyscraper. With a gesture of annoyance, he activated the handle of the elevator, which immediately stopped in front of him, jumped into it and started it moving toward the summit of the immense building, while Williamson went down to the ground floor in the same fashion.

Almost immediately, the anxious faces of Claude, Edmée and Jean appeared on the threshold of the apartment, ahead of that, equally anxious, of the young Indian woman. From the depths of their retreat, their ears, on the alert, had caught the sound of the billionaire's unusual exit. Infringing the prohibition, Edmée had gone into the deserted drawing room. They had all headed for the landing then, having understood that Williamson's intention was to keep them out of the way—

which caused them to suppose that something serious was about to happen.

They were not mistaken. They had only been there for five minutes, consulting one another anxiously with their gazes, when, before their anxious eyes, the paths of the two elevators crossed. A series of detonations departed from the one that was descending, followed by a cry, and then a raucous oath.

The descent continued on the one hand. The other vertical transporter, which had stopped at the floor, opened, and in the midst of a general exclamation emerging from numerous doors suddenly disengaging a surprised population, a bareheaded man bounded on to the platform, his face bloodied, beating the air madly with his arms, and fell almost at the feet of Edmée and Claude, who cried out at the same time: "Montalpé!"

Aided by the mariner and the young Redskin, both of them bent down to help the unfortunate man. Meanwhile, guests and members of the hotel staff hurried down the double stairway in pursuit of the murderer.

The hero of the adventure, however, must have been more frightened than hurt, for, getting to his feet, he started howling in French: "Help! Murder! He's killed me!"

Suddenly recognizing his cousins, he implored them, in a fearful voice: "Protect me! Hide me! The killer will come back!"

"What killer?"

"*Him!*"

"Who's *him?*"

"Don't pronounce his name! Shut up, for pity's sake! He'll kill me again!"

"Damn it! For a dead man, you're making a lot of noise!" Claude could not help remarking.

"Come on, be quiet and let us look at your wound," added the engineer's sister, using her delicate handkerchief to mop up the blood, already quite abundant, that was reddening the dandy's forehead.

"Be careful!" the latter moaned. "The bullet went through my skull."

"Damn it!" exclaimed the former explorer, holding the terror-stricken man still be force. "If your cranium had been pierced you wouldn't be moaning so much. Your wound is a long graze, that's all. There's no reason to scream as if you were being flayed alive."

"You think so?"

"Yes, there, at the top of the head."

"I don't have a fractured skull?"

"I'll admit that you've had a narrow escape. A centimeter of difference in the trajectory and you'd be the late Montalpé."

"De Montalpé, my dear!" rectified the Parisian fop, vaingloriously.

Claude burst out laughing. "The pride is uninjured," he said. "You can see quite clearly that the brain hasn't been damaged. A little iron perchloride lotion and it'll be fine. Jean!"

"Commandant?"

"Fetch a bellboy."

"Done, Commandant; there's one coming now with a first aid kit."

While Claude bandaged the wounded man, Edmée murmured: "How did this happen? What's become of Williamson? My God, where is he?" Her features were distressed. In an emotional voice, she said to her brother: "Claude, leave our bad relative, who scarcely needs treatment except for fear, and run to help our great friend. I'm sure that his life is in danger! Go quickly, with Jean. Find him, protect him…ward off a frightful misfortune that I can sense hanging over him."

"Here's the man Old Sinker summoned," Snow Rose announced, pointing at Williamson, who was coming up the stars, tranquilly.

"Oh!" said Edmée, taking a step toward him. "I was afraid that you'd been killed."

151

"Don't worry, Miss. Things have passed in a satisfactory manner, if not without an unexpected hitch, and I've made sure of my adversary's retreat.

"Ah! My presentiment wasn't mistaken It was a duel, and an odious duel! Oh, it was wicked of you to hide it from..."

She did not finish. Suddenly weakening, she almost fainted in her brother's arms.

"That's extraordinary," murmured the Mining King, with an anxious astonishment. "Miss Edmée waited so intrepidly for execution by the Menominees."

"Her soul is strong in common peril," Claude explained, "but her heart is generous and feeble before a danger run by a friend without her sharing it."

Williamson said nothing more. He was visibly troubled by that nervous weakness, so inexplicable for his psychology, and a hard labor began in his brain, to which the young woman's prompt return to self-possession put an end.

"Excuse that sudden weakness," she said, smiling a little awkwardly. "I don't understand it myself, but it's over. Now, tell me quickly how it came about that those bullets, of which I felt the impact deep within me, and were surely addressed to you, were fired—one of them, at least—at Monsieur de Montalpé."

"You see, Miss, they say that a man doesn't walk toward his misfortune, but that he runs to it. Now, it wasn't only at a run, it was by violence that my adversary's companion took my place in the elevator, in which I was waiting until the exact second agreed before going up to encounter Loeb."

"Hold on, damn it!" cried the man wounded in error. "My murderer had enjoined me, on pain of death, to bring him an answer urgently, and I was nearly five minutes late."

""What answer?" demanded Williamson, staring at him imperiously.

"You're asking too much. I was to find out from a gentleman whether something—I don't know what—was ready."

"Well," said the Mining King, in a harsh voice that was not habitual to him, "since you're so slightly wounded that you can screech and lie like this, why don't you run off and make your report to your master."

"Know, Monsieur Williamson, that Grégoire de Montalpé doesn't recognize any master! Then again, I've had enough of running his errands and spinning like a top in the hands of such a man. The miracle is that he didn't kill me just now, and I don't want to find myself in his presence, and that of his revolver, again. Besides which, you ought to know that I want to break with that bloodthirsty man and attach myself henceforth to your fortune. The mariner in the service of my cousin Rolland ought to have told you..."

"Faithfully," declared the billionaire, in the same tone. "I had postponed my response until now. Here it is: I won't accept into our company a traitor, a spy...or an imbecile."

"Monsieur! I do not accept such epithets!"

"Oh, I won't impose them cumulatively—you can choose. But what I want most of all is for you to liberate us from your presence."

"You're throwing me back into the power of that pitiless man?"

"Of your ally."

"See how he treats me!"

"Error doesn't count."

"I'm doomed, then!"

"That's not my concern. Let's leave it there, please."

"No. I won't leave!"

"We'll leave you, then. Let's go back to my room, my friends."

"I'm not budging from here, and you'll have to come out again. Then, I shall follow you..."

Grégoire de Montalpé did not have time to say any more. At a sign from Williamson, now known to all of the hotel staff, two of the employees had put their hands on his shoulders and were leading him away without his consent, forcibly dragging him to the elevator, into which they pushed him before getting in with him. The dandy protested in vain, his exclamation rapidly fading away into the distance of the lower floors.

"But if I understand the conditions of this fortunately abortive duel correctly," said the young engineer to the Mining King during that forced descent, "your adversary had all the advantages. Descending like that, he could see you for some time, while the metallic floor of his elevator protected him until the two machines crossed paths. How were you able to accept such dangerously unequal conditions?"

Resuming his habitual indolent voice, Williamson replied, smiling: "Bah! What did it matter to me? I have faith in my lucky star, and you can see that it didn't betray me. That's the third time in a matter of days that I've escaped Loeb's attempts on my life, and he's a strong player. 'It's written,' as the followers of Mohammed that you've frequented in the course of your African explorations would say.

"Oh, Monsieur Williamson, don't talk to me about Africa—don't awaken my remorse!"

"Your remorse?"

"For having broken my promise to Senator Dupeyroux. It's today that he was to make his famous interpellation. And when I think that my report was swallowed up with the unfortunate yacht, and that, without it, the senator was unarmed…how he must be cursing me!"

"Perhaps not. Who knows?" And, smiling amiably, the billionaire added: "Perhaps, like me, your Monsieur Dupeyroux has a lucky star. Anyway, it's not your fault, is it?"

"Certainly not."

"Having nothing for which to reproach yourself, expel all vexation from your mind on that subject, and let's think about us." Raising his voice and addressing the small circle of his companions of both sexes, he added: "As it would be ridiculous to try to maintain an incognito that can no longer deceive anyone, we'll be able to get a little air. I'll go to the bank to get a hundred thousand dollars, the dollar being a weapon of attack and defense superior to bullets that miss their target, and of which we've deprived ourselves for too long since we've been on American soil."

"We'll go with you," declared Claude and Edmée, swiftly.

"That's what I want, for it would be wise never to split up. It will procure me the pleasure of employing the few hours that remain to us by showing Miss Edmée around Chicago, which she's doubtless curious to see. Rendezvous in ten minutes in my room, where I'll telephone for an automobile. Until then!"

And, as tranquilly as if no drama had taken place there, he left the landing—where numerous groups, already including a few reporters, were commenting on the "terrible duel" between the Mining King and an unknown enemy.

# Chapter IX
## *The Rain of Gold*

For a simple excursion in the city, to which a certain slowness would add charm and interest, Williamson could have contented himself with one of the large elegantly harnessed carriages or automobiles that the hotel kept consciously at the disposal of tourist clients. If he had preferred an automobile of a prestigious make with a powerful engine, it was not without reason.

As soon as Claude Rolland and Edmée had rejoined him in his drawing room, he asked the latter to do him a small favor in order to keep her occupied momentarily, and he took the engineer to one side.

"Can you drive an automobile?"

"Certainly."

"Good."

"But...we'll have a driver?"

"It might be the case that I'll decide to dispense with him."

"Ah!"

"In any case, you'll need keep a very close eye on the man at the wheel."

"You can't suppose that an unknown driver who might be absolutely anyone, could be...?"

"I don't suppose anything, but I'm wary of everything. Don't be distracted because of your sister; I'll look after her very carefully. Tell your brave Captain Furet to keep his eyes on the young Indian, along with Toby."

*I believe that instruction's unnecessary*, the former explorer thought, smiling involuntarily. To the legitimately suspicious billionaire, he said: "You think that Loeb, having failed to catch you in the trap of that infernal duel, will set up some new ambush for us?"

"The ambush—I don't know what—is certainly planned and perhaps already set. I need no more proof of that than the urgent mission with which he charged your cousin a little while ago. Be assured, though, that as soon as I feel the banknotes in my pocket, I'll no longer be content with a passive defense that will end up by doing us a bad turn, for there's no chance that he'll let up. Not another word. Don't worry anyone, but be ready to understand me at the slightest sign."

"You can count on me."

"I know."

Five minutes later, the little troop, fully equipped, were heading at top speed in the direction of the bank indicated to the driver by Williamson. From there, they went to an agency of the New York *Herald*, into which Snow Rose went on her own—under incessant surveillance, without being aware of it—in order to insert a small ad, the secret of which she wanted to keep.

The Mining King had never seemed to be in such good humor, even aboard the steam yacht *Astrea*, where the presence of Claude, and especially of Edmée, had alleviated his long-standing ennui. It was because, as a man accustomed to the power of money, having had his chest solidly padded with banknotes and his pockets ballasted with dollars at the bank, he felt his strength renewed, and had become proudly confident again.

It was in an almost jovial tone that he said to the young Frenchwoman: "Miss Edmée, it's up to you now to give orders, and dictate the itinerary that your Parisienne whim requires. What would you like to see in Chicago? The pig factories? No, I understand. The monuments? I fear that by comparison with your prestigious Paris, they'll be disappointing. The shores of Lake Michigan, perhaps?"

"Oh yes, said the young woman. "I only glimpsed them from the railway—Erie first, then Michigan—and from a distance. I'd like to see one of those inland seas at closer range."

"The ladies and gentlemen could take a little trip to the former site of the World's Fair, from which there's a superb

157

view over the lake, and where numerous attractions are gathered: music halls, circuses, velodromes and all kinds of sports clubs, including the Aero Club, for which a special factory producing lighting gas has been built, and another producing hydrogen."

"Is that all right, Monsieur Williamson?"

"I repeat, Miss, that we're entirely at your orders."

The auto pulled away at a moderate speed, and then, when it reached a broad straight avenue, launched forward at forty an hour, which soon brought it to the edge of a vast liquid plain, some five hundred and seventy kilometers long and as much as a hundred and forty broad, in comparison with which the largest lakes of Europe are mere ponds.

In the immense gathering of various amusements, it was so quiet, the numerous visitors being thinly spread as they strolled or watched the sports with placid and joyful conviction, that Williamson after a long moment contemplating the lake, saw no inconvenience in the excursion continuing on foot, with pauses in a music hall and on the edge of a golf course, a cricket pitch, etc.

When the little troop emerge from a giant cinema, where they had been diverted to the extent of forgetting momentarily the terrors of the past and their anxieties for the future, they did not find the automobile at the place where they had left it. They only had to wait for a few minutes, for the rapid vehicle did not take long to come to pick up its passengers, but that displeased Williamson, who was not fully satisfied by the excuse furnished by the driver. He decided, in consequence, to resume the effective and direct command that he had relinquished temporarily—in appearance, at least—to gracious feminine whimsy.

With a rapid wink, she showed the engineer a pocket map of the State of Wisconsin, on which he rapidly traced several large zigzags with his finger, whose significance Claude understood immediately.

For Williamson, in fact, the present excursion was merely an adroit feint to put Loeb off the track.

Ostensibly, the little troop was to leave that evening by the Western Railroad. Orders had been left at the hotel to transport the travelers' meager baggage there. In the meantime they were killing time visiting Chicago.

In reality, Williamson was using the excursion to make a real clandestine departure. The auto being a hundred HP,[13] he

---

[13] The author inserts an entirely gratuitous footnote at this point: "The author cannot protest too much here against the incurable malady of our sportsmen that consists of always Britannizing necessary technical terms. "HP" is an abbreviation of the expression 'Horse-Power,' which is exactly similar to our '*cheval-vapeur*,' or, word for word, '*cheval-puissance*.' It is observable that only the expressions are synonymous, not existing between the English HP and our *cheval-vapeur*. That one employs the English expression in a country where English is spoken, as is the case here, is normal, but in France it is simply ridiculous Anglomania. If one objects that the expression "*cheval-vapeur*" is no longer adequate to internal combustion engines which are, in fact, a French invention, let it be replaced by, for example, "*cheval-force*" (CF), but let us not, by borrowing a foreign locution, Britannize, so to speak, our own invention, so fecund and so beautiful, and to which it is necessary from every viewpoint to leave the glory of our fatherland, so fertile in the work of progress." The first commercially viable two-stroke internal combustion engine was, in a way, French, having been developed in Paris by the Belgian emigré Étienne Lenoir in 1859, and describing its capability in terms of "*cheval-vapeur*" [literally, horse-steam] was, indeed, always silly—although "*cheval-force*" is no better (and positively rodiculous if translated literally into English). The problem vanished of its own accord, however, when the comparison with horses was largely abandoned, being conventionally replaced in the context of automobile engines by measurements of their cylinder capacity, and in other contexts by the unit named after the displaced term's inventor, James Watt (thus reflecting the glory of Scotland, alas for the French).

was about to launch it at top speed across country, changing direction so as to avoid and pursuit, and connect with the railway at a distance, in good time to satisfy the peremptory instruction formulated by the young Indian guide.

It was improbable that, until that moment, Loeb and his sleuths had not been taken in. If he had prepared some immediate *coup de Jarnac*, it was evident that the blow, whatever it was, could not fall until they returned from the excursion, between that return and the advertised departure, quite probably at the railway station.

Now, Loeb would wait in vain for the return to the city and the departure, and if he launched himself in pursuit of the auto, it would be at the very moment that the travelers were boarding their Pullman car.

If, by chance—which possibility, at the moment, Williamson was not far from admitting—the chauffeur was under orders and tried to prevent the execution of the plan, excellent by virtue of its very simplicity, we know that the Mining King was resolved to throw him overboard.

Thus, as he climbed into the auto, Williamson said pleasantly to the engineer and his sister: "If you don't mind, we're going to put on a little speed."

"Oh," said Edmée, with a disappointed expression. "Aren't we continuing this amusing and interesting excursion?"

"Yes, but by going on to Hyde Park, a few miles away."

"We're not stopping beforehand at the Aero Club, whose landing-ground I can see over there, surrounded by a fence plastered with posters?"

"On the way back, if you wish."

"What if it's dark? Since we've arrived at the edge of the lake I've been gazing enviously at the colossal sphere of the captive balloon rising up—so high!"

"It goes up half a mile—eight hundred and eighty yards," the driver made haste to inform her.

"What a view one must have from up there, in such clear weather! One must be able to see the whole of the lake, and beyond it, the state to which it gives its name. Who knows whether one might be able to see Erie, the Saint-Clair River and the tip of the great peninsula the Canadian Ontario extends into the lacustrian cranium of the United States?"

"Miss Edmée," Williamson replied, putting on a jovially sulky expression, "I appeal to your sense of justice. If demoiselles have these whimsical desires, which are laws so far as they're concerned, gentlemen are not spared fashionable neurasthenia, and I have to take into account its nervous demands on the temperament. Personally, in an auto, I experience an irrational need for speed. If I don't satisfy it, I sense that I shall become peevish for forty-eight hours. Just grant me thirty minutes to calm that unhealthy irritation. I promise you that we'll make the ascension that appears to be tempting your heart immediately thereafter."

Edmée pursed her lips, not without chagrin. "Are you quite sure," she said, with an enigmatic smile, "that this little crisis is really neurasthenic, and not simply egot..."

She stopped dead. Her gaze had just met her brother's, and she had read therein...that something was at stake. "In fact," she exclaimed, laughing, "as you wish. After all, deep down, I don't care about the famous ascension anymore."

"I expected no less of you, Miss," said Williamson, seriously. And he turned to the driver, who was staring at Edmée, doubtless astonished by such a sudden change of mind. He showed him the road that led due south and ordered, in a dry tone: "Forward! At forty-five and hour!"

The man seemed hesitant. "That's the maximum my engine can manage," he observed.

"I know."

"I've never yet demanded that speed of it. I won't take the responsibility, and I can't guarantee anything."

"I'll pay for any damage to the auto...and there's five hundred dollars for you if I'm satisfied."

"I'll try."

In a matter of seconds the automobile reached the long fence alongside the aerodrome where Edmée had wanted to make her first excursion toward the zenith; in a few more seconds, it had been surpassed…when all of a sudden, the driver cut the ignition and applied the brake.

"What's wrong?" interrogated the billionaire, a trifle rudely.

"What I feared. I can hear a rattle that worries me. It must have overheated. I need to take a look."

"How much time do you need?"

"Five or six minutes, I think."

"I won't give you any more."

The vehicle stopped, the driver jumped out, and Claude Rolland got out with him.

The man exposed the engine, looked. Scrutinizing it with minute attention, and hence with a slowness that appeared to irritate Williamson, watching from his seat.

"You can't find anything?" Claude asked him.

"No, nothing. Everything's working normally. It's doubtless a loose bolt that needs tightening. I'll go underneath."

Armed with a monkey wrench, he slid under the automobile.

The engineer had scarcely raised his eyes than he met the imperative gaze of Williamson, obviously reproaching him: *What are you doing? You're interrupting your surveillance!*

Claude threw himself flat on the ground. He saw the chauffeur busy tightening a bolt, who said to him: "The gentleman can see. It's what I thought—a little looseness in the thread. It's fixed."

The man crawled out from under the vehicle while Claude stood up. The latter saw that the Mining King was standing up in his seat, pointing in the direction in which the vehicle was heading.

"What's that?" he demanded, curtly.

*That* was a black mass of people marching along the road, heading for the Exhibition site that the travelers had just quit.

"The ones in the lead are carrying a banner," announced Jean Guitard, making use of his keen eyesight.

Unhurriedly resuming his seat after the engineer, the driver said, disdainfully. "It's a troop of the Salvation Army, who march singing hymns, supposedly for the purification of these places of amusement, which they qualify as dens of iniquity. Don't take any notice of them. They'll move out of the way."

He put his hand on the gear-stick, but Williamson stopped him abruptly.

"Turn round!" the commanded. "Go the other way. Take us to Evanston instead of Hyde Park."

"Because of those people?"

"Do as you're told," said the billionaire.

"Oh, as you wish. The road north is as good as the road south."

Starting it in motion, the man turned the vehicle around. When it was heading in the right direction, he put it brutally into fourth gear, and without anyone having been able to anticipate the insensate action, leapt out on to the road, where the acquired velocity laid him out on the ground.

The leap might have been fatal. The voyagers did not even have time to make that reflection when a violent detonation resounded, and the auto lifted up as if it were about to take off.

But for the composure and promptitude with which the engineer bounded into the driving seat, cut the ignition and maintained the direction, there would have been a catastrophe. Under the firm and skillful handling of Claude, the auto, mastered, came to a halt.

"It's a burst tire," he explained.

"By the driver, when you took your eyes off him," said Williamson, in a dull voice.

Turning around swiftly, he saw the man, fifty paces away, get to his feet and draw away, limping, still suffering the effects of his voluntary fall.

"Scoundrel!" growled the billionaire. "I promised to pay you well for your services. Here!"

His arm extended, holding a revolver. He fired.

The chauffeur beat the air with his arms and fell backwards.

A clamor in the ranks of the Salvationists responded to that execution, and the troop started running.

"Quickly, everyone out!" Williamson commanded. "Run to the aerodrome!"

As the little company, out of breath, reached the southern end of the fence, they perceived another mass of people, running flat out, coming from the north.

"Those," announced the mariner, "have a big triangle at the end of a pole by way of a flag.

"It's decidedly serious," murmured Williamson. "Loeb doesn't waste any time! The Knights of Labor now! We must at all costs reach the entrance to the Aero Club before those people do."

They started running again, Claude and Jean supporting—almost carrying—Edmée, who was incapable of maintaining the pace.

They arrived level with the captive balloon, the dome of which, gilded by the rays of the sun going down in the west, emerged gigantically above the palisade. At that moment, the leader of the fugitives realized that it would be impossible to reach the entrance, still more than three hundred yards away, in time.

"Halt!" he commanded. "Backs to the palisade and get enough breath back to make our shots count. I think we can hold them at bay long enough for those inside to come to our aid."

"Counting on others is borrowing on the inheritance of the living, always a bad move," philosophized the mariner. "Only counting on oneself is more reliable. This accursed fence is more than two brasses high—no matter; let's try. Without commanding you, Commandant, brace yourself. I'll put Toby on your shoulders. Climbing over the two of you, I can reach the top. Then you'll see!"

Acting while talking, the nimble matelot hoisted himself up to the top of the fence.

Inside, there was a narrow roof, under which equipment was stored, including suspended coils of rope. To grab one of them was a matter of seconds. He threw one end over the palisade, shouting: "Hold on!" As agile as a squirrel, he used that point of support to resume his place at the top of the planks.

"Send up Mam'zelle Edmée!"

In a trice, the young woman, lifted up with delicate energy, was deposited on the interior roof, where Snow Rose joined her, in the same fashion, in a matter of seconds.

For the men, Jean contented himself with mooring his rope solidly to one of the joists of the little roof and letting them climb up, while he occupied himself with getting the young women down to the ground, where everyone was gathered when the first vociferating crowd arrived and stopped, momentarily disconcerted, beside the fence.

Several employees of the aerodrome had run toward the travelers, who had introduced themselves into it by somewhat unorthodox means. At their head was an individual clad in a jacket with dull metal buttons and a helmet with a flat peak, decorated with a badge that depicted an aerostat in gold filigree. It was that individual who shouted to them: "What are you doing? Who are you?"

"I'm Williamson, the Mining King."

"Ach!"

"Pursued...no time to explain...give us shelter...out of range of the miscreants."

"The only shelter I have is the nacelle of the captive balloon, whose captain I am."

"I'll buy it, Captain."

"It's not for sale."

"Yes it is! Ten thousand dollars? Twenty thousand? Here they come!"

"But an aerostat nacelle isn't a fortress. There's no more precarious shelter."

"Excellent, on the contrary—and we'll climb out of range."

"Today's ascensions have finished."

"There'll be an extra one."

"I don't have my staff."

"We'll make do. Go on, take the banknotes. Quickly, let's go!

"So be it," said the Captain, taking the wad of bills that was twice the value of the aerostat. He addressed the club's employees: "You loosen the ropes of the nacelle. I'll operate the winch myself."

Alas, rapid as the negotiations and the embarkation were, they had not been as rapid at the two cohorts, now reunited, who had traversed all the obstacles and invaded the field. As Williamson had anticipated, the Knights of Labor had reinforced the first troop, fusing into a single legion; the individual banners had vanished, to give way to long streamers, on which was displayed the communal, frightfully significant motto: *World Defenders*.

That was the old idea and the old formula so actively and adroitly reawakened by Jonathan Loeb: the idea and formula of the implacable hatred of popular self-preservation against Old Sinker and all those who might serve his criminal genius.

And that crowd headed straight for the captive balloon serving as a retreat for the fugitives.

"Release all!" shouted Williamson.

The balloon oscillated, and...that was all! A hundred hands had seized the attachments, representing a human weight of seven tons, which retained the balloon, ready to launch into the atmosphere, on the ground.

A few dolorously critical seconds went by, but it is extreme peril that provokes ideas of genius, and Williamson had one. Standing up before the howling horde he raised his two fists full of dollars, which he hurled with all his strength into the crowd, shouting: "Yours!"

The effect was devastating. Under the rain of gold, which he renewed three times in different directions around the vast nacelle, their hands instinctively let go of the ropes to seize the sovereign manna that was falling from heaven...

166

Abruptly liberated, with such force that the steel cable, tightened too soon, snapped, the liberated captive launched forth into the sky like a cannonball, carrying Williamson and his fortune, along with his five companions, far away from Loeb and his acolytes.

Five? No; it is necessary to say "six companions." There was one person who had grabbed hold of the ropes to retain the nacelle and who had not let go during the rain of gold launched by the billionaire. That one had been carried away into the air like a wisp of straw.

In spite of the fury of his fourth disappointment, Loeb uttered a kind of hiccup of laughter on seeing the unfortunate Grégoire de Montalpé flying toward the zenith, hanging beneath the nacelle like a ridiculous marionette, also relieved of the weight of his wallet, which his implacable master had made him hand over.

# Chapter X
## *The Latter Day Saint*

Let us take a leap—a truly American leap—of some twelve hundred and sixty miles, as the crow flies, and enter the famous metropolis, at least so far as its inhabitants are concerned, of Salt Lake City, situated in the north of the state of Utah, about ten miles south east of the Great Salt Lake on the Jordan River linking that Lake to Lake Utah.

At the back of a vast courtyard, on the stone steps, tinted green by damp, of a vast house offering the ugly aspect of a single-story barracks, an obese man with a fleshy and thick-lipped face, clad in a dark ulster with a long black jacket hanging over trousers of the same negative shade, coiffed in a slightly furry and prodigiously tall top hat, shod in robust clogs, was scolding five women who were escorting him in submissive attitudes.

This five women, the youngest of whom was not twenty and the eldest certainly about forty, clad in black costumes whose style dated back at least a third of a century, where the dejected spouses of the Latter Day Saint, the great pontiff of the Mormon sect, the patriarch of that essay in religious Orientalism in the midst of the desert of the Far West, the absolute and tyrannical master of the New Jerusalem, as the inhabitants of the city of the Great Salt Lake considered it to be.[14] That

---

[14] This depiction of the Church of the Latter Day Saints is of course, as bizarrely inaccurate and ludicrously insulting as the depiction of the Salvation Army. The Church had, in fact, abandoned polygamy in 1890, and although it was deeply in debt at that point, the adoption of a tithing system had ensured that it was thriving financially by 1910. By that time, its members were increasingly taking prominent roles in such national political movements as the Women's Suffrage movement and the Temperance movement. Far from it being an authoritarian

Saint, that pontiff, that patriarch, that master, the husband of the five wives, the grotesque fat man dressed as we have just seen—because it was raining heavily—closed his huge umbrella, and left his muddy clogs on the threshold.

"Mabel," said the Saint to the oldest member of his harem, a tall ugly woman as stiff as a plank, shivering in her mantle under the icy downpour, "I ought to make you serious reproaches for your coquetry. You want a new dress...at your age! You're not thinking enough about the poverty that the Lord, in his mercy, imposes upon us for the expiation of our sins, and that after having once known the seven fat cows, we're now under the reign of the lean cows! Don't get angry, I'm not saying that for you.

"As for you, Betsy, your accounts are very neatly written, but full of errors. You've recorded as fifty dollars the fine to which I condemned Andrew Sweetish for having permitted his only wife, under the fallacious pretext that she was too rudely beaten, to flee to the land of the Infidels. It was a hundred dollars that I demanded of him, and it's a poor price, in view of his difficulty in living. Betsy, no more favors or...errors of that sort. Such a great sin, when women are so desolately scarce in the New Jerusalem, merits no pity, especial when, as Andrew has, one dares to rejoice in having become solitary again, which is only permitted to children and old men fallen into decrepitude. And then, times are hard...and I need cash.

"Meg and Bella, both receive my anathema for have managed so poorly, one of you the kitchen for the satisfaction of my palate, and the other the keeping of my house, which is not in accord with my dignity as a Latter Day Saint.

"As for you, Maud, your youth is no excuse for taking so little trouble to please me. A little more zeal, if you please, in your privileged functions as secretary! Go put on your beauti-

---

institution, many Mormons were members of the Utah Social Democratic Party, carrying forward a long-standing cooperative tradition within the Church.

ful white negligee made of silk and lace, for which I sent away to San Francisco, and wait for me in my study. We have all day to occupy ourselves with matters of Religion, and know that a wife can never be too beautiful when it's a matter of the Lord and his wife."

The four older women had meekly bowed their heads under the mercuriality of the Master. Young Maud, very irreverently, made a grimace significant of the lack of attraction that the favor of spending a long day in private with her illustrious, vast and mature husband had for her.

The sonorous vibrations of the bell at the main entrance, agitated violently, put an abrupt end to that scene of multiple domesticity. The Saint's Olympian eyebrows furrowed.

"By Abraham! Only an impious man would dare to ring like that on my venerated threshold. Maud, go and see to it. Put the infidel in the parlor and come and tell me what he wants." Addressing a magisterial gesture to his other wives, he ordered: "Go inside!"

Five minutes later, Maud came into the study and handed the Mormon pope a visiting card on which he read: *Jonathan Loeb, chief of the general staff of the Salvation Army.*

He started so violently that his abdomen quivered five or six times before resuming its normal equilibrium.

"One of the great chiefs of that invading and damned sect dares…!"

His indignant expression disappeared, however on reading the two handwritten lines, which were evidently much more agreeable to him.

"Bring the stranger in," the Saint commanded the bewildered Maud.

"Here?" she queried. "Where not even the most notorious of the faithful are allowed to enter?"

"Refrain from judging, brazen hussy…and do as you're told."

It was sitting in an armchair that was too high for his short fat legs, further elevated by the semblance of a stage, enveloped in the tails of his long black coat and with his "stove-pipe" hat on his head that the pontiff of the Mormons greeted with an ample suprasacerdotal gesture the Salvationist general—whose generalship was only the slightest string of his redoubtable bow.

The Saint's welcome was doubtless not to the taste of the newcomer, for the relied to the exaggerated gesture full of junction in a curt and hoarse voice: "No mannerisms, if you please. They waste time and words—time and words as valuable as gold…when they're mine."

"Speak—I'm listening."

"Not like this. Leave your sham throne; you're mistaken if you think it will impress me. We're working in the same cause, my friend: the profitable exploitation of credulity and human fanaticism. The founder of your church had a desire to give Oriental liberties to Occidental Christians; in order to be able to defy Christian laws with impunity he made himself an apostle. In the same way, our late Marshal, in order to conquer and omnipotent and fortunate situation, created a sect that, thanks to his appropriated means of military organization of its propaganda and its faithful, is in the process of making an oil-stain on the surface of the world."

"Alas!"

"Good—there's a frank sigh! Salvationism is a seed-bed of old women, while Mormonism demands a plethora of young ones. So much the worse for you if we're harming your interests. It's the struggle for existence—every man for himself. But that's too many superfluous words. Come down from your splendor. Let's sit down together, like good colleagues, for I need to talk to you, and for both our sakes, no ear should catch what we say."

The Saint hesitated momentarily; then, ceding to his visitor's reasoning, he gave him satisfaction.

Then Loeb said: "You lack women, and the gold in your coffers is diminishing…"

"What makes you think that?"

"I don't think, I know."

"It's a calumny!"

171

"Peace, damn it, or we'll never finish. I also know that Mormonism is breaking up. From numerous deserters..."

"Oh, it's from those accursed wretches! In spite of the terrible punishments with which I threaten perjurers, I realize that defections..."

"Are increasing from day to day, eh?"

"Since you're so well-informed. I won't feign a confidence that escapes me. The New Jerusalem is in trouble."

"You're under no illusions about the cause, are you?"

"Of course not! I only have five wives, when my predecessor had twenty. I'm also obliged only to have one official one, in order not to be at war with the whole of Utah, and to call the others maidservants. If we were prospering, I wouldn't hesitate to maintain our fundamental dogma by the force of independent practice, but..."

"Instead of increasing, you're thinning out."

"How do you expect it to be otherwise, without reestablishing slavery with regard to the sex that's depriving you of its indispensable support? Four-fifths of the men of the Faith are reluctantly monogamous, and the rest are languishing in an involuntary celibacy that takes away their only reason for staying with us."

"You need..."

"Well, yes, we need women, and gold to attract them."

"Indeed. On that subject, I can propose a bargain to you."

"Which is?"

"To furnish you with a woman, a pearl such as Salt Lake City has never seen."

"I'll finally be able to attain the half-dozen?"

"You haven't lost the taste...and gold..."

"Much?"

"Enough to recruit a regiment of...amazons!"

"Isaac and Jacob be praised! How much?"

"Seventy-six thousand dollars."

"By Job's dung-heap—my mouth's watering. And from where does this celestial manna come?"

"From Chicago, in a straight line, for that's the key. A man withdrew from a bank there, four days ago, exactly ninety-six thousand dollars, of which he's spent twenty thousand to make the journey."

"He must have been throwing handfuls of gold to the crowd along his route, then."

"You don't know how right you are, except that it wasn't on the way but on departure that he threw the handfuls. But let's stop talking in enigmas. These are the facts: a genius vomited up by Hell, intends to provoke the end of the world..."

"By the holy prophet Daniel, that would be the abomination of desolation...if it were possible."

"Can one assign limits to the forces of evil? Anyway, impossible or not, all of the American north-east—Maine, Vermont, New Hampshire, Massachusetts, Connecticut, Rhode Island, New York, New Jersey, Maryland, Pennsylvania, Ohio, Michigan, Indiana, Illinois and Wisconsin—is astir. Secret meetings have taken place, and I've been charged with finding the monster and annihilating him before he can attempt the demonic work."

"That's practical. While laughing at the pretention, it's still good to suppress the audacious person in advance, just in case."

"Listen to the rest. The accursed one has summoned to an unknown meeting-place where he's hiding, for some experiment that might, if nothing else, provoke a disaster, a man who is carrying with him the power of gold. That's the man I mentioned to you."

"It's necessary to prevent him reaching him, that's all."

"I've tried three times, in vain, to block his route, and I've come to ask you to help me."

"In an endeavor that is certain as agreeable to the Lord as it is profitable to Mormonism...personally, I'm all yours."

"Good. This man, who is accompanied by four men, one an adolescent, and a Redskin girl...

"Oh—there's another woman?"

"That one I'll keep, for she's the guide, the only one who knows the retreat of the man I have a mission to exterminate."

"Hmmm! She might be colored, but if she comes here, it will be difficult for her to get out again!"

"Don't worry about that. I'll take charge of it."

"In sum, you want me to keep all these people?"

"I want you to get rid of them for me…for good."

"That's more serious, but possible…except in one case…"

"What?"

"If they become Mormons—for then their lives would be sacred."

"The Mormons are in your absolute dependence, aren't they?"

"I'm the master and judge of all the faithful."

"Then I have no anxieties: you won't Mormonize, at the very least, the one that I have in view."

"We have terrible means to force conversions."

"Incapable, in spite of everything, of bending certain obstinacies."

"We'll see about that…when you've put these individuals in my hands."

"They'll be yours when you want to take them. Before then, in return for a gift that I've brought you, gratuitously—which is to say, without keeping anything for myself—I want you to make a formal engagement, which is a condition *sine qua non*…"

"Which is?"

"Not to demand anything of the man in question except for what he has on him, and to be inexorable in his regard, even if he promises you a hundred millions."

"By the poverty of Agar, is he that rich?"

"You can see that it's already given you pause for thought, and that I was right to take my precautions. You'll content yourself with the seventy-five or seventy-six thousand dollars, or you'll get nothing. Choose!"

"I'll take the guaranteed sum."

"Good. But I need a guarantee. You'll have to authenticate and sign this."

Loeb held out a piece of paper to the Saint, on which the latter read, not without an intimate frisson:

*I forbid all those faithful to the Religion to trouble on the matter of my death the bearer of the present document, Jonathan Loeb, chief of the general staff of the Salvation Army. I have killed myself voluntarily in his presence to expiate my violation of a formal agreement into which we entered.*

"What does this mean?"

"That you recognize my right to blow our brains out with impunity if you fail, in any respect, to fulfill the terms of the agreement we've just made.

"And if I refuse?"

"I'll take the celestial manna elsewhere."

The Saint reflected, a conflict taking place within his brain between lesser and immediate cupidity and vast but eventual cupidity."

He very quickly fell into line with the old proverb that a bird in the hand is worth two in the bush.

He certified the document as read and approved, and added the sacred seal to his signature.

"Are you satisfied?"

"Yes."

"And you'll deliver me these impious individuals for conversion?"

"When you've put at my disposal the means of finding them."

"You don't have them, then?"

"As good as. Listen: they slipped through my fingers, so to speak, in Chicago, by virtue of the rupture of the cable of a captive balloon, in the nacelle of which they'd taken refuge. The balloon leapt up eight or nine thousand yards, but one of the people is a skillful engineer, who was able to render himself master of the aerostat, which came back down to a moderate height and, pushed by an easterly breeze, set off toward the setting sun. I've had its position signaled to me by telegraph continually, for everywhere."

"Your correspondents can't have mistaken one balloon for another? There's so much aerial navigation nowadays."

"No. One of the travelers, who fears me and wants to keep on the right side of me as long as I have custody of his paltry funds, has taken care to identify the aerostat by throwing notes addressed to me over the side by night. I've been able to track the balloon until it passed over the Wabash Mountains at Ogden. It flew very low over that paltry city, following the line of the railway track that traverses the Great Salt Lake for a distance of thirty-five miles."

"In which they've doubtless drowned!" exclaimed the Saint, alarmed.

"They must have done everything possible to avoid it and come down on land, being unable to get over the Lake Side Mountains, in the Great American Desert, with what denouement I leave you to imagine. In any case, I have proof that they haven't crossed the desert. After landing, having no food, the fugitive troop must certainly have set out to reach the Great Salt Lake, where their only chance of encountering a few people and help lay in following the shore."

"What if, on the contrary, they headed west, into the desert?"

"No, Williamson, a great traveler, knows only too well..."

"Williamson!" exclaimed the Saint, with a start. "It's a matter of Williamson, the Mining King?"

"Yes, since my tongue has let the cat out of the bag."

"Oh, if I'd known...!"

"Too late. You've signed and I'll hold you to it!"

The obese patriarch nearly collapsed in despair. He was about to protest, quite uselessly, against the surprise, which he considered as shady dealing, when Loeb imposed silence on hm. Someone knocked softly on the door.

The Mormon pope, with a heart-broken expression, answered that appeal, in which he recognized the light hand of his youngest wife.

Through a narrow gap in the doorway, Maud informed him that a band of seven faithful, two of whom were women, dying of hunger and cold, had been picked up by Hugh Neumann, a salt-farmer at Lake Point. Neumann was a Mormon of Silesian origin, rich enough to possess three wives, fifteen sons and a dozen daughters, which made him the most important person in the Church after the corpulent Saint—who, moreover, in spite of his quintuple marriage, had no descendants.

Loeb and his worthy partner looked at one another; Williamson and his companions had thrown themselves into the net; they had not put their enemy to the trouble of finding them.

Hugh Neumann had come to ask where he should take the people he had picked up.

"To my Cabin of Proofs on the bank of the Jordan," the polygamous patriarch replied. And as Maud went away, he explained to Jonathan: "There's no better prison. No one has ever come out without being duly Mormonized."

"What about the others?"

"The river," replied the gentle apostle laconically, with an odious smile.

# Chapter XI
## *The Cabin of Proofs*

For forty-eight hours—or, to be strictly accurate forty-seven hours—the fugitives escaped from Chicago, Williamson, Claude and Edmée Roland, Captain Furet, Snow Rose, the ever-correct and tremulous Toby, and their involuntary, if not entirely unintentionally, companion on the aerial voyage, Grégoire de Montalpé, whose dandysism had fled under the rude tyranny of the implacable master to whom the unfortunate had give in himself, have been prisoners in the Cabin of Proofs.

About what happened during the four days and four nights of their journey from the famous city on the shore of Lake Michigan to the similarly famous—albeit from another viewpoint—capital of the sad land of the Mormons, it is sufficient to say a few brief words, interesting as they have might been with regard to adventures. The situation into which hazard, rather that the implacable hostility of Loeb, had delivered them this time, requires our story to be distracted as little as possible.

The departure from the aerodrome in Chicago had, as we know, by virtue of the ascensional force of the aerostat, very insufficiently ballasted, had the brutality of a fall in reverse.

Although they were all stunned and suffocated, like their companions and Toby, Williamson, Jean and Claude had conserved their composure. Although the first two did not know what to do in order to ward off the danger of rising like an arrow to altitudes where low atmospheric pressure leads to death, the first concern of the third, less of a novice in aeronautical matters, was to find the cord of the valve. When he located it at last, he clung to it desperately—and only just in time, for they were all on the point of losing consciousness.

The aerostat descended again rapidly toward the breathable layers.

As he strove to discern the terrain through the sparse clouds that were traveling between the aerostat and the ground, in order to discover the moment when he ought to arrest the descent, Claude discovered Grégoire de Montalpé swinging in the void, suspended by one arm from one of the lateral mooring ropes of the nacelle, which had, fortunately for him, formed a virtual knot around his shoulder at the moment when it had been whipped away by the sick of the vertiginous ascent.

Abandoning the cord of the valve, the engineer began, with the aid of the mariner, to haul the unfortunate and uninteresting incompetent into the nacelle where he remained inert for several hours before coming to, with a rather intense alarm.

The sympathetic practitioner of wild sprees, quickly showed evidence of great devotion by introducing surreptitiously into the sacks of ballast notes addressed to the person whose domination was so burdensome to him but from whom, as we know, he had been unable to free himself. That was because Loeb had, by means of threats, forced Grégoire to confide his funds to him, and Grégoire, very anxious on the subject of his treasury, was doing everything he could to draw the custodian of his fortune into the wake of the balloon. By introducing his notes, rolled up into balls, inside the ballast sacks, among the prospectuses that the ingenuity of American advertising had inserted therein, he was able to convey messages to the balloon's tracker via the fugitives' own hands

As soon as the aerostat had been equilibrated at an altitude of a thousand yards, in a current heading due west, Williamson and his companions had a discussion. Should they descend as soon as possible? That was not the billionaire's opinion. He wanted to take advantage of the unexpected means of locomotion furnished by circumstance to distance himself from his redoubtable adversary, and, thanks to the velocity of the wind and the rarity of roads practicable for an automobile, the further west they went, at least to try to shake him off once and for all.

The sovereign mistress of the situation, in that regard was the Indian guide. When consulted, Snow Rose declared that the route was good, and that she would tell them when it needed to be interrupted, provided that she was kept up to date with the names of the regions they traversed.

It was decided, in consequence, to continue the aerial navigation for as long as possible, while drawing nearer to the ground from time to time in order to inform themselves about the inhabitants they might encounter in proximity to aggregations of population.

They traveled in that manner all through the night following their evening departure, and then all though the following day.

Nothing is comparable to, and nothing is as delightfully restful as, the silent peace that the adherents of aerial navigation experiences in the bosom of the atmosphere. It seems to the aeronauts that they have forgotten all the quotidian miseries, great and small, of terrestrial life, including the earth itself.

That special influence made itself felt with regard to Williamson more than any of his companions, doubtless because he was naturally less adept than them at escaping his overly important personality in order to let his thoughts vegetate and his heart beat freely. For him, therefore, the entire journey was merely one long conversation with Edmée Rolland, in which he ingenuously gave vent to the increasingly strong emotion that he experienced in the presence of the young woman—who, as we know, had long ceased to consider him as an overgrown brat spoiled by a great fortune for which the difficulties of his early life had not prepared him. If he experienced an increasing enthusiasm for her, she, for her part, saw blossoming in him, one by one, strong and simple qualities that he was almost naively grateful to her for bringing to light.

It was not a flirtation between that young woman and that man, still frankly young, but something better: an awakening within the man of a new man, as superior to the old as a flamboyant sun is to the pale night star, by virtue of the action

180

of a beautiful feminine soul that took an interest in its work much more intense than it realized.

Similarly, there was no longer a flirtation between the good and brave matelot Jean Guitard and the lovely and brave Redskin, but infinitely more: an honest, loyal, naïve and spontaneous tenderness. Both of them had received the mutual "thunderbolt" during their first dramatic interview in the Menominee Reservation. All the time that the operations commanded by Claude Rolland left to "Captain Furet" was dedicated by the latter to his sentimental romance, and all the time that Snow Rose thought she could consent to distract from her role and guide and the apostolate of the scientific faith she had acquired from the lips of Old Sinker was given to giving her reply, in all confident sincerity, to the inflammable mariner.

Toby did his best to be of service to the engineer transformed by necessity into the captain of an aerostat. When Claude judged that he could grant himself a few rare and brief moments of repose he did his best to assist the mariner who had become the first mate, maintaining a vigilant watch and being ready, at the slightest disquiet, to wake up the Commandant—who had never merited that title more.

As for Grégoire de Montalpé, needless to say, he was kept in such rigorous quarantine by everyone that he made few efforts to break the legitimate ice that he sensed around him. Besides which, if the dandy had a firm footing in society, he was no more an aeronaut than a mariner, and he suffered prosaically during the voyage in the sky from airsickness, just as he had suffered on the Atlantic from seasickness—which did not prevent him from committing the infamous perfidy of letting Loeb know the course the balloon as following by means of short notes slipped into the sacks of ballast, but did not encourage him to take any interest in the strange and troubling theories of which the ardent faith of the young Indian was the echo.

It would have been necessary to follow the existence of the little troop hour by hour to note the continual similarities between life on earth and the intimate life of the Earth-

Monster that Snow Rose continually identified, with regard to everything and nothing, as evidence of the similar vitality of the planet.

The violent incidents of the struggle between the two human powers named Williamson and Loeb do not permit us to relate those disquieting theories in as much detail as they merit. We cannot go more deeply into the strange parallel that she established in the course of that aerial journey between the sensitive atmosphere of the globe and what the occultists call the "astral body" of human beings, that sort of nervous emanation of being, invisible and yet so existent that it is perceptible at a distance. And with what acuity the atmosphere—and, certainly, through its rigid skin, the body of the Earth—perceives those sensations! It is troubled, stirs and writhes under the slightest influence of neighboring beings, and it is not only the light spasmodic breath of the sun that it senses, and instantaneously translates the effects, but the magnetism, the nervous manifestation common to all the living colossi—relative to us, of course—that populate the universe.

But let us pass on—very regretfully, because, like Claude, Edmée and even Williamson, although long prepared for those vertiginous concepts, we would be profoundly stirred and impressed by them!

On the evening of the second day of aerial navigation, the balloon had lost so much gas—not so much by virtue of exomosis through its envelope as frequent descents to obtain information about the route it was following—that it was visibly deformed and was only maintaining a relative stability with the aid of reiterated maneuvers and continual sacrifices of ballast. It was evident that it could not sustain them above ground for very much longer when the glistening surface of the Great Salt Lake appeared in the evening twilight.

Fortunately, the easterly breeze remained strong enough, and steady enough, for them to hope that by sacrificing, for lack of mobile ballast, the equipment and even parts of the nacelle, they could avoid a fatal descent into the bosom of the bitter waves. Claude Rolland acted with so much skill, propriety and prudence that a fortunate result was obtained; the liberated captive was even able, by a supreme effort, to go through a low-lying pass in the Lakeside Mountains and came to rest definitively, after a long and perilous drag, on the sands of the Great American Desert.

Then a terrible ordeal commenced for the castaways of the air, in which only the energy of some and the instinct of self-preservation of the others permitted them to triumph. After having resisted as best they could forty-eight hours of privation of food and water, isolated in arid and uninhabited terrain, the unfortunates found themselves in darkness, with the prospect of perhaps having another twenty or thirty miles to cover before encountering any help.

Without losing a moment, they set forth, retracing their route in the direction of the lake, just as Loeb had reasoned and anticipated. Fortunately, an abundant rainstorm permitted them to slake their devouring thirst and recover sufficient strength to reach the eastern slopes of the Lakeside Mountains, and, by going southwards through the foothills, the few houses of Dunstein, where they were able to restore themselves as best they could.

From there, after a few hours of indispensable rest, they reached the shore of the lake and followed it, walking painfully until the fall of night, which they spent shivering in the open.

The next day, they finally found the road from the desert to Salt Lake City, and the point where it turns around the north of the little chain of the Stansbury Mountains, made their only meal in Grantsville and, in the darkness again, ran aground in Lake Point, where the Mormon farmer Neumann picked them up, in order to take them in a cart—preventing them from taking the railway in spite of their protests—to Salt Lake City...and the Latter Day Saint.

That individual—who has certainly seemed grotesque but at whom one would be wring to smile, even in the Old World, for it is only in his form—had resolved to receive those he referred to, by antiphrasis, as his "guests" in a manner to impress them, with a view to their future conquest.

He summoned a few notable households—which is to say, as polygamous as the present emaciation of the sect permitted. The ladies put on clothes with tempting pretentions; the gentlemen submitted temporarily to the humble role of servants. And when Williamson, sufficiently recovered from the frightful fatigues of the four previous days to attempt to clarify the new and once-more-disquieting situation of the little troop, imperiously demanded to be put in the presence of the person who was arbitrarily detaining a free citizen of free America and his friends, it was in an indescribable parody of a harem that they were introduced—a harem in which, in a gold-spangled robe, the Saint was the supreme Pacha.

It was thus, to a world-weary individual like Williamson, Parisians like the Rollands and de Montalpé, a widely-traveled young man like Jean Guitard and a civilized Indian who, by virtue of atavism, was astonished by nothing, that the Saint hoped to make the charms of Mormon life appreciated!

All the suavity of that setting did not prevent the high priest of occidental polygamy from signifying to his "guests" that his duties as the supreme apostle of the Mormon faith obliged him to attempt their conversion by all means possible, and that, to his great regret, he could only part from them when it had been proved to him that he had no chance of saving their souls.

Williamson having protested that he did not have time to waste with such nonsense the obese patriarch added that, in order to be agreeable to him, he would arrange from the work of persuasion to proceed by giant strides, and not prolong the proofs beyond forty-eight hours.

In order to demonstrate the consideration that he intended to show to visitors who, he had no doubt, would have the wisdom to become his dear sons and daughters in Mormonism, he wanted to cede to them the very room in which he had just welcomed them as persons of distinction..

It was a rather vast room with only one visible entrance, with, by ways of annexes, two small rooms devoid of exits. One large window illuminated it, overlooking the River Jordan from a sheer height, which was deep and rapid at that point, full of turbulent eddies that would extinguish any idea of an exodus by the liquid route.

It was there—without neglecting a frugal but sufficient sustenance, mysteriously delivered—that the little company, imprisoned in great secrecy, completed the forty-seventh hour of detention under the pretext of proselytism out of the forty-eight that the Saint had fixed as the extreme duration of the "proof."

Now they understood the value and the only too rigorous exactitude of that word. In the beginning, Williamson and his companions had suffered without overmuch alarm that attempt made, in their respect, on right of people to individual liberty. Harassed and exhausted, they experienced above all else an immense need for repose, which, on bunks that were almost sufficiently comfortable, they spent the first twelve hours in such physical annihilation that none of them found the leisure to think about what they all considered, at first glance, to be a perfectly ridiculous contretemps.

When they awoke, the found a basket full of victuals, to which they did great honor, while wondering how it could have been delivered to them. Before going to sleep, in fact, the prisoners had build a barricade of furniture against the only entrance, which was still intact.

As they finished their meal, rendered relatively cheerful by the wellbeing they felt, they heard a noise, and at one point in the partitions serving as walls they saw a large envelope swinging without any apparent form of support.

*Are we in the home of Robert Houdin?* wondered the Parisians.

*It's sorcery!* Toby and the pretty Redskin thought.

"That," murmured the matelot to himself, "is as odd as navigating at twenty knots, keel in the air. Hmmm...have to see!"

Williamson did not even take the futile trouble of any conjecture. Practical above all, he went to take the envelope, which yielded to the first solicitation of his hand, and opened it in order to discover its contents.

They were as many copies of the dogmas and rigorous regulations of the Mormon sect as there were prisoners, with, at the bottom, a formal certificate of conversion awaiting a signature.

To the set of printed sheets was appended a manuscript bearing advice that was singularly reminiscent of an ultimatum:

*You only have another thirty-four hours to decide. Know that no one but a Mormon has ever got out of the place where you are.*

Silently, the prisoners took cognizance of the printed sheets, on which each of their names was accurately inscribed in the margin, although only Williamson had declared his loudly—without anyone appearing to suspect what that name was worth.

The mystery was further complicated, unless Loeb...? But it was considered implausible by all of them, except de Montalpé, that the enemy, so fortunately thwarted in Chicago, could have picked up their trail again so soon.

Leaving his companions to discuss those matters in low voices, not without some anxiety, Jean Guitard, primarily inclined to action, first wanted to assure himself that there was no means of escape. After having interrogated the walls with his first—almost all resonant but offering no indication of a hidden door—he noticed the grooves of a small trapdoor in the ceiling, between two joists. With the skill of an acrobat and the composure of an able seaman, he formed a pyramid out of tables and chairs, and succeeded in reaching the ceiling, but the trapdoor resisted all his efforts.

Nevertheless, it must logically be up above that it was necessary to explore. Leaning out of the window, he observed a rope hanging from the roof—well out of reach, of course. With a few handkerchiefs torn into strips he manufactured a

cord, to the end of which he tied two of the pieces of iron cut-
lery that had been supplied with the meal. With the aid of that
improvised grapnel, he succeeded after several fruitless attempts, in drawing the rope toward the window, to the interior
of which he attached it. Then, raising himself up over the void
by the strength of his wrists, he reached the roof, broke the
glass of a skylight and found himself in a loft contained a
large quantity of straw and discarded or broken utensils.

There was no exit from the loft but a trapdoor, whose
heavy bolt he withdrew. It was by that route, disappointingly,
that he set foot once again on his fragile scaffolding and rejoined his companions.

"No means of taking advantage of darkness to escape via
the roof, as I'd hoped," he told them, dejectedly. "On the three
sides that don't overlook the river the building is surrounded
by smooth walls fifteen or eighteen feet high. No illusions are
possible; this really is a prison, and a serious one. No point
thinking about the river, with its only-too-visible turbulence;
the best swimmer would down in it.

"Oh, if we only had several nights in front of us to weave
cables with the straw that's up there, I'd construct a raft and
we could get away by the liquid route, thumbing our nose at
the turbulence, but with only one poor night before us, we
can't undertake such a long-term endeavor."

In order to acquit his conscience, however, the young
mariner unscrewed the bolt of the trapdoor to the loft and
wove a solid rope with the straw, long enough to establish a
facile and sure means of communication—for a good climb-
er—between the room and the attic.

Nothing is as depressing as isolation under the latent,
imprecise threat of a blow whose nature one cannot foresee,
any more than the manner in which it will be struck. So, for
the prisoners of the collective, the hours went by with both
hectic rapidity and desperate slowness. They would have liked
to be able to hold them back, and yet they seemed to last for
centuries. Williamson, especially, was agitated.

"Why don't they tell us in good faith what they're going to do with us?" he repeated, incessantly. "Better a grim threat, even mortal, than this waiting!"

None of them, except for the tearful Grégoire, had considered for a second the idea of giving in to their jailer's ultimatum. Setting aside any question of religious commitment, was the Mining King about to place under the domination of a Latter Day Saint and settle, in the fullness of youth, his independent life as a nabob in that odious region of the Great Salt Lake? Such a hypothesis did not even warrant being formulated. Were French citizens like Claude, Edmée and Jean Guitard going to become Mormons, and by intimidation? Could Edmée, most of all, a sincere Catholic, swell the grotesque harem of some farmer as fat as the one who had captured them, rather than rescuing them, at Lake Point? The question could not even arise, any more than that of the young Indian, so ardent and fanatical a disciple of Old Sinker, suffering the same fate.

Such modest valors, such strong and superior humanities, were not accessible prey for the base and brutal proselytism of a Mormon pope.

That evening, the question continually formulated, aloud or mutely, by Williamson, received its response—and what a response!

After a summary and frugal supper, hastily absorbed by pale starlight—for no lamp or candle had been left at the disposal of the internees—the prisoners had lain down silently on their bunks, although not to sleep, for they were too acutely anxious for the arrival of slumber to calm their nervous exasperation. Suddenly, a dry click resonated in one of the partitions, making them all sit up.

Williamson struck a match, by the light of which—without anyone having come in, so far as they knew—they all saw a piece of parchment pinned to the wall by a dagger, and bearing the significant words: *No more than eighteen hours! Our Lord will enlighten you! Sign or die!*

This time the threat was undisguised.

"Ah!" exclaimed Claude Rolland, dully. "If that wretch Neumann, at Lake Point, hadn't taken advantage of our weakness to disarm us, we could attempt to break down that door and open up a passage, revolvers in hand, to flee this accursed city!"

"That would be futile folly, even armed," said Williamson coldly, "for now I'm convinced. Taking our weapons without touching the banknotes I have on my person might have been the work of a fanatic, but this imprisonment without my being robbed, without any allusion being made to the question of money, and no one wanting to seem to suspect the importance of my person, which is not unknown in any corner of the United States any more than in any major center in the world, proves that the head directing this assault knows exactly what I'm worth and intended to avoid the purchase of visible guards, which is always easy when price is not an issue. This is abnormally clever."

"From which you conclude?"

"That the new blow has indisputably been struck by Loeb, whose dispositions have undoubtedly been made, outside as well as within."

"Come on," Claude objected. "It's impossible for that Argus to have eyes everywhere. There are multiple currents in the atmosphere, and we could have found one that carried the balloon southwards or northwards as easily as due east. Even if he affiliates are innumerable, he could only proceed by elimination, which would not have permitted him to be informed so rapidly of our actual direction."

"Unless we took care to guide his search from on board."

"You don't believe, at least, that I've betrayed you?" de Montalpé protested, forcefully. He bit his tongue immediately, but it was too late.

Williamson replied with cold irony. "I didn't ask you for that confession, Monsieur. The advertisements that the sacks of ballast contained would have sufficed, without you, to mark our trail."

*That's true! What an error!* thought the two cousins at the same time, but giving very different meanings to their regret. Claude was deploring his carelessness, Grégoire the futility and danger of a treason that had already caused him so much anxiety and had delivered him into the peril of immediate reprisals.

Cry of anger that rang out in the scornful silence struck terror into de Montalpé's entrails. The Indian woman had just understood the role played aboard the nacelle by Rolland's malevolent relative. Atavism reacted spontaneously on the civilized individual. She ran to the dagger fixed in the wall in order to make it a weapon of just vengeance, while Grégoire, breathless with terror, hid behind Edmée.

But the dagger was firmly embedded. The vindictive Menominee miscalculated the force of her gesture, and, disconcertedly, extracted nothing from the wall but a broken blade.

"Oh, Mam'zelle Snow Rose," the mariner reproached her, softly and tenderly, "Why were you so hasty? A weapon that our enemies had given us, and which, with a little patience, we might have had in good condition!"

"Snow Rose," said Williamson, tranquilly, in his turn, "We are above the office of executioners in the cause of justice, with which Loeb had charged himself. Isn't it evident that if the master Monsieur de Montalpé has chosen had not wanted to get rid of a follower he now judges to be useless, he would have taken steps to ensure that he did not share our imprisonment?"

Williamson was preaching indirectly to a convert. Grégoire was informed as to the amenity of Loeb's sentiments in his regard, and was very well aware that, now that Loeb had custody of his money, he was at least indifferent to the life of the man to whom it belonged. So, he resolved, in order to escape both the dangerous domination of Loeb and the fate that awaited him, to sign, as soon as the first light of dawn permitted him to do so, the certificate of conversion imposed by the Saint.

Three times during the night the same macabre advice was given, in the same symbolic fashion. Each time, with silent and patient effort, it was the mariner who detached the pitiless parchments, and at daybreak, Williamson, Claude Rolland and Toby each hid beneath their clothing a blade whose temper had been assured by experiment.

As soon as the sun rose, dead on time, the unfortunates saw the conditional condemnation renewed by the same mysterious means—except that, to the great chagrin of the brave Jean, no symbolic weapon fixed the ultimatum to the wall on this occasion.

You can imagine what such a day must have been like, after such a night. After exhausting themselves in vain searching for a means of escaping their destiny, they had recognized the inanity of any attempt. So the forty-seventh hour of their detention found them dejected and desperate, and when the last warning—*Beware! In one hour you will be Mormons or dead!*—appeared on the ensorcelled partition, no one looked up, knowing only too well what it contained. No heart among them had weakened; all of them were determined, when the moment came, to sell their lives as dearly as possible. Their nerves were jangling, their brains, overworked by anguish, seemed to be voids within their burning skulls.

They were no longer talking. What was the point? They were no longer even thinking. They could do no more...

And mechanically, they counted the seconds, adding up the minutes.

Then, the material imminence of the crisis provoked an almost violent reaction.

Edmée was the first to rise abruptly to her feet from the chair in which she had been slumped, next to the table, squeezing her temples with her fragile clenched fists. She went to her brother, placed her hand on his shoulder and said, in a slow, grave voice: "Brother, you love me truly, don't you? Well, as I have no weapon, when the fatal moment comes, before striking yourself, kill me."

"Edmée!"

"Would you want your sister, when your blood has been shed, to become the living prey of these monsters?"

Williamson jumped up. "Oh, Miss Edmée, don't talk like that! You, so beautiful…you,, whose soul is so noble, whose heart is so good…you, who are grace, charm, purity, intelligence and valor personified…you, who have no equal, fall into the gross hands of the repugnant and grotesque chief of this sect—that shall not be! You, die! You, who are made for life, for happiness, to reign as a sovereign over humankind…you, wanting to die…wanting no longer to be, very soon, anything but an inanimate statue in order to escape the claws of these predators! Oh, I will not have it! I will not have it! I will not have it!"

"Alas," said Edmée, moved to the bottom of her heart by the exaltation that transfigured the man she had known so cold, so disillusioned, so scornful of his fellow humans, and of women in particular, "what can you do to oppose our fatal destiny?"

"I shall do…I don't know what I shall do! But I want you to live, and to live happily! And I want to live in order to see you live, and live happily! I want you to live, Miss Edmée, because…because you have made me experience what I did not know that my heart could ever experience…because I admire you above all others…because I venerate you…because, in sum, I love you!"

"What a moment for such a confession!"

"Well, exactly—it's when a man sees himself on the threshold of the eternal unknown, when he knows that he might perhaps have only a few more moments in possession of his terrestrial thought, that his soul bursts forth in the brightness of truth, inundated by the supernatural light that shows his sentiments in their true grandeur, and reveals them in their powerful intensity. And it's under the empire of the serene truth that dazzles and guides, imposing itself imperiously upon him, that his voice, obedient to the command of a superior will, translates that truth of that sincerely great and totally liberated soul.

"For a long time—yes, a long time, for in the existence we've been leading for several days, the hours have been days and the days months—I've understood that a complete transformation has taken place within me, of which you are the cause and the goal. But my consciousness, still fogged by all the tenacious errors of my pride and my false past experience, resisted all the intimate forces that extended toward you, refused to admit something so beautiful and so natural, and prevented me from seeing clearly within myself.

"Today, confronted by death—perhaps imminent, unless we receive some miraculous aid from God—at this poignant moment when neither the soul, nor the heart, not the mouth can lie, I repeat to you, Miss Edmée, that I love you."

Edmée gazed at him with a heart-rending smile, and said, emotionally: "Believe, Monsieur Williamson, that your words descend into my utmost depths, and that they are engraved there forever...which is to say, for the few moments that it is still granted to us to be able to see and hear one another...but I'm a Christian; these supreme moments ought no longer to belong to the earth. Let me pray."

She knelt down.

A scene of a similar nature, if not similar expression, was taking place a few paces away between Snow Rose and the brave young mariner Jean.

They did not have to make the confession that their eyes, and then their mouths, had confided even before leaving Chicago. Their mutual tenderness was determined to protest against the evidence, still wanting to believe, in spite of everything, that their lives might still be saved....

Jean Guitard, devoted as he was, forgot about Claude and Edmée, whom he cherished both profoundly and respectfully; for him, at that moment, nothing any longer existed but the almost furious determination to get the adored Indian woman out of that fatal cabin and that deadly city.

He had to do something...

But the minutes went by, flying on the dial of the large antique clock whose tick-tock caused the partition wall to vibrate.

He uttered a muted growl of exasperated despair, seized Snow Rose in his arms and carried her to the thick straw rope that he had fabricated, which was hanging through the gap of the trap-door in the ceiling, obliged Manitoba's daughter to cling to is back, and, charged with that precious burden, climbed up to the loft. From the loft he intended to go out on to the roof, and from there, by the grace of God…it would be necessary for him finally to invent some means of escape, since he loved Snow Rose and it was necessary for him to save her.

As the two of them disappeared into the loft, the clock chimed.

It was time.

Williamson, Edmée, Claude, Toby and even de Montalpé, although his hand was on the point of the cowardly submission that he considered as an aegis, raised their heads at the same time, their faces contracted by an inexpressible anxiety, and instinctively retreated to the wall opposite the only door, through which they were expecting…the unknown!

The door opened.

The Saint appeared—alone!

What! He had the incredible aberration of presenting himself alone? He was not Daniel, however, to renew the Biblical miracle of the lions' den.

After two seconds accorded to surprise, Williamson and Claude exchanged a glance, gripping the hilts of the daggers concealed within their clothing.

They had waited too long. Just as they launched themselves forward, the panels of the wall behind them pivoted, giving passage to six Mormons who, after treacherously seizing the male prisoners by the neck, knocked them brutally down on their backs and, pressing their knees into their breasts, rendered it impossible for them to attempt the slightest defense.

The Saint smiled; the operation had been executed perfectly.

He made a sign to the two unoccupied "faithful," to whom he indicated the trapdoor in the ceiling, and, aping courtly mannerisms ridiculously, headed toward the astounded Edmée.

"Miss Rolland," he said, in a honeyed tone, "welcome to the New Jerusalem. You are the first Frenchwoman to enter the seraphic choir of my beautiful Faithful, all of whom you surpass in personal ornamentation. An envied honor is reserved for you, whom the Lord has blessed; it is the roof of the Latter Day Saint himself that will shelter your felicity. Mabel, Betsy, Meg, Bella and Maud, who already know that they will be your servants even more than your companions, are waiting for you on the threshold of the cabin to take you to your new dwelling in great ceremony. On the way, they will explain your duties and my tastes. Don't worry, I'm not very demanding! Your hand, divine Edmée!"

And he extended his toward the young woman, who shuddered in disgust and, before anyone could stop her and prevent her action, leapt to the window, opened it wide and cried, with her foot on the sill: "One more step by you or your men and I'll throw myself in the river!"

Anxious as well as nonplussed, so much did Edmée's tone testify to the unshakability of her decision, the obese pontiff dared not advance any further, and signaled to the two men who were in the middle of ascending into the loft, on their mission of pursuit, to stop. Gently, he sought to soften the resolute Parisienne.

"Enough!" the latter commanded him. "I swear before God, who will forgive me, that you won't take me alive!"

Without taking her eyes off the Saint, she climbed on to the window-sill. Between her and the abyss there was no longer room for the slightest movement.

"Don't jump!" begged Loeb's accomplice, taking a step back.

"Don't jump!" repeated, like an echo, a young and warm voice that seemed to fall from the sky. "Don't jump, Mam'zelle Edmée—here I am!"

From the trapdoor of the loft, sliding down the straw rope, "Captain Furet" brought his heels down on the skull of the higher of the two Mormons who were in the process of climbing up it—who, stunned, fell on to his comrade, who let go and fell backwards on to the floor.

"And two!" proclaimed the mariner.

He reached the floor almost at the same time as them, threw his arm around the throat of the Saint with a single bound and put the barrel of a revolver to his temple, threatening: "If any one of you budges, I'll shoot!"

The advice had come to late…for the Mormons. With a single impulse, at the sight of the danger run by the patriarch, they had turned their heads and half risen to their feet, rendering, for a split second a partial liberty to the felled prisoners—who took advantage of it.

In the blink of an eye, Williamson, Claude and Toby—the last-named opportunely aided in his weakness by the valiant Edmée, had disengaged themselves from the relaxed grip, seized the throats of their aggressors, knocked them down in their turn and were holding them immobile with the threat of daggers held above their hearts.

"A change of view, eh, Papa?" mocked the matelot, under the nose of the Saint, who was white with terror. "You didn't expect that? Nor that my little Snow Rose would have had the presence of mind to hide her shooter from the search of the rogue who disarmed us in such a cowardly fashion at Lake Point. It's necessary to go gently, fat Papa! Orders, Monsieur Williamson!"

In the tone that was always calm in the midst of the most violent crises, Williamson remarked: "What's become of Snow Rose? We're going to need her."

Stifled cries and the sound of a brief struggle on the floor above replied to him.

Jean Guitard uttered a cry of rage and despair. Someone was attacking, up above, the woman he loved, whom he had disarmed in order to save everyone, and for whom, under the pain of losing all those for whom he had once again shown his devotion, he might have liberated the Saint from the mortal threat in order to fly to the Indian's aid.

At Snow Rose's first exclamation he had almost launched himself forth...but, heroically, with an anguished sweat pearling on his brow, he had remained at his post.

"Have no fear for her," Williamson said to him, who now understood what the mariner must be suffering. "She's too necessary to Loeb for him to allow any harm to come to her."

"Is it him who's grabbed her, then? Oh, woe betide him! I don't know if I can refrain from blowing out the brains of the ape who's trembling in my arms! I could give chase to the abductor!"

"Don't kill that man, Jean!" Edmée begged.

"Don't kill a man who might be useful to us, Captain Furet! But I have a strong desire to get rid of the one who's under my knee. I need to be free in my movements without delay."

"I'll take your place, Monsieur Williamson," Edmée declared, resolutely. "I understand that there are times when a woman's hand mustn't hesitate before the horror of bloodshed, if it's necessary for the common salvation I'll guarantee that the man won't budge until Jean can come to relieve me."

"With a simple energy, she matched her words with action, leaving Toby alone, face to face with his enemy—who did not attempt to take advantage of the groom's weakness, because he knew that any assault would pass a death-sentence on his chief and his companions.

Rapidly, Williamson took over Jean's revolver and his role. The latter, with a terrible gleam in his eyes, relieved Edmée of the dread of being constrained to plunge steel into living flesh.

From then on, things moved swiftly, for Williamson commanded as a harsh and inflexible master. Under his dictation, the Saint was obliged to write:

*I deplore the violence carried out in Salt Lake City against Mr. Williamson and his friends at the perfidious instigation of Jonathan Loeb, and humbly leave it to the generosity of the Mining King to spare myself and the Mormons legitimate reprisals. I order all those of the Faith to give aid and assistance, in full obedience, to the said Williamson, and will punish with the chastisement of perjury any Mormon who attempts, in any fashion whatsoever, any action that might be prejudicial to him.*

*The Latter Day Saint*

Then he demanded that the latter order his six men into one of the rooms with no exit, including the two injured men who had not yet recovered consciousness, and placed Toby on the threshold, revolver in hand, a dagger being sufficient henceforth for the Yankee king to suppress any whim of independence on the part of the Mormon pope. The latter obeyed without hesitation.

Finally free to think of himself, poor Captain Furet sank into a chair and began silently to weep his worthy amorous tears. The loft had fallen silent again. What had become of his beloved Snow Rose?

"I can see her!" Edmée suddenly announced, from the window. "That's surely her, thrown into the bottom of a boat that Loeb is rowing himself, alone, with great strokes of the oars. And wait! She's got free of the gag—which Loeb has immediately reattached—but she had time to utter a cry...no, not a cry! A word!"

"What word?" demanded Williamson, urgently, without letting go of his hostage. "A name, perhaps?"

"I don't know," said the young woman...it ended in an *o.*"

"Think!"

"It was something like *fricot*."

"Frisco!" cried the Mining King, exultantly. "Oh, the worthy girl! Captain Furet, don't measure with your eyes the distance that separates us from that river mortal to swimmers. I now know where we'll be able to find your Snow Rose. And Loeb will become my guide! Let's not lost a single minute—they're precious."

The, addressing the Latter Day Saint, who was very depressed by the turn that the adventure had taken, Williamson said: "You're nothing but a base scoundrel, a mere accomplice in this ugly affair, and the scorn I have for you goes as far as pity. Your excuse, if there is one, is to have wanted to bring, at my expense, a momentary prosperity to your sect, which, as all America knows, is crumbling like an old rotten wall.

"First of all, you're going to return our weapons, or furnish us with others, if your Germanic Mormon has appropriated our little arsenal for himself. Then, as befits important visitors who have given Salt Lake City the too great and entirely involuntary honor of the presence, you're going to conduct us respectfully to the railway station and you're going to wait until the first train we can catch has carried us away for us to relinquish the guarantee of your presence.

"That done, you'll refrain from any annoyances still possible, and, that way, you'll render us a service. Now, as Williamson has never received a service for which he hasn't paid handsomely, you'll receive in your hand, at the moment we hear the signal to depart, a check for twenty thousand dollars."

That program was followed in every detail. Soon—with what a sigh of relief!—the little troop quit the New Jerusalem for good, including Grégoire de Montalpé, who had nearly ended his days as a Mormon.

That scarcely creditworthy socialite had truly had more luck than he deserved. It was fear alone that had stopped in his throat the proclamation of his apostasy, at the moment of the surprise attack in the tricked-out cabin—which he judged it appropriate to keep secret when he saw things turn so promptly and so unexpectedly to the advantage of Williamson and his relatives.

He was, of course, the only one not to have mastered his aggressor, but he had understood that all danger had disappeared for him, the Mormon who had flattened him having been condemned to inertia under pain of provoking the death of his Saint and his coreligionists.

Loeb still had his wallet, to be sure, but now that he had obtained the desired guide, he would be able to find and hatefully put to death this Lobanief, the cause of all the trouble. So casually abandoned by Loeb, de Montalpé would have the misfortune of having to share the suspended inheritance with his cousins, but he knew that half would be more than sufficient to compensate him for his losses. That was all that could be pulled out of the fire, and he would have to settle for it.

# Chapter XII
## *The Broken Thread*

Eight days have gone by since Williamson and his friends left—triumphantly but after having endured inexpressible suffering—the city of the Mormon popes. They have been in San Francisco for seven, for it was definitely "Frisco"—the popular diminutive of the name of the State Capital of California[15]—that Snow Rose's last cry had given as a rendezvous to those to whom she had faithfully attached herself, because they were the ones summoned by her piously venerated master, the demigod, the prophet and the genius that she placed so high above other men...in other words, Old Sinker.

For a week, the Mining King had been strewing gold around generously, mobilizing police officers and private detectives, scouring personally or through the intermediary of his companions the whole city, from dives to palaces, and all the surrounding agglomerations on the shore of the vast closed by of the Pacific, especially Oakland, its sister city—and had not found a trace, not a single clue to the whereabouts of Loeb and his prisoner.

It was certainly not for lack of trying. If Williamson, temporarily occupied with some other concern, had sometimes shown a slight slackness in his research, poor Captain Furet, now pale and exhausted, mad with chagrin, always on his feet, no longer sleeping, only eating what was strictly necessary not to collapse for lack of nourishment, incessantly imagining some tiny new trail, had spared absolutely nothing in the attempt to find his beloved.

The engineer had also gone on campaign very energetically, albeit with no more success. His ardor had been subjected to a pause, however; the steps taken in the first few days only having yielded negative results, he had understood that

---

[15] The State Capital of California is actually Sacramento.

the discovery of Loeb and the Indian, assuming that they really had come to Frisco, would require long days, if not weeks. He had told himself that his personal attempts, as a foreigner, could scarcely add to the chances of success, when the local police, official and unofficial, were working on it. In addition, a case of conscience had imposed itself on his intransigent honesty.

He had not been able due to *force majeure*, to fulfill his promise to Senator Dupeyroux, and the non-reception of his report must have been a disaster for the latter. But might not his sojourn in San Francisco, which would, in all probability, be prolonged, permit him to repair that disaster to some extent?

Dupeyroux might have been able, not having received the promised oratorical "bomb" in time, to have the famous interpellation postponed, a postponement perhaps announced by the desperate cablegrams that had been unable to catch up with the little troop during its journey across the North American continent. If, from San Francisco, Claude was able to cable, if not a complete report like the one swallowed up with the unfortunate *Astrea*, at least sufficient elements to form a basis for the virulent attack projected by the parliamentarian, the disaster would be partly averted, and the former secretary would at least be conscious of having done everything humanly possible to keep his promise.

What if it had the good fortune to arrive in time! And why not? From the collision within sight of the Sandy Hook lightship to the present moment—which is to say, forty-eight hours after his arrival in San Francisco—that frightful series of dramatic events, in which the travelers had seen death at terrible close range four times, and which was sufficient to fill the entire life of a modern adventurer—had only lasted, in total, twelve days, and the term fixed for the interpellation was only five times twenty-four hours in the past.

Claude no longer had his notes, of course, but the facts, dates and figures registered in his excellent and faithful memory were sufficient to edify a very appropriate and hurtful series of accusations.

The young explorer therefore decided to leave to others the ingrate and disappointing labor of man-hunting and to shut himself away, pen in hand, in order to acquit his debt. As he could do nothing without Williamson, for whom the expense would be aggravated by the telegraphic traverse of the vast United States, he explained his project to him.

To his great surprise, the latter turned him down, not without some vehemence. He suggested to him that a parliamentarian in want of a portfolio would not miss an opportunity to scale the heights of a ministry because his documentation was wanting; and that in a week he had had plenty of time to fill the gap with serious information—or not, if he had not even bothered to solicit it, because all the disappointed ambition and rancor, or even some dilettante ironist, might have shown him that the comedy of the political kitchen amuses everyone, and excites indulgent disdain. In any case, what did it matter whether one brought to the tribune solid arguments or baseless enormities, given that the orator is addressing himself to others even more ignorant than himself, and, in consequence, incapable of discerning the true from the false, the political result being the same?

And the Mining King, in a vein of sarcastic humor, concluded with the sally: "In any case, my dear friend, it's probably better for your senator that things turned out as they did. Armed with your work, drawn from sources of truth and experience, he'd probably have failed, because, to the ignorant, the truth appears implausible, whereas, if he stuck to adroit deceptions seasoned with a few facetious quips, it's a good bet that your Monsieur Dupeyroux, if he isn't completely stupid, is vaingloriously enthroned in the ministry he covered."

Claude dared not persist, and, as a distraction from the remorse of his conscience, threw himself wholeheartedly into the search for the undiscoverable.

It goes without saying that His Opulence the Mining King was staying at one of the most luxurious and expensive hotels reconstructed on the still smoking ruins of the tellurian disaster in which—no one has forgotten the frightful seismic catastrophe—the superb city engendered in a few years by the demon of gold had collapsed.[16] He had a vast apartment for his exclusive use on the first floor overlooking the mouth of the Golden Gate. The similar apartment on the next floor up was occupied by Claude, Edmée and their faithful Jean. Grégoire de Montalpé had been disdainfully relegated almost to the eaves, where he was literally cloistered, deeming it imprudent to collaborate in a search whose success, in addition to risking putting him back under the hand of a pitiless master, ran exactly counter to his own interest, which was not to impede Loeb's vengeance. Only the death of Old Sinker/Lobanief, in fact, would permit him to get his hands on his inheritance—henceforth, alas, to be shared.

If the hotel was an appropriate official residence for the dignity of the Yankee majesty, however, it was too public for the conferences inherent to the nature of police work, to which Williamson, Claude Rolland and Captain Furet were devoting themselves with various energies, and young Toby too, who had gradually recovered from the traumas of the previous days and was visibly resuming the formal correctness that had been singularly compromised by the hectic terrors that he had endured since the shipwreck. For business meetings they had chosen the bar of a modest "posada" situated near the southwestern exit from the city, on the road that, after the last few houses of the great maritime city, extends along the extreme foothills of the Santa Cruz Mountains, heading toward the suburban township of San Bruno.

Rendezvous there were frequent, but, more often than not, Williamson sent Toby in his stead. A very powerful magnet retained him in his lodgings: Edmée.

It was not that he dared the incorrectness of aspiring to keep the young woman—obliged to rest after fatigues and

---

[16] The great earthquake that devastated San Francisco occurred in April 1906.

emotions too powerful for her nervous system is not her courage—company in the absence of her brother. That would have been good for the Williamson of before the journey across the United States, to whom the transformed Williamson of San Francisco bore as little resemblance as the beautiful summers of France to the Arctic, or the Clitandre of *Les Femmes savantes* to the ex-King of Dahomey,[17] but a few days had sufficed to mutate the omnipotent and cold egotist, the being of immeasurable and splenetic pride, for whom a scornful impoliteness constituted the acme of originality, into a fearful, respectful, almost modest man, to whom a new and spontaneous intuition to given a grasp of tact, and the most subtle delicacies of the heart.

The beautiful eyes of a woman, mirrors of the noble, valiant and pure soul of an intelligent and refined Parisienne, had worked that miracle. Edmée, like a breath, had melted the heart that had believed itself to be unassailable behind a triple armor plating of gold, ice and scorn for humankind, and which, for its debut in the sweet martyrdom of love, had contracted in the cruel hothouse of a first great suffering.

In fact, Williamson had not waited until the arrival in San Francisco to confirm to the young woman the cry of respectful adoration that, at the poignant moment in the Cabin of Proofs when they had all believed that they no longer had anything to expect but death, has escaped from his entire being, so long concealed. In the saloon carriage speeding toward the Sierra Nevada, the high summits of which were profiled in the west, the Mining King had taken the brother and sister into a

---

[17] Clitandre is the young hero of Molière's *Les Femmes savantes* (1672), whose desire to marry the beautiful Henriette is opposed by the eponymous "learned" relatives, who want to marry her to a "scholar." The French abolished the political authority of the Kingdom of Dahomey in 1900, but were obliged to bring the exiled king Agoli-Agbo back for ceremonial purposes in 1910, maintaining him in a certain celebrity, which did not extend to his looks.

corner, and there, with a simple and timid eloquence, had asked Edmée to consent to share her entire life with him, as she had just shared such terrible dangers.

Very emotional, the young woman had closed her long-lashed yes momentarily, and then, with a grave smile and with a slight gesture of the head, she had replied: "No."

"Why not?" the astounded billionaire had implored, his breast transfixed by a stabbing pain.

"You're too rich, and I'm..."

"What for pity's sake?"

"Listen. Without comparing you to our relative Old Sinker, whose fantastic and immense scientific ambition attacks the worlds that populate infinity and aspires to enslave them—ours, at least—to his will, you, my dear Monsieur Williamson are a power ambitious for supremacy by way of gold, as your great indirect enemy Loeb, is by way of his tyrannical domination of the human herd. Well, my friend, I too am very ambitious..."

"You have the right, adored Miss, to all ambitions; there are no heights of which you are not worthy, and the most worthy!"

"I have only one of them—the highest, in my opinion, to whose conquest a human being of the feminine condition can and ought to aspire: that of happiness in a legitimate love, as perfect as the present state of the thinking race, ruler of Creation, presently permits."

"But my love is at your feet, Miss Edmée, complete limitless and absolute, having no law but to make you a happiness envied by all!"

"I believe that, because I know it. I knew that you loved me before you were aware of it yourself, well before the expectation of the fatal blow excited your soul as far as the confession."

"So why, then, that cruel 'no'—the 'no' that breaks my heart?"

"Wait! The happiness of two people, the only one that I understand and want, is only possible in a shared love in which each of the two gives himself or herself to the other entirely. That is true, especially when there exists between two individuals a disproportion of social condition that, in our case, is pushed beyond the most extreme limits."

"That's not important!"

"It's very important. Suppose that I consent, that we're married, and that one day a dissension erupts between us..."

"Never!"

"On your part, perhaps, but it might be me who renders myself culpable. Then, you would be able to think, if not to say to me, that another ambition is allied to my ambition for happiness...and the happiness would be destroyed. In order that that cannot be, it's necessary that I should be conscious, in a complete and absolute fashion, that the elect of my heart is uniquely that of my heart, and that not the slightest shadow, not the most infinitesimal suspicion of a reflection, can diminish in me the pure frankness of the invincible attraction that draws me toward him."

"And that consciousness?"

"I do not have in its plenitude."

"Ah! You don't love me!"

"Yes, too dear illustrious companion in peril, I experience for you, such as I have learned to divine you and know you in spite of yourself, a profoundly tender amity, but..."

"But?"

"I'm not absolutely sure; nothing furnishes me with the dazzling proof that, in the sentiment that I experience, the Mining King has completely disappeared behind the features of Williamson."

"Is that such a great evil? Oh, how I permit you to unite those two, who are but ne, in your thought!"

"But I cannot permit it. The happiness of which I dream can only be attained if, in the tribunal of my own judgment, I can swear before God that I know I am giving as much as I receive, that I love as much as I am loved. Then, I will not care whether there is a billionaire behind the mask, since I shall only see the elect. Then, he will know that he is truly loved, and can savor ideal happiness in peace, forever exempt from suspicion. But so long as I cannot be sure that my tenderness is what I want and need it to be, I shall maintain the 'no' that my conscience and my sentimental ambition have just ordered me to formulate."

"And…when will that certainty come to you?"

"Perhaps tomorrow, perhaps never. It is my heart that will tell me. If it speaks in the direction you desire, I will tell you immediately. You know that I am frank and honest, and you have my word—my oath, if you wish. Wait!"

"Alas! And that's…your final word?"

"I never have two of them."

"I'll wait. But if your heart rejects me for wanting too much, or if it is too slow in becoming clement, I shall die of it."

Since that conversation, every time Williamson's eyes met Edmée's, they imported: "Is it today that you will tell me that you love me?"

And every time, the young woman's gaze responded: "Wait!"

And it was that waiting that riveted the languishing lover to his sumptuous apartment, which seemed to him to be so ugly and so sad. But up above, on the chaise-longue on which the unique object of his thoughts was resting her dear and adorable feminine fragility, the heart of the beloved might suddenly speak, and he wanted to be there to receive immediately the confession on which his life was suspended—if it came!

That evening, however, Williamson came to the meeting at the posada. That was because Edmée felt better, and had resolved to go there in order to embrace her brother.

At the agreed time, in the corner opposite to one in which three belated clients were finishing their consumption, Edmée and her companion saw Snow Rose's poor inamorata arrived, exhausted, dejected and hardly able to stand up, escorted by Toby.

"Well?"

"Nothing—still nothing! I have however, repeated the tour of the two bays of San Francisco today, asking questions everywhere. It's impossible that it's to Frisco or its surrounding area that the filthy dog of a woman-stealer has brought her! Damn! I have nothing left to do than to go bury myself alive in some convent in Mexico, for I'll never see her again."

"Come on, courage, Captain Furet! You must never despair. I still have hope! Have a glass of brandy, and tell us about our day."

Slightly reanimated by a few drops of alcohol, the mariner began: "You know I told you that I thought I'd picked up a trail?"

"Yes that kind of ancient cowboy—or 'peon,' as they say in this Mexican state of the Union—whom we found so often on our heels, following us, but who fled as soon as we approached him, and whom you intended to try to follow in our turn."

"I said to myself: he must be one of Loeb's spies..."

"That quite probable, in fact."

"Well, no, Commandant. I ended up clarifying the matter. I found out where he lives and informed myself in his regard. He's a fisherman from the hamlet of Purissima, not far from here on the Pacific, a mile south of Half Moon Bay. His name is Santos Miguel and he's considered a harmless lunatic. For about a month, his monomania has consisted of running around Frisco in all directions, without ever speaking to anyone, looking at all the passers-by, listening to what they say, and especially never missing the arrival of trains on the Great Western Railroad, at Oakland as well as San Francisco. He watches the passengers go by, then goes back to wandering or to bed. It seems probable to me that, less crazy than he's believed to be in Purissima, he's a police informer. At any rate, he can't have anything to do with us, in spite of his persistence in our regard, since, having been following that bizarre trade for a month, he can't be spying for Loeb, who wasn't in America then."

"That's true."

"With all that, we're no further forward than the day we disembarked here. I have to don my mourning-dress, I tell you, because I'll never find my beloved Snow Rose, just as you'll never find Old Sinker, since you have no guide."

Poor Captain Furet was in despair.

"It's a crime," he moaned, "to have put a treasure of grace like Snow Rose in the situation of becoming the victim of a ferocious beast like this Loeb! What has he done to that dear creature by now? He might have tortured her, to force her to guide him to the place to which she was only supposed to guide Monsieur Mining King! Courageous as she is, she won't have wanted to betray him in favor of his implacable enemy, whom she venerates and calls Master and genius. And perhaps he'll have killed her, without me, unfortunate and powerless, having done anything to defend her!"

"Come on, my worthy Jean, calm down and reflect! To harm Snow Rose is entirely contrary to Loeb's interests. Be sure, on the contrary, that he'll treat her as a precious hostage, and try to get round her, but will avoid attacking her head on for fear of not obtaining what he desires from her."

"Who knows, Commandant?"

Williamson intervened. "Monsieur Rolland is right, Captain Furet. There's more reason to be anxious, at present, for the fate of Old Sinker than the gracious guide that he gave us, whom we've unfortunately allowed to be abducted, and who has so profoundly touched your heart."

"Oh, Monsieur Williamson, what makes me want to blow my brains out in furious despair, is that I've been the cause of that misfortune, by taking it into my head to leave her hidden in that fatal loft in order to try to keep her out of the hands of that filthy dog of a diabolical Saint!"

"No, Captain Furet, I alone am the guilty party, because, lacking composure at that terrible moment, I wasn't able to foresee what happened and obviate it, within the limits of the possible. In the interest of the strange man who made me what I am, I should not have allowed myself to lose sight for a single moment of the person who was to guide me to him, and whom, by virtue of that fact, he entrusted to me.

"Be careful," said Edmée. "That remorse is almost a reproach addressed to me."

"Oh, Miss Edmée, how can you say that? To reproach you for something when, on the contrary, I'm accusing myself so bitterly for the sufferings that you're endured because of me!"

"Come on," said Claude "let's cease these futile recriminations. I can see that it's up to me, who is untroubled by any intimate emotion, to be calm and practical for everyone. Let's leave the past and, in order to make resolutions for the future, let's envisage the present situation clearly. In that regard, one thing is of primary importance: Ariadne's thread is broken."

"Alas," said Williamson, "to the extent that I'm permitted any other concern by the suspension of my life on a word that hasn't yet been pronounced, that's what upsets me the most. I made an oath to respond without delay to Old Sinker's summon, but it's materially impossible for me to keep it."

"Let's reason it out," the young engineer continued. "That conductive threat, we must try to reconnect at any price. There are two means to do that: the first and most urgently imposing was to try to pick up the trail of our guide. It seems increasingly evident to me that every passing hour diminishes the chances of succeeding in that. The remains the second, which I submit to Mr. Williamson: to inform Old Sinker about the difficulty that had stopped us by the anonymous and secret means that he has given us to communicate with him—the worldwide publicity of the New York *Herald*—and request instructions from him. That might take a long time or a short one, depending on whether Lobanief is far away or close at hand, but it seems to me that it's nevertheless the best thing to do. What do you think?"

Williamson put his head in his hands and reflected carefully, He was about to open his mouth to reply when the door of the bar, now empty of other clients, as shoved brutally and opened with a bang.

Williamson, Edmée Claude and Jean leapt to their feet and stood there for a few seconds, eyes staring and mouths agape, literally paralyzed by surprise.

In front of them, rigid and rugged, the tall, thin silhouette of Loeb was outlined, clutching Snow Rose.

What did it mean?

Laconically, his voice hoarse, Loeb explained:

"I'm returning your guide to you, Williamson, because she's useless. Old Sinker is making a fool of you. I regret having tormented you—for as I've said, I have no hatred against you—and of having given myself so much trouble to end up in a cul-de-sac. I've forced the Indian to confess the whole truth to me. Her mission was only to bring you to San Francisco, and she has no idea where the man I hate is hiding. I refused to believe in that ignorance for a long time; I've set all the traps imaginable for the Indian; I've used all means, and it's necessary for me to yield to the evidence. She doesn't know anything. She can't guide either you or me to the man whose retreat, as I have twenty proofs, she doesn't know. She's useless to me; I don't want to encumber myself with her any longer, and I'm returning her to you.

"Williamson, I'm also ending my war against you. Our struggle, like your journey, is over. The advice on which you set out on campaign, with me in your wake, was a joke in poor taste on the part of the man whose entire life, in fact, is one vast bluff, as is his pretended science. In his regard, I've reawakened passions in the United States that I'll make haste to extinguish. I'm not in the habit of persisting in a still-born affair. I'm cutting my losses and quitting the game, regretting the time wasted."

Throwing a wallet on to the table in front of the friends, amazed by that unexpected denouement, he added: "Give back, I beg you, to that imbecile named Grégoire de Montalpé, what remains of the campaign subsidies with which he furnished me. Follow your path, which I don't envy, having proved to you that I'm stronger by means of domination than you are by means of millions.

"Adieu…and no hard feelings!"

And Loeb, with a shrug of the shoulders that expressed his scorn for having put so much effort into a vain project, turned on his heel and left, leaving his enemies of the day before still immobilized by amazement.

It was Captain Furet, obedient to the supreme law of living beings, who broke the charm. He advanced toward Snow Rose, his arms open wide and tears in his eyes, pronouncing her dear name—and the Indian allowed herself to fall into them, murmuring: "Captain Furet! Oh, my dear!"

Extracting herself very quickly from the candid effusion, with a modest gesture, Snow Rose came to Williamson and said: "What that evil man has just said is true. Old Sinker limited my mission to San Francisco, without any other indication..

"Then…what are we going to do now?"

"I don't know."

"Who might know, then?"

"Old Sinker."

"When and how will he let us know his wishes?"

"I don't know."

"Monsieur Rolland advised me to solicit him via the New York *Herald*."

"It's not necessary. Old Sinker hadn't said so."

"If we do nothing, the situation could last forever."

"Old Sinker will make provision."

"After all," Williamson concluded, "it's up to him, in fact. If, as it seems, he hasn't taken precautions, there's nothing we can do. We'll have made a voyage that, for my part, and even though, time after time, it has brought us frightful anguish, has been the best of my life, for I've discovered something better than America therein.

"My friends, let's go back to the hotel, and live, since we're rid of Loeb, as if we had no other goal than to visit the city, the Queen of the Pacific, come what may…or what might. Will you deign to grant me your arm, Miss Edmée"

They had been walking for ten minutes through the city, still partially reconstructed, when Claude, who was walking beside Williamson, said, in a low voice: "There's the man."

"What man?"

"The monomaniac my matelot says is named Santos Miguel."

"Where?"

"Behind us. He went past the couple formed by Jean and Snow Rose and immediately attached himself to their paces. They're both too preoccupied to have noticed him. I'll inform the mariner."

"Don't do anything, my friend. Total passivity is now our law."

At the moment when Snow Rose and her great friend Jean, following Williamson and Rolland, went into the hotel, the Indian started. Behind her, almost in her ear, a voice had said: "Manitoba."

"My father?" said the gracious Redskin—who was hardly red at all—turning round and finding herself face to face with the Californian fisherman that Jean recognized immediately.

"Menominee," added Santos Miguel.

"My nation?"

"Your name?"

"Snow Rose."

"Finally. I've been waiting for you for a month."

That interrogation was not to the taste of the young mariner. He was about to criticize the manner in which the individual permitted himself to interrogate Snow Rose while she was on his arm when the latter uttered a significant "Shh!" and addressed herself to the supposed monomaniac.

"Is it the great chief of the Menominees who sends you to me?"

"No. It's an old man with long white hair who passed through Purissima a month ago and asked me to carry out a commission, paying me in advance.

"He didn't tell you his name?"

"He said that it wasn't worth the trouble, and that you'd recognize the origin..."

"Of what?"

"The letter I have for you."

"A letter? Why didn't you say so right away? Give it to me, quickly.

"Here it is."

"And that's all?"

"That's all."

"Dear Captain Furet," said the young woman, urgently to the young mariner, "give this man all the dollars you have on you. Mr. Williamson will return them to you."

Jean obeyed. The man drew away, calling down all the blessings of heaven on the generous young people, and Snow Rose ran after the Mining King and his friends. She signaled to them at a distance that she had to talk to him.

Intrigued, the billionaire took everyone into the drawing room of his apartment.

Then the young Indian took the letter from beneath her mantle, where she had hidden it, opened the envelope and took out a fragment of a map, which she handed to Williamson.

The latter had scarcely glanced at it when he stifled a cry of surprise. In the corner was the sign.

"My friends," he said, very emotionally, "Admire the wisdom and the prudence of the man who is summoning me. It was deliberately that he broke the connective thread—a rupture to which we owe Loeb's renunciation and Snow Rose's liberation. At the same time, though, he's taken care to re-knot it, for he's undoubtedly given me this time, via the intermediary and emissary so well-chosen, the indication of the definitive place where we'll find him."

"Which is?"

"I shall imitate the prudence of which he has given me such a marvelous example. I'll tell you as soon as we've left San Francisco."

"We're retracing out steps?"

"Oh no! On the contrary."

"But we're leaving?"

"In two or three days' time. Loeb is still so close! We're going to organize ourselves as if we were going to stay here for some time, and then disappear abruptly. It's the end of our voyage, Miss Edmée. May I flatter myself with the hope that it will make me happy?"

"To one of the questions you asked at the posada a little while ago, Snow Rose replied that Old Sinker would make provision. To the one you're asking I can only reply, at this moment, that God will make provision."

Williamson bowed his head, not without discouragement, but, in spite of himself, with a vague...very vague...hope.

# Chapter XIII
## *The Fantastic Murder*

The surprise at the posada—a surprise of deliverance and partial happiness—followed by that of the letter, had taken place on a Monday evening.

Exactly two weeks later, and, in consequence, on the second Monday thereafter on the incommensurable and implacable Clock of Time, a supplementary liner of the America-Japan Line, after having left the large military port of Yokosouka to port, moored a little before nightfall in the harbor of Yokohama. To general surprise, from that liner of nearly ten thousand tons, whose vast flanks could accommodate more that thirteen hundred passengers, only six passengers emerged.

Having not found, at first glance, a steamer departing from the great California port at his convenience, and wanting to be able to traverse the north Pacific as rapidly as possible, in order to render a repeat of the shipwreck off Sandy Hook impossible, the Mining King had chartered one of the modern giants of the sea for his personal use.

Loeb surely ought to have been a long way from San Francisco two days after his abrupt renunciation of pursuing his campaign of hate, but Williamson was determined not to neglect any precaution, no matter how exaggerated it might seem. To that effect he had ostentatiously rendered a villa in Berkeley, near Oakland, directly opposite the broad entrance to the bays, had transported his friends and hearth there, as if he intended settling in for a long sojourn in California, and, via the intermediary of Captain Furet, had arranged a seemingly-fortuitous encounter with the director of the Transpacific Company.

The latter invited the celebrated Yankee king to participate in the trials of a new ship, which had its coal-bunkers full and set forth, at an average speed of seventeen knots...all the way to Japan.

Claude and Edmée could not be dupes of the stratagem, although Jean Guitard had maintained an obedient silence regarding the step he had been secretly instructed to take, but what about Snow Rose, who was hesitating so dolorously between the duty of returning to the paternal Reservation now that her mission was accomplished and her great desire to see Old Sinker again, in the company of her brave and joyous sweetheart? In any case, she was, intimately, infinitely grateful to the Mining King for having thus disposed of her without consulting her and for having imposed a long voyage upon her "in convoy," as Jean put it, with her dear Captain Furet.

As for Grégoire de Montalpé, Williamson had simply left him in Berkeley, alone with his recovered wallet, which was not too badly breached, the procedures of the dominator of men having been—for that very reason—fairly economical.

In the little group, now so amicable, that was following the fortunes of the Caesar of the dollar, de Montalpé was the only one who, in Williamson's scale-free eyes recalled the moral vileness of the human rabble that his old misanthropy had once generalized. Thus, the presence of the gentleman, who had not even redeemed his sins by a little virile courage, was intolerable to him, and he had deprived himself of it—not sorry, fundamentally, to do him the bad turn of making him miss out on the goal for which he had associated himself with Loeb in Paris.

The surprise of the workers at the port of Yokohama on observing the small number of passengers disembarking from such a large ship come from so far away was completed by the breathless arrival of the United States consul, escorted by the principal authorities of Yokohama, one of the largest of the nine Japanese ports open to commerce.

That was because, on arriving within sight of the coast of the Isles of the Rising Sun, the Mining King had thought he ought to announce the fact by means of a skillfully courteous cablegram. He would have need of Japanese complaisance to reach the rendezvous signed to him, traveling across country in the minimum possible time. Knowing the mistrust of the conquerors of Korea, having experienced it previously, he took his precautions.

It was, therefore, as an important person that Edmée's "suitor"—whom the voyage had left sighing, as before, in spite of the long intimacy of the crossing and a few hopeful glimmers that he had seemed to observe in the young woman's eyes—was welcomed at Yokohama, and it was with quasi-royal honors that he was received in Tokyo.

Given the delicate negotiations between the victorious isles of the Far East and Washington, sage governmental diplomacy considered it an honor to give an extraordinary reception to an individual of primary influence in the great American Republic. Whether he liked it or not in spite of his haste, it was necessary for Williamson to submit, for forty-eight hours, to diurnal and nocturnal festivities, with gala performances, mousmé ballets and sumptuous meals, which were only tolerable because the Parisian grace, beauty and wit of Edmée was magnificently triumphant thereat.

Finally, on Thursday, he was able, with his companions, furnished with all the necessary licenses to travel through the fantastic insular empire, to depart via the Tokyo-Mito-Sendai-Hachinohe-Aomori railway for the north of great Nippon.

It was between the last two stations that he left the railroad and the little troop, mounting horses brought from the capital in a wagon added to the train, set off in the company of reliable guides toward the volcanic chain that gives Japan the appearance of a gigantic antediluvian reptile with a dorsal crest, asleep in the waves, its slumber sometimes troubled by profound shivers.

A grave emotion rendered the voyagers silent as they approached a mountain higher than its neighbors, whose conical summit, partly veiled by light vapors, dispersing liked ripped gauze in the breeze, rose up arid and bare above the cultivated fields, which, in that winter season, dressed its base with a gray and brown checkerboard reminiscent of the fabrics favored by Anglo-Saxons.

When they arrived sat the extreme limit of cultivation, Williamson, after having consulted for the hundredth time the map received in San Francisco, halted the little troop, made them dismount, dismissed the guides and horses, and, following the detailed indications of a large-scale plan drawn on the back of the sheet of paper, beckoned to his companions to follow him.

For two long hours, marching in his wake, they went around the vast cone, scaling blocks of lava solidified in bizarre forms, sometimes disappearing into narrow corridors, going up and coming down again, in order finally to arrive at the threshold of a somber portal, from which a warm breath emerged, which seemed to be the entrance to a disquieting tunnel plunging into the heart of the mountain.

In a voice rendered tremulous by emotion, the Mining King formulated the brief words: "This is it."

Torches were lit and, with a stride as firm as the uneven nature of the ground permitted, they advanced, their staring eyes searching the darkness.

Avoiding the projections of rock that sometimes threatened their heads, they descended a slope that was often steep for more than an hour.

Suddenly, the vault of the tunnel rose up abruptly above their heads. They went into a vast cavern...

A hundred meters in front of them, a luminous dot was shining, which was raised and lowered three times in a sign of greeting.

Their hearts squeezed by an oppressive anguish, they headed toward the beacon.

By the light of their torches, a tall old man appeared, clad in animal skins, his head crowned by abundant white hair falling in snowy waves over his shoulders. He was holding up a heavy lantern at the end of a robust arm.

"Old Sinker!" murmured Snow Rose, in a tone of devotion that was both ardent and almost fearful.

The old man stopped some fifteen paces away. The steel of a large caliber weapon suddenly gleamed in his right hand.

"Williamson?" he interrogated.

"I'm Williamson, and I've come in response to your summons."

"Advance alone!"

The Mining King obeyed, his lantern raised to the level of his face.

"I recognize you," said Old Sinker—and, accompanied by Williamson, he approached the immobilized group and inspected them with a rapid glance.

"Snow Rose!" he recognized. "Why did you come all this way, child? Anyway, it's Destiny." Then, indicating the rest of the group, he said to Williamson: "Who are they?"

"This is Mr. Claude Rolland, an engineer, and his sister Edmée, two noble hearts, French, and your relatives, their grandmother having been a Lobanief. Next to them is a valiant mariner of the same Gallic race, their servant, or rather their devoted companion, an intelligent and intrepid seaman who has saved us all from death three times in the course of the voyage. Finally, my groom Toby, a faithful and taciturn lad."

The strange old man seemed to collect himself. Then he said: "All right. Come."

Following him, the little troop traversed the vast cavern without saying a word. Claude noticed, in passing, that the uncertain light of their torches, penetrating the darkness vaguely, revealed in its depths a series of giant windlasses capable of unrolling tens of kilometers of steel cable.

Having arrived at the wall, Old Sinker lifted up a heavy opaque door made of several bearskins sown together, and the visitors went into a large natural chamber copiously illuminated by several incandescent bulbs.

That redoubt, in which a company of infantry could easily have assumed various drill-formations, simultaneously resembled a laboratory, by virtue of the immense furnace laden with retorts, crucibles alembics, and electric and other heaters; the generating plant of a factory, by virtue of its powerful steam engine and its dynamos; and the study of a geologist who was also an advanced mathematician, by virtue of its collection of minerals of unknown forms and gleams, its blackboards covered with figures and equations, and its colossal table heaped with books and pieces of paper blackened with calculations. Only a heap of furs serving as a bed, a few kitchen utensils and a few stacks of food-tins announced that it was also a place of residence.

Claude's curious gaze noticed immediately, first of all a fissure in the wall into which the fumes of the furnace and the steam engine disappeared, which doubtless communicated, doubtless a long distance away, with the crater, and thus served the endeavors of a single man as a chimney, and then the continuous noise of a trickle of water into a full basin.

Then his surprise, as an engineer, at finding in that profound cavern, in a site distant from any human aid, a laboratory, a factory and a habitation, disappeared. That was because they all saw, fixed to a low part of the vault, an iron chain from which hung a terrestrial globe pierced through by a dagger: the sign.

The engineer—the others not having minds free enough to deliver themselves to observation—did not have the leisure to take his investigations any further. With a grave gesture, Old Sinker had invited his visitors to sit down on rocky outcrops forming natural seats, and, standing up, having slowly caressed his long snow-white beard, began to speak:

"In the fifteen years since we met, Williamson, in very dramatic circumstances. My work, then merely sketched, has passed from the domain of theory into the domain of precise, palpable facts.

"I told you then, roughly and without insisting, that the terrestrial planet is, like us, like everything, a living being, whole pellicular surface we inhabit as parasites

"I charged my intelligent, docile and unique neophyte, Snow Rose, to prepare you with some knowledge possessed by her, for the striking truth that awaited you here. I assume that she has done that."

"Yes, Master, albeit in the insufficient fashion corresponding with my feeble strength."

"I have no doubt, Snow Rose, that the little that it was in your power to say has been well said.

"I told you, Williamson, at the time of our abrupt and definitive separation fifteen years ago that I would summon you after you had enriched yourself more than other men, when I was in a position—in collaboration with you—to be the master of the destiny of the world. That day has come.

"It is you alone that I wanted to instruct and enable to assist at the supreme moment the proof crowning an entire life of effort to discover the Truth. You will know shortly why I am tolerating other presences, including that of these two French people, to whom I am sympathetic as much because they are French as because a little of my blood runs in their veins, and above all because you like them and answer for them.

"So, listen, Williamson, about whom I have not ceased to think since our former encounter, and whom I have made the richest of men, I hope...and listen, all of you!

"Geologists, who, if they had the slightest sincerity, if not modesty, would call themselves simply 'dermologists,' since it is not the Earth that they can discover but only the epidermis of the monster, because it is only the epidermis that they have been able to penetrate to a feeble depth and determine its contents...those, I say, who have baptized themselves, as falsely as pridefully, 'geologists,' have, from the heights of their professorial chairs, informed humanity of a host of errors to which a few rare intellects have refused to subscribe—such as Lord Kelvin, who recently disappeared from the number of insects living on the substance of the Immense Beast.

"They have represented it as a mass of molten minerals surrounded by a crust solidified by contact with the cold of space, without pausing at the impossibility of the resistance of that crust—the thinness of which even they observe—to pressures due to solar and lunar, not to mention planetary, attrac-

223

tions, without taking into account the fact that the rapidity of translation of seismic shocks is far superior to what is achievable traversing a liquid medium.

"It would be cruel for human science to persist.

"That the Earth is solid in all its parts, and that, in consequence, the story of the central broth, transforming the globe into an immense chaotic cauldron, is a myth and a dream, I have known for a long time, because I assured myself of it directly a long time ago."

At that formidable assertion, Old Sinker's listeners raised their heads.

"Yes," he said, tranquilly, it is already ten years ago that I traversed the famous terrestrial crust and I, a pygmy, commenced to delve into the flesh of the monster, boldly compiling an anatomy of the basis of that vivisection. That is why you find me in this region, which I chose for two reasons, one technical—which would have been sufficient on its own—and the other political.

"Technically, it was necessary for me to find a place where the 'hide' was very thin and where the vital organs came, in a sense, to touch it—a place comparable to the human temple, where, almost beneath the thin skin, the artery beats that creates a vulnerability.

"Politically, it was necessary for me to work in a region where the people, mentally very different and very preoccupied with their social development, would let me work without paying any heed to me, a people having, in the mass, very little science and too much superstition to come prying into my solitary labor.

"I found here what I needed: in the ten years since I transported into this cavern the necessary tools and provisions, the simple agriculturalists, even those on the slopes of the mountain, have, I believe, quite forgotten me. As for the limited thickness of the terrestrial dermis, I had rightly anticipated that this tormented ground, punctured by volcanoes, guaranteed a sensitive area and present inflammation of the immense body. I discovered the 'flesh' eighteen and a half kilometers down, a flesh less hard than the skin—and by 'skin' I mean the rocky dermis, not the epidermis, and even less the superficial dirt of twenty or thirty million years, a dermis that we incorrectly label the subsoil, the region of quarries and mines utilized by our existence on the ultimate surface. That flesh is, as I say, less hard than the skin, but of a variable hardness and nature, as the cellular composition of our bodies differs between muscles, fat, nerves, bones, etc."

Old Sinker saw Claude Rolland agitating his fingers with some impatience. "Do you have an objection to make?" he asked, with a certain arrogance.

"No—a question to ask."

"Go on."

"The increasing heat...?"

"It only increases in traversing the envelope, at the inner surface of which it reaches it maximum—which is to say, that of the body, which no longer varies, at least in the limited thickness of that which I've been permitted to reach, and which I firmly believed to be very similar throughout the Monster's mass."

"And that temperature?"

"Is a hundred and forty-eight degrees centigrade."

"How were you able...?"

"To survive there? Certainly not without a refrigerant suit and a provision of air at a respirable temperature. It is not an environment into which a man can introduce his body, which is adapted to environments proximal to the cold of infinite space, without the protection of his industry, nor one where it is prudent to torment the Beast in person. When my tools were operating, I was able to keep myself out of reach, far away in the inert matter that overlies the epidermis.

"Once, however, in spite of that precaution, I nearly failed to return to the extreme surface. My scalpels had attacked and sliced special very distinctive fibers—as I observed later—of a substance and contexture that I shall call 'ambient tissue.' The consequence of that was a general tremor that was translated, in the sunlight, into seismic shocks, which, I subsequently learned, had repercussions, unfortunately mortal for too many human beings, in several regions some distance away from here. I believe I can affirm that I encountered that day a significant 'nervous filament.'

"In addition to that exceptional case, however, I observed, by the evidence of inexplicable pressures to which my implements were subjected in spite of the resistance of their massive metallic alloy, superior to that of modern chrome steel, that the mass is, in general, like our flesh prone to reflexive reactions against anything that troubles its normal harmony. Thus, it was only after my tools had finished their work that I went down to study the results."

"But how," Williamson asked in his turn, "while your strange experiments were taking place here, were you so often able to indicate to me, in America, the existence of mines that..."

"The labor that I carried out here necessitated frequent interruptions, superficial healing, without which my carnal fragment, robust as it is, would not have resisted that superhuman labor. It was then, Williamson, that I undertook expeditions to America, where my expert eyes read the so-called subsoil and threw into your coffers a few more millions of dollars."

"Your fabulous work, then...?"

"Save for an improbable error, is complete. Two months ago, I set my tools at rest, because I had certainly encountered one of the entity's organs."

"An organ?" queried the troubled auditors of the fantastic lecture, in chorus.

"An essential organ, if I can believe the rhythmic beats, at intervals of twelve hours, to which its rather tender and very elastic envelope is subject, which I hesitated to perforate. Is it the Monster's heart? I cannot believe so, given its proximity to the surface. Is it an analogue of the carotid in the human neck, rendered by its outlying position easy to reach? Everything gives me that conviction.

"Then a formidable problem arose before my conscience, whose eventual solution has been simultaneously the torment, the goal, the terror and the desire of my entire life.

"I believe that I am sure of having put my finger on a vital organ of the planetary Monster that carries us. Ought I to surrender my secret in order that others, after me, can push on even further with the study of the living sidereal body that carries us through space in its rolling course, as a swallow carries a spider with hooked feet through the sky from north to south? Or should I mortally wound the rolling giant, taking revenge for the countless voluntary cataclysms that, since the beginning of time, have doomed so many millions of human brethren, as well as billions of inferior animal brethren?

"Its death, doubtless slow, would bring about the slow disappearance of all the parasitic lives that struggle and suffer in order that fewer of them might die. But could there be any more transcendent benefit than that general annihilation, and, as I once said, would not the man who was able to become the 'murderer of the world' be sublimely wise and good?"

Williamson and his companions had risen go their feet, breathless. Lobanief extended his arms in a gesture of supreme authority.

"Wait, before replying!

"I hate the Earth! It is because it has revealed itself to me as the infamous devourer of human creatures that it has enabled me, in one horrible minute, always present in my mind, to divine its living and malevolent nature.

"More than thirty years ago, exiled from my fatherland, I came with my family in search of forgetfulness and repose, to an isolated and almost deserted location far from human grandeurs, which are often very heavy to those who assume them.

"I had bought a small plot of land on the border of Canada and the Union. From the house where I lived, my view extended to the horizon over the calm majesty of the immense and beautiful Lake Superior. I hunted, and I fished in the abundantly-populated Pigeon River, which ran at the foot of my wild property. I meditated for hours or cultivated the sciences, for which I had always had a pronounced penchant, and I relaxed in the bosom of a numerous and tenderly cherished family...

"I was happy!

"One evening, a terrible storm burst over our house, which oscillated but resisted. Then, without there being any volcano, or even mountains, in the most distant vicinity, the ground opened up beneath my dwelling, which I had quit momentarily in order to go to the stables to make sure that my horses had not been carried away.

"It was into an unfathomable abyss, which closed as soon as it had opened, like a demonic rictus, that my house was swallowed up, with my adored wife, two sons already grown up, who were my pride, and an adorable daughter, who was an angel, and my last-born son, scarcely emerged from infancy, who was a cherub!

"Mad with terror, I leapt on to a stallion, whose halter I broke, and I fled, galloping aimlessly, until my mount fell dead, leaving me inanimate on the ground.

"I was picked up by Menominee Indians, who took me to their Reservation, then as vast as a kingdom, and cared for me. It was among them that I recovered my reason, and thus my dolor, among them that I acquired the conviction of the living spasm of the Earth, and the burning desire for cold vengeance was implanted in my soul.

"After thirty years, the hour of that vengeance has chimed. I have seen so many human beings suffer, one after another, due to the Earth, that in avenging myself, even at the price of the annihilation of everything it bears, it is humanity entire that I can and want to avenge!

"It is futile now, you will have understood, to talk to me about the other solution, of preserving the gigantic Beast, which is perhaps nothing but an immense invalid rendered evil by its own suffering, of learning to know its organism in order to care for it, to regulate its functioning, so that the humanity of future ages might succeed in playing the role of benevolent microbes in human and animal organisms

"If I said these things to humans still to new on the surface of the turbulent being, still poorly detached from the animality of their material nature, they would not believe me, would persecute my disciples, and continue for many centuries to come to languish in error and suffering.

"No! The moment has come for my vengeance and for the worldwide benefit of extinguishing all life in the world, by means of the sacrificial murder of the world! A Being as formidable as that, the vital duration of which is measured in millions of centuries, does not die immediately of a small wound, even if it is mortal. The present generation, at least, will have time to complete its career before the monstrous death-throes commence, and your life, Williamson, will be beautiful; the only one informed, having the supreme and sovereign power of gold, you will extract from the end of the world all that it can offer of joys; you will be the last fortunate man—which is what I want, because I love you!

"The moment has come! Lift up your hearts! Watch the judiciary strike of the Avenger of Humankind, the Master of Death, the Murderer of the World!"

The fantastic old man had stopped speaking, but his listeners were still stunned, astounded and terrified...

Only Williamson darted at Lobanief a singular glance, whose fixity seemed to want to read in Old Sinker's soul something that he had not said, something that extended his entire being in an intense and mute interrogation.

The tall old man, who, his expression inspired, appeared to have become even taller, summoned the billionaire to come toward him with a broad authoritarian gesture, into which a nuance of emotion nevertheless intruded.

He said to him: "In spite of the long-meditated precautions that I've taken, the immense action that I'm about to take is subject to contingencies, because our embryonic science can't anticipate everything.

"I'm going to go down in order to judge the force of the thrust that I must deliver to the Monster. Every two thousand feet I've set up a refuge, but in case I don't come up again—

and only then—you must swear, once you have acquired the certainty that the avenger of humankind cannot reappear alive in the sunlight in order to delight in the progress of his murderous work, that you will open this letter, in which is recorded my final revelation and my last will."

So saying, he took from his bosom a sealed envelope, which the billionaire received in a tremulous and distracted hand.

The tall old man fixed Williamson with a long stare in which there was a strange, intense expression...and advanced majestically toward the exit from the chamber into the large grotto, heading toward its dark depths, followed by his stunned guests, oppressed by a kind of tremulous, admiring and quasi-religious horror.

Suddenly, ten arc-lamps inundated that opaque obscurity with light, and, at the extremity of the series of enormous windlasses that Claude Rolland had glimpsed in passing, illuminated the gaping opening of a large fissure, a black and mysterious gulf, to the rim of which Lobanief advanced.

He called to Snow Rose, and, showing her the lever of a commutator fixed into a block of lava, ordered: "At the precise moment that I disappear!"

Eyes dilated, with a double gesture, abrupt and catastrophic, the young Indian seized the lever and nodded her head, saying: "Yes."

Then, Old Sinker/Lobanief shoved, as he jumped into it, a kind of metallic skip or nacelle, which oscillated momentarily directly above the abyss.

In a voice that showed a hint of emotion for the first time, the old man shouted: "*Au revoir*, Williamson...or adieu!"

The windlasses having been immediately set in motion, he plunged into the warm darkness of the gulf.

At that moment, the engineer pulled himself together. "Come on!" he said. "It's frightful and it's insane, all this! We need to stop..."

Detaching himself from Edmée, who was clinging to him, he leapt toward the Indian.

Too late.

Snow Rose had lowered the lever.

He stopped, dazed by anguish.

A sepulchral silence reigned, only troubled by the unctuous friction of the axle-trees of the windlasses in their groves.

Of the six human creatures who were there, none was breathing...

Suddenly, muffled, mysterious and formidable, the sound of a multiple detonation, compounded out of explosions, gigantic cracking sounds and sinister rumblings, as if a thousand cannons had started firing simultaneously in the distant entrails of the earth, rose from the terrible abyss.

At the same time a dense column of vapor surged forth, rendering the intense light of the lamps vague, and the ground shook, oscillating.

Uttering cries of fright, Toby, the Indian, who had been grabbed and was being dragged by the mariner, and Edmée, gripped in her brother's arms, raced toward the corridor through which they had come when they arrived, the only exit from the cavern.

They did not reach it.

A terrible shock shook the grotto, the vault of which collapsed, opening a huge gap in the mountain-side to the sky.

As they fell, the blocks had crushed the windlasses.

Terrified, the fugitives hastened toward the new exit, rendered accessible by the piles of fallen rock.

Only one remained. Standing on the edge of the gulf, extending his arms desperately, Williamson shouted in the silence that had almost been restored:

"Him!... Him!!... Him!!!"

Edmée tore herself away from the fraternal grip, violently. Climbing over the collapsed rocks she ran to Williamson.

"Come!"

"Him!... Him!!"

"A few seconds more and it's death!"

"Run away! Leave me!"

"Those hot and poisonous vapors...that are coming out of it. In spite of the hole, they're filing the cavern...irrespirable!"

"Run!"

"A few more seconds and we'll suffocate!"

"Oh, run, run away, Miss Edmée! I can't...I can't! Him! Down there! Him!!!"

Struggling against the efforts of Claude to drag her away, the young woman begged: "Come, if you love me!"

"I...I can't!"

"Then...then I'm staying—we'll die together!"

Williamson uttered a mad scream and turned to Edmée. "You want...?"

"If you want to die, I don't want to live!"

"You love me, then?"

"Until death!"

"Ah! To live! To live! I want to live!"

With a clamor of wild joy, Williamson seized the young woman in his arms, his strength multiplied tenfold, and carried her away toward the light, toward the sky, toward life. Claude helped him in the climb, difficult with a human burden.

Behind them, in the midst of incessant trepidations, an increasing din rose up, similar to that of a tumultuous tide forcing itself through a narrow bottleneck.

The two men hastened recklessly, but they were out of breath, blinded and strangled by the hot and fetid vapors, whose column now hid the exit.

Fortunately, help was at hand. Jean Guitard, after having set his beloved Snow Rose down on a safe path, came back to aid his dear masters.

After a great deal of effort, and after having thought twenty times over that they would not reach the portal, the little troop was finally reunited in the open air, on the flank of the crater, beyond the emanations of the subterranean exhalation.

Just in time!

A shock, a hundred times more violent than the first, completed the dislocation of the vault of the cavern...

Before the frightened eyes of the fugitives, with a sound that no comparison can approach, the entire vault collapsed, opening a gaping, fuming hole several hundred meters in diameter.

Although, very fortunately, they had only stopped on the part of the mountainside beyond the scope of the vast subterranean cavity, Williamson and his companions nevertheless remained in a situation that was, if not immediately critical, at least very worrying.

Backed up against an outcrop of volcanic rock, unscalable without ropes, ladders and outside assistance, they saw the vast cavity that had opened up in front of them cut off the other direction of escape. They had no alternative but to wait where they were for assistance that seemed unlikely to arrive, exposed to the risk of falling victim to some further convulsion of the mountain.

Their eyes, widened by anguish, could not tear themselves away from the gaping circle, from which smoke was rising, alternately gray and yellow, and from which Williamson was still vaguely hoping that, by some miracle, the tall and disturbing old man who had caused the cataclysm might emerge.

When, after half an hour of anxious waiting, the vapors had finally thinned out sufficiently to allow them to penetrate it with their gaze, it was not Old Sinker that appeared but a lake of thick mud, punctured here and there by bubbles from which jets of smoke emerged, and the overflow of which was pouring into a broad groove that ran down the side of the mountain, destroying in its passage a number of symmetrical rectangular crop-fields.

"It wasn't an artery or an organ," murmured Snow Rose, sadly. "It was only a tumor or an abscess. The master, in losing his life, wanted to wound the monster mortally...perhaps he's only given it relief."

For his part, Williamson, renouncing his impossible hope, let out a long sigh.

"It's really your opinion," he asked Edmée and her brother, "that your unparalleled relative, to whom I owe everything, is definitely dead under that burning scum emerged from the depths?"

"He's dead," replied Edmée and Claude, gravely, in chorus.

Then, the Mining King, with a trembling hand, took the sealed envelope from his pocket, opened it and started reading. At the very first lines he straightened up and uttered a stifled cry. Holding out the unfolded letter to the young people, he cried, with sobs in his voice:

"I suspected it, and wasn't mistaken. Old Sinker was my father!"

The child found and brought up by the Canadian garrison at Fort William was the last-born of the noble Russian exile Lobanief, who had miraculously survived the catastrophe in which the rest of his family, save for his father, had been swallowed up. And when, as a young reporter, Williamson had saved from the Hudson and despair the author and apostle of a discovery or a new scientific faith, the latter had recognized his son. Not wanting any human affection to deflect him from his bitter, fantastic and murderous determination, however, he had resolved, while heaping the greatest terrestrial benefits upon him, to remain a stranger to him, and only to summon him on the day of the frightful experiment, which would be that of his death, when the two would be reunited!

Williamson, his eyes moist, turned to Edmée. "My father," he said, "wanted to give me the mastery of the world, by means of the knowledge of its imminent end. The surety of the progressive and constant diminution of the vital intensity of the world's surface was an element of fortune even greater than the reliable discovery of mineral wealth.

"By an error of his genius…or madness…the Earth, the object of his hatred, swallowed him up without him being able to keep his promise. But he did something better for me. The fact of his supreme appeal put in my cold and egotistical path, and intimately involved with my life, to teach me to know its value, an angel descended to earth with the features of a woman!

"My father hasn't given me the mastery of the world, but may his great shade, which floats here above his Titanic tomb, be blessed! Thanks to him, via your love, Edmée, my soul has finally awakened to communion with the Great Secret of the World!"

# Chapter XIV
## *Conclusion*

For a long moment, Williamson and Edmée, standing side by side and hand in hand, dreamed silently, delightfully and gravely, their gazes wandering over the horizon, no longer veiled by the smoke of the subterranean mud, already cooling.

Claude contemplated them fraternally, while "Captain Furet," with the eloquence of his gaze, gradually dispelled the grave and tragic shadows in the dark eyes of Snow Rose.

Suddenly, above them, an abrupt and hoarse voice shouted: "There they are! They've been surprised and delayed by that sudden eruption of mud. We've arrived in time!"

The six fugitives raised their heads and, at the top of the outcrop of volcanic rock, recognized Jonathan Loeb, flanked by a Grégoire de Montalpé who, having recovered his sufficiency, was more a dandy than ever, accompanied by several Japanese authorities and the highest representative of the United States in the Empire of the Rising Sun.

"You have, on the contrary, arrived too late to encounter the noble genius Old Sinker, who is no more, but very much in time for me, since you've been gracious enough to bring the most important representatives of this Empire and our Republic. If you please, gentlemen, will you give us the means of getting out of the situation we're in and coming to join you?"

Men equipped with climbing equipment rapidly organized the liberation of the six prisoners of the mountain, who were welcomed with the greatest respect by the Japanese and the Yankee diplomat, with a suspicious hostility by Jonathan Loeb, and with a Southern loquacity by de Montalpé, to whom the "official" news of the death of the inconvenient Old Sinker gave a crazy desire to dance with joy.

"It was naughty of you to leave poor Grégoire kicking his heels all alone in San Francisco, when you were heading for the beautiful land of Japan! Fortunately, the worthy Monsieur Loeb hadn't left the place; he'd caught wind of the flight and, having no doubt of its objective, freed me in order that we could come here at the gallop, with the aid of these powerful Messieurs, warned about the catastrophes of which their country, by virtue of facts of which you're aware, might eventually become the theater. Then..."

"Enough!" said Loeb, immediately obeyed.

Williamson went to the American diplomat and, handing him the envelope whose seal he had broken a short while before, said: "I'm depositing these papers in the hands of the senior representative of the United States, which, in the circumstances in which they were given to me, establish the decease of the noble Russian Baron Lobanief, my father."

"What!" cried de Montalpé, who had reasons for not being content with the general surprise. "You're the son of..."

"These papers establish it officially.

"But then...the inheritance?"

"A thousand regrets, my dear...relative. But perhaps you were also ingenuous, in so often thwarting the plans of an...adversary who thought of nothing but getting rid of me?"

"Oh, what a gaffe!"

Williamson addressed Loeb.

"Our paths were different; I dare to hope that we shall no longer be adversaries?"

"Well, we might, in the circumstances, now that we've made one another's acquaintance, even become allies, for I've never been directly your enemy."

"As regards an alliance, it's not that, for the moment, that I desire," the Mining King replied, diplomatically. He took Edmée's hand. "Gentlemen," he proclaimed, bowing slightly, "the new Baron Lobanief, American Citizen, has the honor of introducing you to his fiancée, Miss Edmée Rolland, of Paris."

This time, the unfortunate Grégoire thought he would faint from stupor and jealousy. As pale as his immaculate shirt-front, he stood there open-mouthed, unable to articulate a single word.

Addressing the diplomat again, Lobanief/Williamson went on: "As soon as we return to Tokyo, I shall have the honor of asking you to be kind enough to marry us, in conformity with the law. My mourning forbids any ceremony; we shall proceed with a simple civil ceremony; the others will take place, in accordance with Mrs. Lobanief's desire, in New York or Paris. I beg the Japanese authorities, whose welcome was so pompously gracious on my arrival, to be kind enough, for the same reason, to allow me to pass through Tokyo and Yokohama incognito in order to return to my ship.

"Oh! Let's not forget, in personal happiness, the happiness of others. I desire that, at the same time as the marriage of Miss Rolland and myself, the union should also be sealed of this brave mariner here, whom I shall continue to employ in the position and with the salary of a captain, with Miss Snow Rose, to whom I shall give a dowry of two hundred thousand dollars."

Finally, Grégoire de Montalpé was able, through a throat taut and obstructed by tears, to articulate a cry of despair: "And...and...and me? What...what...what will become of me?"

With an exaggerated and cold politeness, Lobanief/Williamson said: "Your presence here, my cousin de Montalpé, proves that you have a pronounced taste for long voyages. Let's see, my dear future brother-in-law and Director General of my mines, can we not find an exploration or a residency...somewhere?"

"A residency, certainly...I'll take care of it."

"Where?" moaned the discomfited dandy.

"Madagascar."

That was Claude Rolland's only vengeance with regard to Grégoire de Montalpé.

One final amazement was reserved, not for the unfortunate Grégoire, but for Claude.

On arriving at San Francisco, he found a dispatch from France addressed to New York, which had been forwarded by post to the Californian port by reason of the notoriety of the second name contained in the address: "M. Rolland, care of M. Williamson, Mining King."

Claude opened it and read:

*Many thanks. Report perfect. Effects tribune devastating. Ministry slain. Am minister. If politics tempting, return quickly. Reserving situation cabinet chief.*

*Dupeyroux.*

Claude's features expressed such a prodigious bewilderment that his billionaire brother-in-law, who was watching him from the corner of his eye, could not help smiling.

"But...I wasn't able to send my work, since I didn't reconstitute it after the shipwreck!"

"My dear Claude, it was received anyway."

"*My* work?"

"Not entirely. Thanks to the intermediary of the Catholic priest who rendered me a service in New York—and who will get a true cathedral for his pains—I had a critique of French colonial administrative methods compiled by an adroit American humoristic journalist and cabled..."

"And it was a fantasy concocted by trickery that...?"

"Brought down one ministry in order to consecrate another. Don't be surprised. In France, people believe so easily that which isn't serious, especially when one senses a foreign brand on it. I don't advise you to quit me to follow the senator; a man of real value, knowledge and honesty like you would make a deplorable politician, out of favor as soon as you opened your mouth. You'll stay with me eh?"

And, with good hearts, the two brothers-in-law shook hands firmly.

## SF & FANTASY

Adolphe Alhaiza. *Cybele*

Alphonse Allais. *The Adventures of Captain Cap*

Henri Allorge. *The Great Cataclysm*

Guy d'Armen. *Doc Ardan: The City of Gold and Lepers*

G.-J. Arnaud. *The Ice Company*

Charles Asselineau. *The Double Life*

Henri Austruy. *The Eupantophone; The Olotelepan; The Petitpaon Era*

Barillet-Lagargousse. *The Final War*

Cyprien Bérard. *The Vampire Lord Ruthwen*

S. Henry Berthoud. *Martyrs of Science*

Aloysius Bertrand. *Gaspard de la Nuit*

Richard Bessière. *The Gardens of the Apocalypse; The Masters of Silence*

Albert Bleunard. *Ever SMalher*

Félix Bodin. *The Novel of the Future*

Louis Boussenard. *Monsieur Synthesis*

Alphonse Brown. *City of Glass; The Conquest of the Air*

Emile Calvet. *In a Thousand Years*

André Caroff. *The Terror of Madame Atomos; Miss Atomos; The Return of Madame Atomos; The Mistake of Madame Atomos; The Monsters of Madame Atomos; The Revenge of Madame Atomos; The Resurrection of Madame Atomos; The Mark of Madame Atomos; The Spheres of Madame Atomos; The Wrath of Madame Atomos* (w/M. & Sylvie Stéphan)

Félicien Champsaur. *The Human Arrow; Ouha, King of the Apes; Pharaoh's Wife; Homo-Deus; Nora, The Ape-Woman*

Didier de Chousy. *Ignis*

Jules Clarétie. *Obsession*

Michel Corday. *The Eternal Flame*

André Couvreur. *The Necessary Evil*; *Caresco, Superman; The Exploits of Professor Tornada* (3 vols.)

Captain Danrit. *Undersea Odyssey*

C. I. Defontenay. *Star (Psi Cassiopeia)*

Charles Derennes. *The People of the Pole*

Georges Dodds (anthologist). *The Missing Link*

Charles Dodeman. *The Silent Bomb*

Harry Dickson. *The Heir of Dracula; Harry Dickson vs. The Spider*

Jules Dornay. *Lord Ruthven Begins*
Alfred Driou. *The Adventures of a Parisian Aeronaut*
Sâr Dubnotal *vs. Jack the Ripper*
Odette Dulac. *The War of the Sexes*
Alexandre Dumas. *The Return of Lord Ruthven*
Renée Dunan. *Baal; The Ultimate Pleasure*
J.-C. Dunyach. *The Night Orchid; The Thieves of Silence*
Henri Duvernois. *The Man Who Found Himself*
Achille Eyraud. *Voyage to Venus*
Henri Falk. *The Age of Lead*
Paul Féval. *Anne of the Isles; Knightshade; Revenants; Vampire City; The Vampire Countess; The Wandering Jew's Daughter*
Paul Féval, *fils. Felifax, the Tiger-Man*
Charles de Fieux. *Lamékis*
Louis Forest. *Someone is Stealing Children in Paris*
Arnould Galopin. *Doctor Omega; Doctor Omega and the Shadowmen* (anthology)
Judith Gautier. *Isoline and the Serpent-Flower*
H. Gayar. *The Marvelous Adventures of Serge Myrandhal on Mars*
G.L. Gick. *Harry Dickson and the Werewolf of Rutherford Grange*
Delphine de Girardin. *Balzac's Cane*
Léon Gozlan. *The Vampire of the Val-de-Grâce*
Edmond Haraucourt. *Illusions of Immortality; Daah, the First Human*
Nathalie Henneberg. *The Green Gods*
Eugène Hennebert. *The Enchanted City*
V. Hugo, P. Foucher & P. Meurice. *The Hunchback of Notre-Dame*
Romain d'Huissier. *Hexagon: Dark Matter*
Jules Janin. *The Magnetized Corpse*
Michel Jeury. *Chronolysis*
Gustave Kahn. *The Tale of Gold and Silence*
Gérard Klein. *The Mote in Time's Eye*
Fernand Kolney. *Love in 5000 Years*
Paul Lacroix. *Danse Macabre*
Louis-Guillaume de La Follie. *The Unpretentious Philosopher*
Jean de La Hire. *Enter the Nyctalope; The Nyctalope on Mars; The Nyctalope vs. Lucifer; The Nyctalope Steps In; Night of the Nyctalope; Return of the Nyctalope; The Fiery Wheel*
Etienne-Léon de Lamothe-Langon. *The Virgin Vampire*
André Laurie. *Spiridon*
Gabriel de Lautrec. *The Vengeance of the Oval Portrait*
Alain le Drimeur. *The Future City*

Georges Le Faure & Henri de Graffigny. *The Extraordinary Adventures of a Russian Scientist Across the Solar System* (2 vols.)

Gustave Le Rouge. *The Mysterious Doctor Cornelius* (3 vols.); *The Vampires of Mars; The Dominion of the World* (w/Gustave Guitton) (4 vols.)

Jules Lermina. *Mysteryville; Panic in Paris; To-Ho and the Gold Destroyers; The Secret of Zippeliu; The Battle of Strasbourg*

André Lichtenberger. *The Centaurs; The Children of the Crab*

Listonai. *The Philosophical Voyager*

Jean-Marc & Randy Lofficier. *Edgar Allan Poe on Mars; The Katrina Protocol; Pacifica; Robonocchio; Return of the Nyctalope;* (anthologists) *Tales of the Shadowmen 1-11; The Vampire Almanac*

Xavier Mauméjean. *The League of Heroes*

Joseph Méry. *The Tower of Destiny*

Hippolyte Mettais. *The Year 5865; Paris Before the Deluge*

Louise Michel. *The Human Microbes; The New World*

Tony Moilin. *Paris in the Year 2000*

José Moselli. *Illa's End*

John-Antoine Nau. *Enemy Force*

Marie Nizet. *Captain Vampire*

C. Nodier, A. Beraud & Toussaint-Merle. *Frankenstein*

Henri de Parville. *An Inhabitant of the Planet Mars*

Gaston de Pawlowski. *Journey to the Land of the 4th Dimension*

Georges Pellerin. *The World in 2000 Years*

Ernest Pérochon. *The Frenetic People*

Pierre Pelot. *The Child Who Walked on the Sky*

J. Polidori, C. Nodier, E. Scribe. *Lord Ruthven the Vampire*

P.-A. Ponson du Terrail. *The Vampire and the Devil's Son; The Immortal Woman*

Georges Price. *The Missing Men of the Sirius*

Edgar Quinet. *Ahasuerus; The Enchanter Merlin*

Henri de Régnier. *A Surfeit of Mirrors*

Maurice Renard. *The Blue Peril; Doctor Lerne; The Doctored Man; A Man Among the Microbes; The Master of Light*

Jean Richepin. *The Wing; The Crazy Corner*

Albert Robida. *The Adventures of Saturnin Farandoul; The Clock of the Centuries; Chalet in the Sky; The Electric Life*

J.-H. Rosny Aîné. *Helgvor of the Blue River; The Givreuse Enigma; The Mysterious Force; The Navigators of Space; Vamireh; The World of the Variants; The Young Vampire*

Marcel Rouff. *Journey to the Inverted World*

Léonie Rouzade. *The World Turned Upside Down*
Han Ryner. *The Superhumans; The Human Ant*
Pierre de Selenes: *An Unknown World*
Angelo de Sorr. *The Vampires of London*
Brian Stableford. *The New Faust at the Tragicomique;The Empire of the Necromancers (The Shadow of Frankenstein; Frankenstein and the Vampire Countess; Frankenstein in London); Sherlock Holmes & The Vampires of Eternity; The Stones of Camelot; The Wayward Muse.* (anthologist) *News from the Moon; The Germans on Venus; The Supreme Progress; The World Above the World; Nemoville; Investigations of the Future; The Conqueror of Death; The Revolt of the Machines; The Man With the Blue Face*
Jacques Spitz. *The Eye of Purgatory*
Kurt Steiner. *Ortog*
Eugène Thébault. *Radio-Terror*
C.-F. Tiphaigne de La Roche. *Amilec*
Simon Tyssot de Patot. *The Strange Voyages of Jacques Massé and Pierre de Mésange*
Louis Ulbach. *Prince Bonifacio*
Théo Varlet. *The Golden Rock. The Xenobiotic Invasion; The Castaways of Eros; Timeslip Troopers* (w/André Blandin); *The Martian Epic* (w/Octave Joncquel)
Pierre Véron. *The Merchants of Health*
Paul Vibert. *The Mysterious Fluid*
Villiers de l'Isle-Adam. *The Scaffold; The Vampire Soul*
Philippe Ward. *Artahe ; The Song of Montségur* (w/Sylvie Miller) *Manhattan Ghost* (w/Mickael Laguerre)

www.ingramcontent.com/pod-product-compliance
Lightning Source LLC
Chambersburg PA
CBHW060353030726
47497CB00003B/697